Published by Dog Star Publications August 2015.

**The Tragedy Of Life's Cruel Wisdom,**

**By William Of Stratford 1615.**

ISBN 978- 0- 473-33665 - 3

The author welcomes any comments and can be contacted using the following email address: **drzargle1@gmail.com**

# The Sunday Star

## Mr Brian Jones of Stratford last week struck it rich with his metal detector – and in his own back garden!

A treasure-hunting enthusiast since his early teens but fed up with finding just bottle tops and the odd old coin, Mr. Jones couldn't believe his luck when he tried out his new metal detector in his own back garden. Within minutes he noticed a strong signal at the rear of his property and promptly dug up a battered, very rusty iron box containing a tightly-rolled clump of rags. Beneath the rags – which Mr. Jones said crumbled like wet sand – was a long object encased in what looked like a thick block of candle wax. Breaking through the wax Mr. Jones found a rolled-up collection of very old papers covered in tightly scrawled handwriting. His next-door neighbour Mr. Jenkins, a retired English teacher, declared the pages to have been written by none other than Shakespeare himself and the play, called '*The Tragedy Of Life's Cruel Wisdom',* is possibly one of the last known works by the great Bard himself because after the title it clearly reads '*By William Of Stratford 1615'*. If the manuscript turns out to be authentic, it is said to be priceless and beyond the wealth of even multi billionaires.

A delighted Mr. Jones is planning to scan each of the 120 or so hand-written pages and put them online for people to enjoy and for scholars to study. Professor Osborne of Oxford University's Chemistry Department has offered to date the manuscript using the latest techniques and to co-ordinate the research into the manuscript's authenticity. 'It will have to be one of the most rigorous investigations into an historical manuscript ever undertaken', Professor Osborne commented. Mr. Jones has already received offers from as far afield as China and New Zealand for the right to give the first performance but as yet he has made no decisions. The thorny problem of ownership is beginning to blossom into a legal nightmare. Officially anything found in or on Mr. Jones's private property belongs to Mr. Jones, but, some argue, does not a lost play, hand written by Shakespeare himself, not qualify as belonging to the nation? Lawyers have suggested that Mr. Jones may at some future date donate his find to the nation. However, for the moment Mr. Jones is probably the happiest man in Stratford.

Brian Jones says:

*Hello and welcome to my blog. By now you've probably heard of my amazing find and I can hardly tell you how excited I am to share it with you and the rest of the world. If it does turn out to be what I think it is – Shakespeare's last play written in his own hand – it will be sensational. But I'm going to leave that for you to decide. I have received no money for this and I have already refused unbelievable fortunes offered by billionaires from around the world. Why? Well it's because I feel that if this really turns out to be Shakespeare's last play, then it belongs to everyone, not just to me – I just happened to find it. And the idea that this amazing manuscript might become some rich person's private property sticks in my throat. That's just the way I am I guess. I am toying with the idea of leaving it to the British Museum in my will, but as yet I've made no firm decisions. If at any point I do earn some money from this manuscript, I want to say here and now that every penny will be donated to a charity of my choice. Since my mother died of Alzheimer's not that long ago, I may donate anything I get to a charity concerned with dementia. Not sure. So how will this blog work? I will scan and upload the play page by page and see what sense, if any, my fellow bloggers can make. But be warned, from the way it's been written the hand writing is sometimes difficult to read, but with a little practice you get used to it. And just to let you know, I've not read a lot of Shakespeare myself, so I'm going to need your help to get around the language (the last time I listened to Shakespeare was when I was at school and it was read to us by a really wild teacher who locked the classroom door and performed Julius Caesar standing on the desks!). So let's start – here's the title page with what looks like a list of the characters. What I find a bit odd though, is that it looks like Shakespeare himself is in the play – because the first character is 'William – citizen of Stratford'. Would Shakespeare have really written a play about his own life? Queen Elizabeth I is also in it and someone called Sir Francis Walsingham. Anyway here's the first page – enjoy!*

# The Tragedy of Life's Cruel Wisdom
## by William of Stratford 1615.

## Dramatis Personae.

William – citizen of Stratford.

Ann – wife to William.

Thomas Morton – friend of William.

Celine Morton – sister to Thomas Morton.

Hick Morton, Judd Morton, Stelly Morton – all
brothers to Thomas Morton

Queen Elizabeth I

Sir Francis Walsingham – advisor to the Queen

Edward, Christopher – friends of William.

Jonesie, Hans, Robert, Alex – William's fellow
actors/friends at the theatre.

Robert Cecil (Earl of Salisbury) – later advisor
to the Queen.

Jackie – brothel friend of William

Attendants to the Queen.

Henrietta – Lady-in-waiting to the Queen

Priest, Prelate, Bishop of Westminster

Two murderers, guards, prison guards, spies,
beggars, messengers.

Sundry actors in street scenes and at theatre.

# ACT 1

Brian Jones says:
*Now here are the first few lines where someone called Thomas Morton is speaking to himself. Sounds like he's pretty sad.*

The Tragedy of Life's Cruel Wisdom.

Act 1

Scene i

(At night, in a tree Thomas Morton sits,
a noose around his neck)

Thomas: Unasked, this world hath spun me of silk
Yet I shall, in bitter revenge, unspin this flesh
And all my tattered existence free of all its
tarnished innocence.
At sixteen a love beyond love was released
into my veins
Yet at eighteen doth this same agony
Now throw my raw heart beneath the
dancing crowd
To be mucked and spat on.
But why should I care, the multitudes
have only ever
Seen their own blindness as the pinnacle
of their own truth, and I, so close to
death, have no patience to stand on
their pin-headed mountains to mock
at ants and sparrows.
I, instead, see nothing but the true abyss
of my Gillian.
For two malicious years of unfettered
confinement,
My thoughts, my cries have so blanketed
my mind with their.

8

Swamp Dog says:

*No way! This has gotta be a fake!*

 Flynn says:

*Anyone who writes a thing like this must be insane! Or a megalomaniac with a third class degree in deception!*

 Swamp Dog says:

*Right on Flynn!*

 Cecelia says:

*You two cupcakes are being so unfair! What if it's genuine?*

 Brian Jones says:

*I promise you it's not a fake – I found it just as the article in the Sunday Star describes. I'm not trying to make money out of this – otherwise I wouldn't put it online for all to see, I'd be trying to sell it to the highest bidder.*

 Moriarty says:

*The probabilities are it is certainly a forgery. Caution and scepticism. Anyone remember the Hitler Dairies?*

 Swamp Dog says:

*Eat my daddy's balls! I never knew ol' Adolf kept a diary? How can I get a copy? And don't call me a cupcake!!*

 Flynn says:

*Before anyone can say this is a fake or authentic, it will have to be given the most monumental scrutiny – as patient and as precise as a brain surgeon but as rigorous as the Hubble Space Telescope! Besides carbon dating the pages, the wax, the rags and the ink (all these would have to come out with roughly the same date – the beginning of the 17th century), the handwriting will need to be*

*examined, the language analysed and compared with all Shakespeare's known plays. Then if it does appear to be a real find and not another hoax, it would be one of the most sensational medieval archaeological finds ever made!*

Cecelia says:

*But darlings, even if it turns out to be a hoax, who cares as long as it's good? If Shakespeare can still inspire lesser Shakespeares who cares? After all he did say we're all actors strutting our butts about the stage – even you Swamp Dog! I bet you do push-ups in ever-so tight boxers – you muffin!*

Moriarty says*:*

*The first line reads 'Unasked, this world hath spun me of silk...'*
*Silk would have been a fine, rare and exotic cloth in Elizabethan times.*
*'Unasked' I guess would mean without his consent. 'The world hath spun me..' might mean 'made'. So paraphrasing, the first line could mean 'Without my consent the world made me into a fine, rare person?' Any ideas?*

Swamp Dog says:

*@Cecelia – I do push-ups – and I also open gay walnuts like you between my teeth. 'The world has spun him' means he's turning so fast he's all mixed up, confused like – and he didn't ask for it, so he's pissed off. That's how I see it.*

Molotov says:

*For christ's sake it says he's in a tree with a noose around his neck – it's obvious he's about to top himself ! He's suicidal – not confused!*

Olga says:

*Moose around neck? In tree? Did English have this wild animals long ago? I am thinking moosies is vegitarians, no?*

10

Swamp Dog says: *This proves it's a fake! Shakespeare could never have seen a moose! They only grow in Canada!*

 Moriarty says: *But the word "moose" first entered English in 1606 - so who knows what Shakespeare saw? The word is borrowed from the **Algonquian languages**, and according to early sources, 'moose' is likely derived from 'moosu', meaning "he strips off "*.....

 Cecelia says: *'He strips off'! On stage? With a moose!? No way! Shakespeare must have had a real sweet-and-dirty mind! What a darling! So bold!*

 Molotov says: *The poor quality of these postings is tragic. If you can't read hand written text accurately then please don't waste other people's time by posting trash because you have misread, misunderstood or can't grasp the meaning of the words of your own language.*

 Swamp Dog says:
*There's nothing wrong with my language – you ape!*

Brian Jones says:
*I must agree with you Molotov. Also I'm afraid the postings are becoming too much to handle. I've had over 300 in the last few minutes and many are so far from the topic they have become quite stupid and irrelevant....So I'm going to be very selective and allow postings from only those who have something relevant to say about the text. Also if we go through every single word as it appears this blog will balloon into the stratosphere, so I'm going to select comments to post only after a character has completed their lines. So be warned! Here is the rest of Thomas Morton's opening speech.*

Encrypted passions that every heartbeat hath blurred
the night into conscious day and each day
into sickening night.
Yet, as I impenitent lay in my cell, thou, William,
hast wired out fathered and thrown
An infinite distance between us,
And it hangs like a colossal dagger in the sky
Not knowing if to point at ecstasy or at the
outpouring of tumultuous imbecile.
But all this while, my love, thou hast said nothing.
Thy silence hath cast and seeded the world of all
dreams,
For it and it alone hath spawned the termination
of my could,
A cruelty for which there are no trite exonerations,
no sweet-guilded excuses, no flower-wrapped
verses,
For it is a cruelty far beyond the infinite malice
of all the stars.
With love's consuming pain I fell to my knees
And swallowed the flames of thy vast,
unbridled sex
And for this alteration, this bright triumph of
existence,
I have been murdered many times over.
But no more.
No more shall these trite deaths cheat me
of death's final release.
And so I kiss the rose that soon will
My heavy soul scoring across the gaping thresholds of
hell.
2.

Moriarty says:
*It's not really a 'speech' – it's called a soliloquy....*

 Swamp Dog says:
*That's bollocks! A 'silo' is where they store grain!*

 Moriarty says:
*OMG!*

 Cecelia says:
*Poor sweetie! He sounds really stressed! What's an 'Encrusted passion'? And it looks like he's all mixed up between night and day, AND at night he gets sick! Well no wonder! It says he's 'in a cell' – a prison! I'd be scared! But at least he has William with him – a friend, someone to hold onto while he's throwing up.*

 Swamp Dog says:
*But it says this William guy has 'wived and fathered' – well, unless he's got flying sperm, how can he have kids behind bars?*

 Cecelia says:
*Hi cupcake! I didn't know you could read so well!*

 Swamp Dog says:
*Fuck off Cecelia! And FFS stop calling me cupcake!*

 Molotov says:
*There is a big difference between understanding what individual words mean and understanding the meaning of several words put together. This guy's been jilted by his ex – William – who's gone off with a woman and had kids. That's why he's depressed.*

Cecelia says:

*But it seems he's frightened of silence and he's been having bad dreams – he says he's had the* 'worst of all dreams' *about* 'spawning termites' *and a* 'colossal dog in the sky'. *Poor sausage, he's having delusions in prison. Makes me want to reach out and cuddle him.*

 Swamp Dog says:

*Has he got Aids or something? Because he says there's a* 'cruelty beyond the stars'?

 Moriarty says:

@ Swamp Dog - *Aids did not exist in the 17th century. As Molotov has already pointed out, this part has all to do with his disappointment at being rejected for a woman. What he's saying is that the cruelty he feels is way worse than the infinite malice of the stars.*

 Swamp Dog says:

*But that's stupid – stars can't be angry! They're just fucking stars! Never did like Shakespeare – he just makes crap up!*

 Flynn says:

*But this is certainly not Shakespeare! You're all assuming this stuff is genuine! It's without doubt a scam. Mr. Brian Jones is probably some frustrated Sunday newspaper poet who's spent years writing stories in the dismal language of journalism, and who has now concocted his poetic raison d'être and is trying to reveal his true soul to the online world without revealing his real identity. For all we know 'Mr. Brian Jones' is 'Mrs Belladona Juice-Bag', a would-be author who's written a dozen books of hopeless poetry and had each one rejected by every publisher on the planet. This pathetic scam could be his or her last throw of the dice before being carried out on a stretcher and slid into a literary grave.*

Brian Jones says:

*Thank you Flynn for exposing me and my forgery to the world! But you couldn't be more wrong if you'd tried! I've never written a poem in my life and I've never written for a Sunday newspaper. I've been a humble public servant with a passion for treasure hunting ever since I was a kid when I dug up a gold bracelet on Southend beach. The money I got for the bracelet paid for my first metal detector and I've been hooked ever since. But sometimes I have wondered if I am the victim of some prankster. Has someone planted this iron box in my garden knowing that I'd find it with my detector? It was quite deep (about half a meter down) but there was no sign that the earth had been disturbed by someone before. A chemistry professor from Oxford was here yesterday and asked for samples of the rags and wax – he said he was going to carbon date them. It could take a few weeks he said.*

 Swamp Dog says:

*Half-way down the page he says 'with love's coming rain he filled his knees'? – Does this mean with love's coming rain he filled his pants? It doesn't make any sense?*

 Cecelia says:

*Silly cupcake! It's obvious! He can only ' 'fill' his knees', if his knees are empty. It means he feels himself to be a 'hollow' man, unworthy and of little value. But love's rain is coming to fill him up and make him feel better.*

 Swamp Dog says:

*But then it says he swallowed fire – so either he was being tortured or he'd eaten some red-hot chilli sauce. Did they even have chillies in those days?*

 Moriarty:

*Sure did. Chilli peppers were first brought to Europe after Columbus's second voyage in 1493 – so they'd been around for at least 100 hundred years.*

Swamp Dog says:

*What the hell does 'unbrindled sex' mean?*

Moriarty says:

*'Brindled' means 'with spots or streaks'. So I guess 'his unbrindled sex' could be a reference to his genitals being clean and without blemish? Perhaps it's a hint saying he was a virgin?*

Molotov says:

*OMG you people are so dumb! He's describing giving William a blow job! It reads 'unbridled sex' – in other words 'wild, free sex', 'sex without limits' – like when you take the bridle off a horse and it goes running madly across the field because at last it's free of constraint.*

Wrecking Ball says:

*Are you now saying he had sex with a horse? Before it was a moose! Shakespeare sure was a big time, filthy bastard!*

Cecelia says:

*Poor sweetie! How cruel! He says he's been murdered just for giving his friend a blow job! That's so unfair!*

Swamp Dog says:

*How do we know it wasn't this William who murdered him? If some guy tried to give me a blow job I'd tear him to pieces!*

Olga says:

*Shakespeare has sex relation with horse? This is English joke, no? What is 'blow work'? Do you need permit?*

Wrecking Ball says:

*Makes no sense!!! If he's dead how can he be talking!!? Dead's dead! Unless he's a ghost? There's lots of ghosts in Shakespeare.*

Molotov says:

*You people just don't get it do you? The guy speaking – this Thomas Morton – has somehow been imprisoned for having sex with William and he's suffered so much abuse from those around him that it feels like he's had an emotional and psychological death. And every time someone rubs his past homosexuality in his face it's like he is being murdered all over again. He feels so abandoned and rejected he's sitting in a tree about to kill himself. He even says he will 'kiss the rope that soon will swing his heavy soul across into hell'. Now do you get it!? Brian could you upload the next page please?*

Brian Jones says:

*I must apologise Molotov, but for some reason my 'EDIT' button isn't working. I've tried several times to delete many of the posts above. You seem to be the only one trying to read the words accurately. As for myself I've always found poetry difficult to understand because of the way the words are put together. But you seem to be doing a good job. Here are the last few lines of Act 1, scene i.*

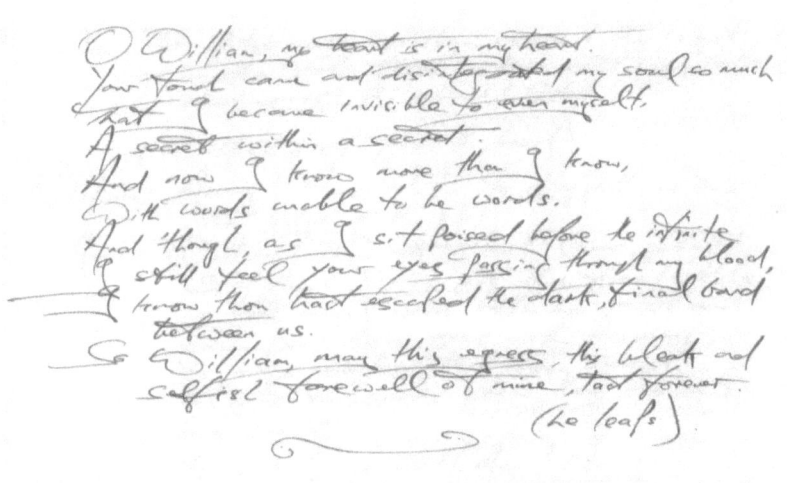

17

Swamp Dog says:

*I get the feeling Brian Jones doesn't like us on his blog. Where's the freedom of speech in that?*

Cecelia says:

*My thoughts exactly cupcake! It's a horrible feeling not to be wanted – it's rejection – when all we want to do is contribute to this wonderful discovery.*

Wrecking Ball says:

*Hey cupcake! Do you have moobies like me? I wear a D-cup.*

Swamp Dog says:

*Will you guys stop calling me cupcake!*

Molotov says:

*'My heart is in my heart' is very enigmatic. Is he saying no one can see his true self?*

Cecelia says:

*He really needs to phone a friend.*

Moriarty says:

*Maybe it's like a collapsed lung – his heart's collapsed inside itself?*

Molotov says:

*If you mean collapsed with sorrow then I'd agree. But if you're thinking of some medical condition I'm not sure Shakespeare would have been so knowledgeable or so crass – especially as this guy is about to hang himself in the dead of night.*

Swamp Dog says:

*He says when William came and touched him, he went gaga. But doesn't that depend on where William touched him? I mean if William grabbed Thomas by the arm – that's nothing – but if he grabbed Thomas by his Viagra Falls – that's enough to make any man run for the hills!*

Cecelia says:

*Sweetheart! – I'd just run after you!!*

Wrecking Ball says:

*But how can you become invincible to yourself just because someone grabs your goolies? If someone took my goolies hostage I wouldn't exactly feel like Superman set free.*

Molotov says:

*FFS! Read the words! It's doesn't say 'invincible' it says 'invisible'! Through William's touch he became invisible to himself. Today I guess we would say he 'fell apart'- especially when William became sexually intimate. Thomas became a 'secret within a secret' – this could, I suppose, mean super shy? or super embarrassed?*

Wrecking Ball says:

*It's anal sex!!! – a 'secret in a secret'!!*

Moriarty says:

*He says he 'knows more than he knows' – which could be his way of saying he's stumbled upon something dangerous?*

Molotov says:

*You mean like in Genesis when Adam eats the 'Forbidden Fruit'? What do you make of the next line – 'With words unable to be words'? It's probably the strangest thing I've read in years – in one way it sounds so potent, so tragic, while in another it's almost like he's saying he can't express himself – as though he's been struck dumb.*

Swamp Dog says:

> *Anal sex would strike me dumb for sure! I'm 65 and never done it!*

*Wrecking Ball says:*

> *The stupid bastard's drunk! He says so himself in the next line – 'as I sit pissed before the infinite'. To find the courage to kill himself he's gone and plastered hisself – that's what's happened.*

Moriarty says:

> *I don't think it says 'pissed' – it looks more like 'posed'? But what does 'posed before the infinite' mean? Maybe he thinks he's taking a position – a bit like how a high diver poses at the end of the diving board before springing off?*

Molotov says:

> *I'm sure it reads 'poised' because there is, I think, a tiny 'i' before the 's' – and it would make more sense for him to say 'poised before the infinite' because he's just about to jump, and the 'infinite' to him must be synonymous with 'death'.*

Moriarty says:

> *I think you're right – I can just see the 'i'. But then in the next line what does 'I still feel your eyes passing through my blood' mean?*

Molotov says:

> *But it's all part of one phrase – 'And 'though, as I sit poised before the infinite I still feel your eyes passing through my blood....' Not sure, but it might mean that even as he is about to die, he still feels deeply his love for William and William's love for him. What do you think?*

Ezekiel says:

> *God has written this is an abomination: 'Ye that follow the road to Sodomy, shall die beneath the rocks of hell and heaven, for neither place shall be as a refuge for this abomination of the flesh.'*

Swamp Dog says:

*O fuck off and shag a cactus! We don't want any of you religious fruitcakes trying to push your abominations up our arses! Just go and wank over your Bible!*

 Ezekiel says:

*The lingering smell of intercourse shall hang about the sodomite as dung doth staineth the hindquarters of the cattle. And ye shall not be spared when the earth is torn asunder by the breath of Almighty God!*

 Wrecking Ball says:

*Spare me your sanctimonious shit - you turd in a bottle!*

 Moriarty says:

*@ Molotov: I see what you mean, which sort of makes the next line – 'I know thou hast escaped the dark, final bond between us'– more understandable.*

 Molotov says:

*What Shakespeare's saying – I think – is that this 'dark, final bond' is the life-long commitment of marriage between, in this case, two men. But William has 'escaped' this dark love that dare not speak its name, because he opted for social conformity and marriage with a woman and had children. And now, since William is 'released' from this bond, Thomas too wants his release but is about to do so by choosing to take his own life.*

 Cecelia says:

*Shakespeare always makes me feel so sad.*

 Swamp Dog says:

*He's always OTT serious. It's like he sees good and evil even in baking a cake, or washing a pair of socks.*

Cecelia says:

*All Thomas needed was a big hug and none of this would have happened.*

Ezekiel says:

*What Thomas needed was to repent his sins and beg Our Lord Jesus for mercy - 'Forgiveness, saith The Lord, is the rarest fruit of sin, it showeth compassion for the weakness of man and yea! none are outside the bosom of God'.*

Wrecking Ball says:

*@ Ezekiel: You're like someone straining to suck your own tits! – you pathetic excuse of a human! I bet you dream of world domination as you pull the legs off spiders. If I knew where you're hiding I'd come and rub my moobies in your face!*

Cecelia says:

*I'm not hiding – I'm waiting!*

Molotov says:

*I find the very last line quite chilling because Thomas wants his death to never be forgotten – he says 'may this....selfish farewell of mine...last forever'.*

Moriarty says:

*I think he's saying when he dies he wants his death to last forever?*

Molotov says:

*But death is forever?*

Moriarty says:

*Not if you're religious – I think this is Thomas's way of saying there is no afterlife, no heaven, no Christianity, no God. In fact isn't he, with these words, proclaiming himself to be a sixteenth century atheist?*

Molotov says:

*A good point. But would someone at the end of the sixteenth century really do this? Stand on the threshold of death and radically deny the existence of god?*

Moriarty says:
*Why not?*

Ezekiel says:

*The kingdom of heaven is there for all to grasp – but only the pure of soul can be blessed and allowed to enter. For it is written 'those that spread their seed from man to man shall have their eyes roasted on the spit of God's eternal anger, and neither shall they nor any man who hath defiled themselves with the excrement of another be welcome in the house of the Lord.'*

Wrecking Ball says:

*You religious dingbats really do get high on the smell of shit, torture and ejaculation of 'seed.' You hate sex and the body, yet you're obsessed with sado-masochistic ideas. You're sick. You're like grey maggots in an open wound.*

Molotov says:

*@ Moriarty: Another way of looking at this last line is that he wants this farewell, this gruesome act of suicide, to be so awful, that it lasts forever in the minds of those he leaves behind – almost as though he's trying to punish them by leaving them to cope with the pitiful tragedy of his death. Perhaps this is why he calls the act a 'selfish farewell'?*

Brian Jones says:

*Thanks Molotov and Moriarty – you're doing a good job. Not sure about the others. Edit button still down I'm afraid. Anyway, just uploaded the beginning of scene (ii) – there seem to be lots of exclamation marks between William and someone called Ann (probably his wife) - which I guess means they're having a row?*

Scene ii

(A bedroom, William and Ann asleep. William suddenly springs up terrified, clutching his throat.)

William: Arrrg! Away! Get me more breath! Arrrg!

Ann: William! What is wrong.!? Speak!

William: Arrrg! The devil is standing on my throat! Away! Arrrg!

Ann: There is nothing there William! Thy throat is free!

William: His pointed tail is whipped and wrapped upon my neck! Let me go!

(William tears off his nightshirt)

Ann: William stop!

William: He's choking me Ann! Arrrg!

3.

24

The Redeemer says:

*Shakespeare writes that the Devil is standing on his throat - this is exactly the fate of all sodomites! Before they can rise, still dripping from their deed of filth, Lucifer is set to choke them in their beds!*

Moriarty says:

*But he's in bed with his wife – it says so at the top, if you could just read it carefully!*

Cecelia says:

*Oooo! She's on top!? Naughty!*

Wrecking Ball says:

*Not another turd in a bottle!*

The Redeemer says:

*This blog is pure pornography and should be taken down ! You are all advanced sodomites of the first order!*

Wrecking Ball says:

*And since you're a retarded sodomite of the second order you can piss off and go fuck yourself with a carrot!!*

The Redeemer says:

*Very eloquent Wrecking Ball – though I'm not afraid, like you, of good, righteous sex with my wife. You want – no, you need – the total perversion of sexual love! As you dive into the depraved anus of yet another man, God is watching you, cursing you and sending his instructions to the Devil. Shakespeare knew this, which is why he is punishing himself for his past wickedness with Thomas. And you will be next if you don't writhe for mercy in the dead of night and prostate yourself before the Holy Trinity!*

Cecelia says:

*O sweetie! I think you mean 'prostrate'? Sigmund would be so proud of you!*

Molotov says:

*@ Brian Jones: The sooner you can fix your edit button the better – this blog is getting too cluttered with lunatics who are not only illiterate but who have agendas they should be burning off behind the walls of an asylum.*

Brian Jones says:

*@ Molotov: I couldn't agree more. I'm really sorry, but I've tried everything. The site administrator thinks there is a virus in my computer which has for some reason disabled the 'edit' command from my computer to their system. Who knows? But rather than deleting the entire blog I want to continue because some people (you and Moriarty for example) are at least trying to unravel the meaning of Shakespeare's words.*

Flynn says:

*There you go again Brian Jones – still trying to fool the rest of us that Shakespeare wrote this unreadable trash and not you! It's a nice try but it won't wash! Once you have been exposed for the fraud you are, there will be no place left on planet Earth where you can avoid the ridicule of your peers. I suggest you try the rain forest as they've probably not yet heard of Shakespeare.*

Brian Jones says:

*Great to have you – and your honest way of talking – back on the blog!*

Molotov says:

*Scene (ii) opens with William imagining he's being strangled by Satan in his bed. But Brian can you please upload the next page as I can't tell where William's hysterical awakening is going.*

Brian Jones says:

*I think Wrecking Ball was right about Shakespeare loving ghosts, because further down the next page it says in brackets that the ghost of Thomas Morton appears at the foot of the bed. Here's the upload of page 4.*

Ann: For pity's sake William cease! This is just another ~~false twist~~ in the wretched, false ~~dontine of~~ thy mind! Stop!

(William falls from the bed)

William: Arrrg! Ann help! He draggeth me onto the edge of the pit!

Ann: William! Thou art abed! Come, get up! ~~Stop this!~~ It is just the ~~frail~~/bubble of ~~thy~~ mind which hath so ~~burst out~~ ~~crumpled~~ thine eyes with poisonous, visionous madness that thou ~~seest~~ ~~belching~~ vulcanoes where there ~~are only~~ bed-sheets!

William: He holds me still Ann! Away!

Ann: ~~Get off~~ William! There is no God-sent devil ~~about~~ thy neck!

(Ann pulls William back onto the bed)

William: Away! Strangle someone other than I!

27

Ann: Get up William! There is no God-sent
devil about thy neck!

(Ann pulls William back onto the bed)

William: Away! Strangle someone other than I!
Away!

Ann: William look at me! The devil hath gone!
I bit at his slimey tail as he ran!

William: If not the devil, then whose evil, swift
cunning doth tighten about my throat!?

(The ghost of Thomas Morton, a noose
around his neck, appears at the foot of
the bed)

Ye gods! He airs and beckons! Ann! Look!
His face is set to shatter my soul!
He hath come to strip my bones of their flesh!
Hence!
4.

Wrecking Ball says:
*His wife Ann is shouting about his false teeth!*

Swamp Dog says*:*
*Where's it say that?*

Wrecking Ball says:
*She shouts 'cease' and then 'This is just another false tooth in the wretched, false dartiness of thy mind'? Isn't this a spelling mistake? Shouldn't it be 'dirtiness' of thy mind? It would make more sense.*

Moriarty says:

*Sorry, but I read it as 'darkness of thy mind'.*

*@ Molotov: Page 4 seems to be more of the same hysteria all the way down to where the ghost appears.*

Molotov says:

*Yes, but the coincidence of William's imagined strangulation and the suicide of Thomas is confirmed when the Thomas's ghost appears with a noose around its neck. What I think Shakespeare's saying here is that even in death these two men are connected by the love that once existed between them – Thomas's ghost is trying to pull William with him across into the eternal death he has chosen. Ann, on the other hand, seems to act like an anchor holding William down in the reality of this world.*

Swamp Dog says:

*Wrecking Ball – you geriatric! Put your specs on! It says 'twist' not 'tooth'! But you're right 'false dirtiness of thy mind' makes more sense given the fact he's in bed with his wife but secretly wants to be in bed with his bum buddy ?*

Cecelia says:

*I feel for both Thomas and William because they are both choking yet one's dead and the other's alive. And Ann's a bitch! While her poor hubby's being strangled she just shouts at him! Mean cow! I don't see why William should have a 'dirty' mind – he may be in bed with a woman but they are not actually doing anything are they? Because he's in the middle of choking to death, 'darkness' fits perfectly.*

Olga says:

*Hallo, I am Russian lady high class. I have beauteous inclines and my valleys are precipitous. I look at men with large columns and great wealth. I give warm fluids with 100% skin. I wish close contact. I have rich vibrating treasures. Please show your desires for my text numbers. Low costs for worn genitals. Hurray while stocks last!*

29

Moriarty says:

*@ Molotov: That's a neat way of looking at it because Ann shouts that in his 'visionary madness' he is seeing 'belching vulcanes where there are only bed-sheets!' Ann is like the voice of common sense, someone whose understanding of the world is grounded in the reality of everyday life.*

Molotov says:

*And the contrast is even stronger when you remember just how superstitious people were in these times – if the milk turned sour they crossed themselves because they seriously believed they had been visited by the devil. So Shakespeare could have credibly written Ann's role as a superstitious wife who truly believed William was possessed by Satan. Instead he portrays Ann as a hard-nosed realist who refuses to take any of this nonsense – she even says she 'bit at the devil's slimy tail' to make him leave. Brian, any chance we can have page 5?*

The Redeemer says:

*In answer to William's question on page 4 – 'If not the devil, then whose evil, swift cunning doth tighten about my throat!?' It is God's divine, swift cunning that is around William's throat, punishing him for ramming his seed into the stinking anus of another man – a place of utter sickness, a pit brimming with vile, loathsome corruption, a stew-hole choked with fermenting excrement and crawling with maggot-ridden filth beyond all description. And ye on this site with lustful intent, be warned, if with your tongues you lick the anuses of the wicked, they will turn and mount thee like dogs and spill into thee the poison of Gomorrah to the end of thy days. Repent now!*

Wrecking Ball says:

*Holy fuck! The Redeemer seems to be working up quite a sweat! Bet he gets a hard-on writing this crap.*

Brian Jones says:

*@ Molotov: Page 5 is now up. There seems to be a startling development because, if I've read it correctly, Ann – William's wife – exposes her breasts on stage! See what you think.*

Ann: Will look at me! Only I am before thine eyes! Look! Here are my naked breasts! They and they alone William are the only reality in this all-tangible world!

William: I see him still! white-grinning between thy breasts!

Ann: Thou seest thine own inverted mind! Awake I say!

(She strikes William across the face. The apparition vanishes)

William: The — the pit hath... closed... I live... ...my children?... do I have children?

Ann: Yes! All three such sweet babes!

(William takes Ann by both shoulders and stares into her face).

William: Thomas... Thomas, I can't.

(Ann shrieks and strikes William hard. She sits on his chest and beats him.)

Ann: You man-bitch! You counterfeit queen! How dare thee! Thou flimsy-penised whore! Why dost thou mouth thy steamy madness at me like this!? Art thou trying to turn snakes into giraffes! Men into stones! and raindrops into wild, fierce- -dancing women!?

31

Molotov says:

*Clearly William's hallucination persists so strongly that, out of sheer desperation, Ann places herself in front of William and opens her nightgown to show her husband the one naked reality that could, she hopes, snap him out of his delirium. However, it doesn't work because William says he can still see Thomas 'white-grinning between thy breasts', and it is only when she strikes William 'hard across the face' that the apparition disappears and William's sanity apparently returns.*

Swamp Dog says:

*Shakespeare makes Ann do a full Monty on stage!*

Olga says:

*What means 'full Monty'? I am thinking it is English idiom for 'full mounting'? I am Olympic champion in full mounting. I give discounts and do special mountings with caviar. Would you like to text me?*

Swamp Dog says:

*What's a 'pithath'? After Ann clocks him across the kisser, William says 'the pithath closed' He's not a miner by any chance?*

Cecelia says:

*Silly cupcake! I think it's two words 'pit hath' – but you're right it's not written very clearly, so you're forgiven. Next time I'll slap your wrist.*

Moriarty says:

*@ Molotov: But then William calls his wife 'Thomas', so his delusion is obviously as strong as ever. Ann goes wild with anger, again strikes him and then sits on his chest and beats him!*

Cecelia says:

*Ann is an absolute bully! Her poor husband is strangled and terrified by a ghost and all she can do is slap him about! She shows no sympathy, no love, no tenderness – just hysterical, selfish anger. I hate her!*

Olga says:

*I do also slappings and beating and other lusty specials. Text me now if you are hot.*

 Molotov says:

*@Moriarty: She is obviously so outraged with jealousy and disappointment that she loses her self-control and releases her anger physically and verbally against her husband. It's as though she can't believe William is still so compulsively deluded that he can actually mistake her for Thomas. I guess Shakespeare wants us to assume that Ann knows all about William's former lover and their obsession with each other, because she calls William a 'man-bitch', a 'counterfeit queen' and a 'flimsy-penised whore'. Rather than mincing her words she instead minces his masculinity.*

 Moriarty says:

*And at the bottom of page 5 Ann shouts -'Art thou trying to turn snakes into giraffes!....and rainclouds into wild, fierce-dancing women!' What's that about?*

 Wrecking Ball says:

*It's obvious, he's got a fear of snakes and he wants to dance in the rain with naked women. In other words she's telling him straight that he's a randy bastard with the hots for giraffes. Shakespeare's weird.*

 Olga says:

*'Flimsy-penised' – No worry, I make all soft erectiles rise to full glory and mountings. Text me for quote.*

Molotov says:

*@ Moriarty: I think Ann is goading William – saying something like 'if you're so mad and you can see things in the afterlife that no one else can – go on! – let's see you 'turn men into stones' and 'snakes into giraffes' etc. Almost like she's shouting at him 'What are you trying to prove? What are you trying to do to me with this madness of yours?' But we need to see the next page to get the full picture. Brian, we need page 6!*

 Brian Jones says:
*OK*

 Moriarty says:

*OMG! Have you seen page 6? Ann's tirade continues for almost the whole page!*

Again and again how dare thee! How canst
thou vent that cursed, disease-driven name
into my face!
Less than a name — a bound, a wretch, a nothing
who magicked thy wholesome, virgin
seed from my head!
What!? Dost thou want thy loins forever to
crawl with the Antichrist!?
Wilt thou always fire and scream and eat
the very earth this spineless, empty 'Tom'
hath defiled!?
Even though I have lain here in our bed,
My body stained with thy babe's very blood,
Yet you, in this dream-madness, you let this
'thing', this abstract speck of nothing,
To everyday gut the enthroned love from my
heart!
The more thou lovest this dubious 'him', the more
thou despiseth me as a woman!
But be thou doubly seemed William, if
thou dost not
Sever this wretch from thy soul,
thou wilt forever drain the whole firmament
of my mind
Of all its love and life for thee!

William: But why Ann dost thou rage so at a
mere ghost? Art thou jealous?

Ann: Ha! I jealous! I shall tear my
flesh into pieces of sulphurous fire
before I word to jealousy!

William: O Ann hold! Thou wast made to
terrify humanity!

6.

The Redeemer says:

*Ann is a noble woman who speaks the truth for she sees this sodomite's loins crawling with the Antichrist.*

Wrecking Ball says:

*I bet every morning you brown-nose your god's butt-hole so much you can only smell shit everywhere you go! Get a life.*

Molotov says:

*@ Moriarty: From what I've read Ann seems to continue trashing not only Thomas but also William's memory of their homosexual relationship. But the telling conclusion comes, I think, when she proclaims that William 'let's this 'thing [she can't bring herself to call Thomas by name] to everyday gut the enthroned love from my heart!' So we can see that this issue of William's gay past has remained an unhealed wound ever since the day they were married.*

Moriarty says:

*The last lines of her speech are a threat because she warns 'if thou dost not sever this wretch from thy soul, thou wilt forever drain the whole firmament of my mind of all its love and life for thee!' She's quite a woman!*

Molotov says:

*You're right. This shows that Shakespeare wanted to portray Ann not as a cosy, shy wife who looks after babies and bakes apple pies, but as an intellectual boxer, a fighter capable of harsh, uncompromising eloquence - the type, perhaps, who in earlier times, would have been burnt as a witch.*

Cecelia says:

*She is a witch! I for one would burn her. She's a cruel, hard-hearted woman who doesn't deserve a good husband and babies. William is a tormented soul who needs tender care and kisses. He's seeing visions of his best friend who's just committed suicide and all she can do is wobble her tits in his face and punch him! Only a witch could do such a heartless thing!*

Moriarty says:

*William then accuses her of jealousy – but I can't make out what's written above the erased part in her reply. What's it look like to you?*

Molotov says:

*But now notice how sane William seems – it's almost as though their roles have reversed. He almost taunts Ann by asking 'why do you rage so at a mere ghost'? And notice he says 'a mere ghost', implying the sight of dead Thomas's spectre is nothing to get flustered by – whereas only moments before he was shitting buckets because he thought Thomas had come back from the dead to 'strip the flesh from his bones'. By comparison Ann is now beside herself with anger so much that when William taunts her with being jealous, she rages that she would rather 'tear my flesh into pieces of sulphurous fire' before she'll 'bend' to jealousy. She has now become the irrational one.*

Moriarty says:

*William then utters an almost pitiful cry for her to stop, saying 'thou wast made to terrify humanity'.*

Cecelia says:

*You see – she's a monster! Just like I said!*

The Redeemer says:

*She is no monster! She is fulfilling the role that Nature intended all women to fulfill – she is a wife and servant to her husband and a mother to her children! How? Because in her anger she is refusing to be cowed into some sort of second class person who allows William – even in his imagination – to indulge in contagious homosexuality. She well knows that sodomy is blasphemous and that each time a man penetrates another man what he is really doing is breaking God's divine commandment and satisfying the Devil's lust.*

Wrecking Ball says:

*She is not, like you – Redeemer – a thorough, fucking moron! What happens when you get an erection? Does your brain burst out of your ears with excitement?*

Molotov says:

*'Thou wast made to terrify humanity!' is a chilling accusation to say to anyone – but more especially to your wife! – the one person whom you are supposed to love without reservation. William must feel so shaken by Ann's blistering outburst that he can't take anymore and just wants her to stop.*

Moriarty says:

*We need to see if their argument is resolved. Mr. Jones we need page 7 please!*

The Redeemer says:

*Don't forget that it has been scientifically proven that homosexual seed is highly infectious – just like mad cow disease! It sits in the anus and crawls about confused and embittered and causes intense itching desires. The seed then creeps into the blood and finally gets to the brain where it triggers a dramatic change in personality. For example, a good-looking, healthy youth with blond, curly hair and a pleasant smile, when infected, starts to show all the dark symptoms of having been sodomised. He may start to swear, to drool and be constantly 'playing' with his hands inside his trouser pockets. Hair may begin to grow on the palms of his hands, on the soles of his feet and between his toes. He may become cross-eyed and disorientated and his ears may start to stick out from the side of his head like spoons.*

Ezekiel says:
*Take down this blasphemous blog Brian Jones or there will be consequences!*

Wrecking Ball says:
*What are you going to do? Ask your sky fairy to send a thunderbolt and zap his privates?*

Brian Jones says:
*My privates are quite secure Wrecking Ball – thank you. In the interests of freedom of speech, page 7 will be up as soon as I can stop laughing.*

The Redeemer says:
*Especially beware of the youth who takes melons into his bedroom – this is a sure sign of vegetable lechery. If the youth indulges in intercourse with vegetables, dark rings will begin to appear beneath his once beautiful eyes and his cheeks will start to look hollow and lifeless like those of a skull. His strident, glowing, perfect body that once impressed his friends will begin to sag and smell like a bowl of limp sauerkraut and slowly he will come to look like a nervous, oppressed lunatic twitching with homosexual guilt.*

To shake men's blinded hearts!
To stab the darkness and strike at their mistakes!
Sweet Ann forgive me!

Ann : ~~If~~ I do rage Will it is because I have
~~gained~~ an almost colossy of a man;
the vastness of my ~~fear~~ doth shew the vastness
of my love for thee. Do not Will cast it
aside as ghosts.

William : Heaven ~~loud~~ me! Methought I was betrothed
to the night yet, in ~~truth~~, I was wedded
to the Sun.

Ann : Then ~~let me~~ light stretch out beyond the
opaque stench of this grave ~~then digest~~
~~for thyself~~
Use not, William, thyself to see, but without
thine eyes and, between thy teeth, burst
their apparitions ~~and falsehoods~~,
For with this grievous distemper thou canst not
see ought but the tantalising chaos of
despair!

William : Spare me Ann! Say no more!

Ann : Will I .... (she stops aghast) .... Will thy
neck!

William : Ann do not ~~terrify~~ me! What is it?

Ann : Thy reddened skin shews a bruised circle of
violence! Was I so rough with thee?

William : Nay sweet Ann, not thee. Then it must be
~~true~~, I have been swung from a gibbet!

Ann : Only from the gibbet of thy mind William.

William : Bring me a glass — I must see!

(There is a loud knocking at the house door. Ann
goes to the window and calls down into the street)

7.

40

Molotov says:

*@ Moriarty: So William's full reply looks like: 'Thou wast made to terrify humanity! To shake men's blinded hearts! To stab the darkness and strike at their mistakes!' And then he begs forgiveness. With these dreadful words William seems to be describing all of womankind who can somehow see into men's desires and motives better than men themselves. What, I think, Shakespeare is really implying here, is that, when it comes to self-knowledge, men are emotionally blind whereas women are the insightful, intuitive ones – that special half of humanity who at least have the courage 'To stab the darkness and strike at their [men's] mistakes!' What do you think?*

The Redeemer says:

*And this too is a scientific fact – the sperm of the masturbator are crooked and swim in circles, hunch-backed and deformed with sin.*

Wrecking Ball says:

*Gawd! So that's what the lump on my shoulder's all about! And here's me thinking I had muscle growth.*

Moriarty says:

*@Molotov: Possibly, or it could be that he's just saying these things because he's frightened of losing Ann. After all she does seem, in this scene at least, to be like an Amazon, an anchor holding William's life together. And don't forget, since his homosexual episode with Thomas, William has fathered 'three sweet babes' with Ann, so there must be a bond between them which, one would expect, he's anxious not to break – or is this too naive?*

Wrecking Ball says:

*@ The Redeemer – I'm not going to give you the satisfaction of trying to reply to your psychotic rant. All I will say is that religious zombies like you should be buried alive in their own shit, with just their noses sticking above the surface – so they can forever smell the stench of their own ignorance and lies.*

 Swamp Dog says:

*Couldn't agree more WB – I think The Redeemer has been missing a few good shags in his life. It's obvious he denies himself the very thing he secretly wants – one good, monumental fuck.*

 Brian Jones says:

*Please people! Can I ask you to stick to the topic and aim of this blog! We are meant to be reading a lost play by Shakespeare, not arguing about masturbation and zombies!*

 Moriarty says:

*@ Brian Jones: Pity about your virus disabling your delete function. My guess is most of your followers will skip the trash and concentrate on the manuscript pages you upload. But what I find a little odd is that apart from myself and Molotov there don't seem to be many taking this discovery seriously? I mean where are the thousands of Shakespeare scholars around the world? Why aren't they queuing up to post their thoughts – even if they think it's not genuine, let them say why not. Have you heard anything from the Oxford professor who's carbon dating the pages?*

Brian Jones says:

*@ Moriarty: Not yet. He's only had the samples for a week or so. He said that three independent laboratories will each carbon date the samples so that they can compare their results and that could take at least a month. Though he did say that his lab might have a preliminary result soon. What do you make of page 7?*

 Moriarty says:

*Not sure – but Ann comes across as one almighty woman. She hardly allows William space to say anything!*

 Molotov says:

*You're right, her words seem to tower over William with cruel, breathtaking honesty! She says that her rage is a measure of her love.*

 Moriarty says:

*I don't understand this love-rage thing - 'If I do rage it is because I have gained an almost-colossus of a man' ? What's Ann trying to say?*

 Molotov says:

*I think it's again Shakespeare trying to invoke the idea in his audience that women are more insightful, more intuitive – that Ann discerns in William some greatness, some potential which he himself cannot see. And the reason she is so outraged is because William seems to have become blinded to his own abilities by all that has happened in his past life – especially with Thomas.*

Cecelia says:

*An 'almost-colossus' means he's of small stature – for all we know he might even be a dwarf. And she's angry simply because she loves him so much. There's a lot of love in Shakespeare.*

Wrecking Ball says:

*What crap! There's hardly a single snog anywhere in Shakespeare! Where's the love in Macbeth – there's blood and lies all over the stage? Where's the love in Hamlet – there's just poison and ghosts blowing wind up peoples' knickers? And come to think of it, there's not one mouthwatering snog in all of Romeo and Juliet!*

Cecelia says:

*But love is more than kisses Wrecking Ball! I think you need some tenderness in your life.*

Molotov says:

*In William's answer we can get a glimpse of the truth because he says he thought he was engaged ('betrothed') to the night, but was 'wedded to the Sun'. In other words he thought he was going to marry someone dark and chaotic but instead he was married to Ann, a woman whose sharp, bright light (insight) remorselessly exposes William's shortcomings, his blindness, his weaknesses and foibles. It's almost as if the character of William has become a mouth-piece for Shakespeare's own opinions regarding women.*

Cecelia says: *She's still a bully.*

 Moriarty says:

**The next piece of script in Ann's reply is too squashed together for me to read –** it looks something like *'light stretch out'* **and** *'opague...grave'.*

 Wrecking Ball says:

**It's too fucking scribbly! I mean what does** *'Then letmc lignt streth auf heyard the opague stend oc this grave thou olisseet far thuseef'* **mean? You want us to stay on topic with stuff we can't read! Bollocks!** **@ Cecelia: You wanna give me some tenderness? I'm open to offers.**

 Molotov says:

**If you look at what went before, Ann's reply makes perfect sense. William exclaims he was married to the Sun, so immediately Ann replies** *'Then let my light stretch out beyond the opaque stench of this grave thou diggest for thyself'.* **Again Ann is saying 'Let me see for you.' She even goes further in the next line and says** *'Use not, William, thyself to see.'*

 Swamp Dog says:

**Does she say he has to bite his own eyeballs!?**

 Molotov says:

**Indeed she does** – *'rip out thine eyes and between thy teeth burst their apparitions and falsehoods'.*

 Swamp Dog says:

**That's gross!**

 Moriarty says:

**Ann doesn't really mean it literally. She's trying to help William get rid of his delusions.**

Molotov says:

*She calls his delusions a 'grievous distemper' which makes him see only the 'tantalising chaos of despair'.*

Moriarty says:

*Is she – or Shakespeare – implying here that despair is tempting him to fall apart – a bit like tempting him to have a nervous breakdown?*

Molotov says:

*Well 'tantalising chaos' could mean she thinks William is vulnerable, that he can be enticed by his delusions to let go of his personality and embrace despair. Hard to know exactly, but the effect Ann's words have on William is devastating because he pleads with her to 'Spare me Ann! Say no more!' – as though she is some executioner holding a knife of words against his throat.*

Wrecking Ball says:

*Holy crap! She's now seeing ghosts! It says 'She stops a ghost!'*

Cecelia says:

*You silly cupcake! It doesn't say 'She stops a ghost!' It says 'She stops aghast' – because she's seen something shocking on William's neck.*

Swamp Dog says:

*Hey! I'm cupcake!*

Cecelia says:

*Don't be jealous Swamp Dog! And anyway, I thought you didn't like me calling you cupcake?*

Swamp Dog says:

*I sort of got used to it.*

Cecelia says:

*O you sweet, shy muffin! I could chew you up!*

Molotov says:

**Yes, Ann notices a red mark around William's neck – a 'bruised circle of violence' as she calls it. William's answer is that he must really have been hung from a gallows, but Ann counters with – yes, you have, but only from the gallows of your mind.**

Wrecking Ball says:

**Because he's mad – right?**

Molotov says:

**Not exactly – he's just suffered a terrifying hallucination not because he's mad but because of the strength of feeling he had – or still has – for his former lover, Thomas Morton – a lover who, just minutes before, has taken his own life.**

Moriarty says:

**@ Molotov: Which begs the question if Ann can see some red swelling around William's neck, then how can the hallucination belong to only one person? Ann could not see the ghost of Thomas but she can see the mark around William's neck – which is evidence that something supernatural has happened.**

Wrecking Ball says:

**Or she could be just as mad as he is – right? I mean they both seem stuck in orbit around a fluffy mouse. Shakespeare could be just pulling the wool – right?**

Cecelia says:

*Sweetie, this is probably not Shakespeare, but a very itty-bitty imitation of him. The real Shakespeare would have used richer language, you know with loads of strange, half-forgotten words that no one uses anymore, like 'exsufflicate', or 'dungy', or 'twiggen'. Whoever wrote this piece only has a modern vocab at his or her fingertips.*

Molotov says:

*Correct. Somehow the writing feels too contrived, almost as though it has been 'Elizabethanised' on purpose. And the other thing I've noticed is that the ideas and thoughts in this play are somehow expressed in too straightforward a manner. For example, there is no struggling for a meaning, no long, tortuous syntax to unravel as there is in real Shakespearean dialogue. I know in what I've written above, I've often referred to the author as 'Shakespeare', but the more I've read the more doubtful I've become. Put simply, the dialogue is too easy. Shakespeare had a much more complex way of writing, he was very fond of a style where statements seem to bite their own tail – the very thing which makes real Shakespearean dialogue so taxing and so exciting.*

Brian Jones says:

*@ Molotov: Sorry to perhaps dent your doubts, but Professor Osborne from Oxford – the guy doing the carbon dating – has just emailed me to say that the tallow used in the metal box has a date between 1585 and 1610. This would place the tallow in the correct century. But he says we must be cautious and wait for confirmation – or otherwise – from the other two labs dating the tallow. However, if you think the writing is not that of Shakespeare then whose is it?*

Moriarty says:

*This is just a thought, and please shoot me down if you don't think it's worth considering. But is it possible that Shakespeare did write these pages and the reason the language is so 'easy' is because when it was written Shakespeare was in his declining years? Maybe he had lost his linguistic versatility, become less articulate – he might even have been suffering from Alzheimer's or some form of dementia that robbed him of his mental agility? We just don't know.*

 Molotov says:

*The date of the tallow doesn't really say anything conclusive because if this is a forgery, the forger could easily have got hold of tallow from the sixteenth century (a stock of very old church candles?). The real test for me will be the dating of the paper and ink. This is what revealed the so-called 'Hitler's Diaries' to be such amateurish forgeries. If both the paper and, more especially the ink, are confirmed by all three labs to be from the latter part of the sixteenth century, then I'm back on board.*

 Brian Jones says:

*@Molotov: But why do you say 'and more especially the ink'?*

 Molotov says:

*Because it is entirely conceivable that a forger somehow found blank paper from the sixteenth century – in an antiquarian book for example. There are plenty of libraries around the world with volumes from this period – how do we know if the forger didn't get hold of a copy with enough blank pages on which to write? The dating of the ink is however crucial because I do not believe it is possible to get hold of ink - that's still usable - which was made in the sixteenth century.*

Passion Fruit says:

*This story of Thomas and William has touched a nerve in my soul that is still raw and painful. I have refrained from commenting until now because my own situation is very precarious – let's just say I've often blindly tip-toed on both sides of the line that separates life from death.*

 Cecelia says:

*You poor thing! You must keep well away from that line! Can I help to keep you safe? Tell me about when you came out?*

 Brian Jones says:

*@Passion Fruit: Maybe you would do better on a different thread? I'm sure there are blogs out there that would help you to express yourself.*

 Passion Fruit says:

*I was always out but didn't know it. I was born, so my parents told me, under a ruby moon and they called me Jack – a name I have always hated. But by the time I reached fourteen I just knew I had to make the move to Susanne or I never would. I knew that if I didn't call myself the name which seemed to be calling out to me from my innermost heart, I would live the rest of my life avoiding the fake portrait of myself in the mirror. I would always see myself as a stranger to myself, a fraud, a manikin frozen with disgrace. So one day I became Susanne.*

 Moriarty says:

*@Passion Fruit: This blog is about a play that might turn out to be the last thing Shakespeare ever wrote for the theatre. Not sure how your life story fits in?*

Cecelia says:

*Of course Passion Fruit's life story 'fits in' – you dough ball! She said William and Thomas's plight has burnt a hole through her solar plexus – as it has mine. She belongs with us!*

Passion Fruit says:

*Thank you Cecelia – as you can guess 'acceptance' has been a major issue throughout my entire life. When I was a kid, and long before I reached any realisation about my sexuality, it used to feel like there were millions of tiny, seismic tremors and shocks, all unmistakably piling up along fault lines in my body and that it was just a matter of time before the crust, the mask of my identity ripped apart and let out the leviathan within me. At the time I was still in short pants and so I didn't, or couldn't, know what this anxiety was all about. In the bright chaos of my childhood mind I felt I was destined to be anything my imagination wished.*

Cecelia says:

*Not too sure about the leviathan bit, but I think I know what you mean. I always wanted a child, always longed to be a mother but it just didn't happen and now it's too late – I've stopped laying eggs! So was it only when you were fourteen that you realised you wanted to be Susanne?*

Wrecking Ball says:

*Cecelia! I thought you were about 28 with smooth hips and firm apple breasts! But now I read you've got a pear-shaped bum and tits dragging the ground! No matter how much tenderness you give I just don't think my manhood could ever rise to the challenge!*

Molotov says:

*@Brian Jones: Brian could we have a look at page 8 please before I go mad and abandon this blog.*

Brian Jones says:

*Dear Molotov I understand your frustration. I am trying to find a fix for my blocked delete function, but the virus is proving to be inaccessible. In the meantime please try to ignore the posts off topic. Here is page 8.*

Ann: Who is it darest wake the living with the dead!? Gabriel! Wherefore comest thou at this dread hour?

Gabriel: Ann! Let me in quickly! The Morton's will have their claws into William's face! Hurry!

(William and Ann both descend and let Gabriel inside)

William: Your voice speaks of bloody revenge, what dreadful matter has happened Gabriel?

Gabriel: The youngest Morton, Thomas, he more than older beloved William, was found hanging in the wood by his sister - Celine. The Morton father, spitting blood and fire, is even now on his way here, strong-armed with brothers and clan all blind in anger to aid the family of its ill-perceived shame! William you must flee this very instant!

William: I cannot I cannot leave Ann and my children to have their throats to mass, ungodly slaughter!

Ann: William! No as Gabriel says! Gabriel will at speed and wake our father and the family! Tell them what has occurred and raise them here with haste, well-armed and prepared to save their daughter's and grand-children's lives. Hurry!

Gabriel: William fear not, I will use the shield of my soul and body to protect Ann and the little ones - that I promise thee. But do not take the main road. Use the forest tracks thou knowest so well and go only afoot at night until Oxford. Adieu! (exit Gabriel) 8.

Moriarty says:

*Looks like Ann's brother Gabriel has arrived to warn William he must make a run for it – the Morton clan is coming for his blood.*

Passion Fruit says:

*@ Moriarty: You see! William could be me – I was also a fugitive!*
*@Cecelia: Yes, it was only when I hit puberty, at about fourteen or fifteen, that the whole universe of my personality shifted dramatically towards Susanne and the being of woman. Almost overnight I fell in love with myself and the whole feminine world. I adored the way women could flaunt and celebrate their bodies, the way they could push their breasts into the faces of mankind, wear eyelashes and eyeliner, wear gorgeous lipstick and paint their finger and toe nails blue, green or red. For the first time in my life I realised how women could attract and play with the narrow-minded desires of men, and of just how 'primitive' men were with their silly compulsion to fill holes. In particular I dreamt of growing my hair into a long, sensuous river down my back, and when, eventually, I did sense my tresses swinging against my naked shoulders, the feeling was so delicious I almost cried.*

Molotov says:

*Notice how Ann again comes across as the decisive pragmatist. She orders Gabriel to fetch help while at the same time tells William to do as Gabriel suggests. Any chance we can have page 9 Brian?*

Brian Jones says:

*Page 9 looks like the end of scene ii in Act 1. I like Ann's last lines.*

Ann : William! Come dress quickly! I'll prepare a sack!

(William dresses hastily with heavy coat and boots etc, while Ann takes a large sack into the kitchen and throws provender inside for the journey. When he is ready they embrace.)

William: I will aim for London and lose myself in its multitudes. I will find employment and send thee what I can, and when all this tearful chaos has past I promise I will return. Kiss me children everyday with my love, let them not forget me. Ann, thou art the certainty of the Sun with its axis deep embedded in my heart. Without thee and without my love for thee, I would but cruise and tumble through the impenetrable obscurity of space like some meaningless fragment of death.

Ann : Tush William! Such wild flatteries will delay your life! You must hurry! Go across these dank fields yonder! Go! Go!

William : One flesh and again one flesh is love's tender price,
One flesh and again one flesh is man's game of dice.

(exit William)

Ann : O Will!
In the threat of night thou must turn from thy loving wife,
In the threat of night to find thyself and save thy life.

9.

Cecelia says:

*@Passion Fruit: You're right many men are very simple-minded around sex. Have you ever noticed the creepy similarity between sex and sport? So often the sport involves getting a very obvious small, 'white' ball into a very obvious 'hole' – and when this happens the men go orgasmic! Just look at the way men behave in football – each player is like a single sperm engaged in a bitter, life-and-death competition with his rivals – he's got to battle his way around obstacles, fight, cheat, swear and literally do anything just to get the precious 'white' ball into that gaping 'hole'! Then they flaunt their big muscular legs and wear brightly coloured boots on the end as though what they are really doing is trying to display the bright, red swelling at the top of their penises! Somehow it's so pitiful to see all these highly coloured penises running around desperately try to get their seed into the big hole – and when this finally happens, the men fall down, hug and kiss each other as though experiencing some collective, tribal orgasm.*

Molotov says:

*After all the practicalities William almost blurts out his true feelings for Ann and what she has truly come to mean in his life. He seems to realise he may not see her again but nevertheless he confesses that she has become some sort of profound anchor and that without his love for her he would* 'but cruise and tumble through the impenetrable obscurity of space like some meaningless fragment of death'.

Passion Fruit says:

*@ Molotov: I once felt like that – a meaningless fragment of death...but chance intervened.*
*@ Cecelia: But what about golf?*

Cecelia says:

*Exactly! Just look at golf! Does the shape of a golf club not remind you of anything? And what about the 'white' golf ball dropping into the discrete, little 'hole', and the golfer waving his 'club' high in the air as a sign of his orgasmic triumph? – is it not all so clearly a benign substitute for intercourse?*

Moriarty says:

*But Ann seems to chastise William in a friendly way telling him that such flattery will 'delay' (?) his life. Not sure if it's 'delay' or 'delas' – but 'delay' is the only one that makes any sense here. What I don't understand is William's parting couplet where he says 'One flesh and again one flesh is love's tender price, One flesh and again one flesh is man's game of dice'? Is he saying this to himself or to Ann? It's unclear.*

Molotov says:

*I think he could be saying this more as a parting clue for the audience. I interpret it as meaning love's 'tender' cost is the physical union of two people, but who you actually end up having a sexual relationship with – regardless of gender – is very often a game of chance? What do you think?*

Moriarty says:

*But are you sure this 'one flesh and again one flesh' is a reference to a sexual union?*

Passion Fruit says:

*@ Moriarty: If two people make 'one flesh' it can only happen when they are naked together – to me it's obvious.*
*@ Cecelia: OK, then what about tennis – your theory doesn't work?*

Cecelia says:

*Don't you believe it! Tennis is a little like homosexual foreplay – the white globule of seed/egg flies backwards and forwards as though neither side wants it, but when one player get the ball 'in' and the other player 'misses', again the winner drops to his or her knees and rolls around on the floor as though in a barely controllable state of orgasm. I know in all these cases people will say it is the 'release of tension' – but isn't that exactly what a sexual climax is all about?*

Molotov says:

*@ Moriarty: It's a reference from the Christian bible which has become an unmistakable euphemism for sexual union.*

Wrecking Ball says:

*Holy crap! I go away for a bath and when I return everyone's talking about tennis, sex and the bible!*

Olga says:

*'Euphemism' is English joke for orgasm – no? I can do also sex euphemes at special price.*

Moriarty says:

*Ann's last lines are pretty neat – 'In the threat of night thou must turn from thy loving wife, In the threat of night to find thyself and save thy life.'*

Molotov says:

*Me too. I especially like 'to find thyself' because maybe it's a passing reference to the Socratic 'know thyself', and William, of course, who might have problems around his sexual orientation, is leaving his wife and three small children, to not only 'save' his life, but also to discover what type of sexual person his really is, where on the sexual continuum does he feel he belongs?*

Cecelia says:

*@ Passion Fruit: What did you mean when you said '....but chance intervened'? What happened when you became Susanne?*

Passion Fruit says:

*Well Cecelia, when I reached sixteen I knew what I wanted. But I was absolutely determined not to see this change in my identity as some violent, ugly breaking point, or as some inconceivable catastrophe or unmentionable scandal. No way! I was going to welcome it, rejoice and celebrate. For me it was going to be like my first menstruation, the first sign that my body was awash with fertility – or something like that. Anyway with these crazy ideas in my mind I knew puberty was going to be my one chance to undergo a delicious metamorphosis. At night, as I lay in the dark wrapped in my duvet, I imagined myself as a chrysalis, a cocooned, new embryo being magically rearranged. So when the moment came for me to emerge, I knew I wanted to do it with so much splendour and vivacious glamour, that the whole world would bite its tongue with awe and admiration.*

Moriarty says: *Brian! Hurry! Scene (iii) please!*

Brian Jones says:
*Sorry for delay – having uploading issues – will upload it asap.*

Cecelia says:
*So did the world bite its tongue? How did you come out?*

Passion Fruit says:
*When that wonderful morning came it was a normal school day. Both my parents – who knew nothing about my decision – had already left for work, so I was alone in the house. My school was just a half an hour's walk from where we lived so I wasn't rushed. The school didn't have a uniform so I could wear more-or-less what I liked – and that morning that's exactly what I did. From long, secret practice I pulled on a pair of black tights, then a short, clinging denim skirt. With a bit of fiddling I fixed on a bra and padded out my breasts with little rolls of tissue paper. Then I threw over my head a long black jumper which I pulled in at the waist with a thin, bright red belt that matched my flat, ever-so-sweet red leather shoes. O god, when I look back at how sexy I was that day! I could almost cry. Anyway, next I fluffed out my hair so that it looked a little wild, applied eye-shadow and a hint of eye-liner and then smeared a touch of sandalwood oil where my jumper met my neck. Susanne, I said to myself, would definitely not choose a gaudy, glitzy red lipstick – so instead I used a faint red glaze. The final touch – which gave me a real feminine sparkle – was a pair of tiny, silver, so-discrete stud ear rings that caught the light like beautiful, miniature stars. Susanne, I now felt, was ready – I was coy, pretty and utterly delicious.*

Scene iii

(At night, a forest track)

William: How far have I come?
But is not the more yielding question — how
far with love have I come?
Or should I not say 'How far 'in' love
have I come?'
Or how far 'to' love? Or 'from' love?
Or 'for' love?
Perhaps 'towards' love would suit better.
Strange how each tiny preposition gives to each
'love' its own ~~new~~ new, oblique understanding,
As though mere words, just by using here and
there a tricksy prefix, suffix or crude con-
figuration of epithets, can push so many
meanings in so many directions. But can love
have a language built from utterance?
What words then can enshrine poor, sweet
Thomas, my first ever love? What const thou,
Thomas, now be ~~someone else's~~ someone else's breath?
O Thomas, as a bird which hath crashed
against the glass, how fell like a soft
angel to my pillow and lay stunned and
shy in my arms, thy tiny heart racing with
love's ~~all-honeyest~~ pain. Wherever thou art,
Thomas, know I loved thee so truly that,
had ~~not~~ the world despised us, I would
have gladly wedded with thee into whatever
~~dark~~ bliss exists beyond eternity.
And Ann and our ~~sweet~~ babes, my second
one. When first we met I was an almost-dead
fist, a ~~bare~~ youth, down and falling apart in
the surf, yearning for air, gasping for just one
breathless atom of meaning in this chaotic,
~~mucky~~ sewer called life! So why Ann didst
thou love me so? I was nothing, I brought nothing
and I remain nothing, so why—                    ©.

59

Moriarty says:
*It's another long 'silo' Swamp Dog!*

Cecelia says:
*Moriarty! You're being mean!*

Swamp Dog says:
*If we ever meet, Mori-fucking-farty, I'll tie your foreskin to a rocket.*

Wrecking Ball says:
*Don't worry Swamp Dog, Mori-fucking-farty sounds like a dry wanker – the sort of person who couldn't have an emotional relationship with a sock.*

Brian Jones says:
*Gentlemen please!*

Cecelia says:
*@ Passion Fruit: So what happened when you got to school?*

Passion Fruit says:
*When I walked through the school gates my heart was hammering so much I thought it was trying to get inside my head and make me blush even more than I was. I suppose I expected whistles, cat-calls, oooos and ahhhhs but nothing happened, the kids in the playground just milled about in groups as normal. No one seemed to recognise me, I was just another new kid.*

Molotov says:
*Scene (iii) starts with William alone in a forest at night still obsessed about love. It's almost like he's trying to make sense of his own position by trying out all the prepositions he can sensibly fix to the word love.*

Moriarty says:

*But then he suddenly seems to give up and declare that language is not sufficient to capture what love is. That's what I make of the line – 'But can love have a language built of utterance?' It looks like William is trying to find the right words, not just to describe his own feelings of love, but to understand the whole 'thing' of loving someone else.*

 Molotov says:

*You're right. This was a train of thought that Shakespeare often explored especially in his sonnets, that love was beyond the reach of language, that trying to express in words what love is, actually spoils it.*

 Cecelia says:

*But surely someone must have recognised you? What about your friends? or the teachers?*

 Passion Fruit says:

*Well, yes they did eventually. A big sixth former, who I'd seen around but didn't know, came up to me and asked in a friendly way, 'Hi, I'm Andrew – you new?' Of course, inside I yelled out 'Yes I'm most definitely NEW!', but instead, I said nothing and just smiled, nodded and scanned the playground for someone I recognised.*

 Swamp Dog says:

*What's a 'fumigation of epithets' mean?*

 Wrecking Ball says:

*Isn't an 'epithet' a laxative? Then William's got the skitters. Well, he is alone, at night, in a forest – stands to reason. I think that's what Shakespeare really wants to say. Roaming around in the pitch dark in the sixteenth century –  it's enough to give Tarzan the heebie-geebies.*

Molotov says:

*This problem of the limitations of speech to describe human emotions, is repeated half-way down the page when William asks 'What words then can enshrine poor, sweet Thomas, my first ever love?'*

 Cecelia says:

*@Molotov: I guess love has inspired more poetry than any other emotion?*

*@ Passion Fruit: But someone must have recognised you when you went into class? What happened at morning registration – your new name, Susanne, wouldn't have been in the register?*

 Moriarty says:

*But then I do like the following rhetorical question when William asks his memory of Thomas 'What canst thou, Thomas, now be but someone else's breath?' – as though the spirit of the dead lives on in the mouths of the living.*

 Passion Fruit says:

*Of course not – I went and sat in my old place, but this was only after a near riot broke out in the corridor. But the name-calling started outside. I walked across the playground towards Kate, an old friend of mine from primary, but before I reached her some boy screamed out 'O shit! Look at Jack!' Then more voices full of surprise and almost panic, began to shout things like 'O my god! He's a trany!' 'Jack's a trany!' 'Ratch man! Jack's a trany with a fanny!'*

 Cecelia says:
*You poor thing! It must have been so horrible! Adolescents can be so cruel! What did you do?*

 Moriarty says:
*William likens Thomas to a bird that 'fell like a soft angel to my pillow'.*

Ezekiel says:

*The only fallen angel here is Satan! His tongue reaches out from the sodomite's anus to mock at the world of the righteous! And ye that indulge in the same hissing laughter, ye that lap seed from the tips of each other's genitals, yea that draw seed down thy throats, have defiled the pure soul the Lord God gave thee! These two men, William and Thomas, are full of homosexual poison and are thereby damned for all eternity to blister in Hell. Brian Jones, be warned, good Christian men have you in their sights. If you do not take down this shameless depravity, the consequences will be harsh indeed.*

 Wrecking Ball says:

*Do the world a favour Ezekiel – go shag a meat-grinder.*

 Molotov says:

*@ Brian: Maybe you should take these threats seriously? We all know what fanatics can get up to. This is the worst form of religion because it has no respect for human dignity. It has its own definition of what and how humans should behave – a definition that is meant to enslave and subjugate all other definitions. If I was in your shoes Brian I would be careful and maybe think of looking into some police protection?*

 Brian Jones says:

*Thanks for your concern Molotov, but I think this play – which might possibly be Shakespeare's last – belongs to everyone and no amount of threatening or bullying will stop me from showing it to the world. If we have the freedom to think but don't have the freedom to say what we think, then it's like being free inside a prison. That's what I think anyway. As for the gay thing – if two people love each other, they love each other, and that's the end of it. I have no right to judge it as 'good' or 'bad'. Live and let live has always been my motto.*

 The Redeemer says:

*This is the arrogance of the libertine! God dictates, we obey! All else is heinous sin!*

Swamp Dog says:

*Is a 'libertine' a fruit like a tangerine?*

 Wrecking Ball says:

**You bet Swamp Dog! His clothes just peel off revealing his naked skin oozing with juice and seed! Just the thing for Ezekiel and the Redeemer!**

 Passion Fruit says:

**What did I do? I blew a kiss at one of the boys taunting me and he ran off screaming across the playground. But the girls were great. They surrounded me to shield me from the boys and their comments, then they asked me about my clothes and ear rings, but more especially they all wanted to know about my breasts. But before I could tell them I was using padding, the bell went and we started walking into the main building for registration.**

 Molotov says:

**A fair and humble philosophy to live by Brian.**

 Moriarty says:

**Have you read what William says about his love for Thomas – it's quite moving? He says (to the Thomas in his imagination) that if the world had not despised them, he would have gladly married 'with thee [Thomas]** *into whatever dark bliss exists beyond eternity'.*

 Molotov says:

**I suspect William's conscience must be sorely troubled because in the last – what twelve hours? – he has learnt of the loss of his first ever lover to suicide – a person he abandoned because of the social stigma. Now, suddenly, he's had to abandon his wife and children and flee his home town. He knows he is a hunted man and here he is, hours later, going blindly through the darkness towards London, where he knows no one, talking to himself, reviewing what love has done to his life so far. There's a bitter-sweet sadness here that's somehow hard to define.**

Cecelia says:
*So what's this riot you wrote about? What happened at registration?*

 Passion Fruit says:
*Well upstairs, near my form room, there was a much bigger crowd of boys hanging about waiting for me, and when I appeared on the stairs they all began whistling and shouting insults. Then, naturally, my form teacher stuck his head through the door to see what all the commotion was about, but when he saw me he froze as though he'd suddenly been doused in liquid nitrogen. 'Jack?' he half-whispered to himself, but I didn't answer. Instead, trying to be the super calm queen, I walked passed him and went and sat in my usual place next to Jason.*

 Moriarty says:
*And further down he describes the state he was in when he met Ann – it looks to me like he's saying he was an 'almost dead fish...falling apart in the surf'. My guess is he met Ann on the rebound?*

 Molotov says:
*There's probably more to it than that because they seem to have married in a hurry – maybe Ann was pregnant? Also in a small town the pressure to conform must have been enormous and certainly would not have encompassed tolerance of a gay relationship with a sixteen year old youth. When William was robbed of Thomas he probably did fall apart emotionally but he was savvy enough to see that to be socially accepted he needed to be involved with a woman and, if possible, to marry her. But just look at the cynical, almost despairing way, in which he describes life: 'I was... a bony youth....gasping for just one breathless atom of meaning in this chaotic, murky sewer called life!' He's in his early twenties and already he's describing life as a sewer! He's growing up fast. Normally you'd expect such profound existential disillusionment to be the prerogative of wise, old savants with white beards, not a young, healthy man on the threshold of adult life.*

Cecelia says:
*I bet Jason was thrilled!*

Passion Fruit says:
*No way! He was terrified! He yelled out - 'I'm not sitting next to a bum fucker!' and sprang out of his seat and stood against the wall. I got up, went over to him and whispered 'Jason, don't be afraid, I'm not interested in your bum – maybe later, when we're alone', and I stroked his cheek! – god I was such bitch! But he was such a tempting victim! He stood there, his eyes bulging with terror, staring at the ceiling, speechless and with a face like wet paper! But just then the head teacher arrived.*

Molotov says:
*In such a state William asks himself why Ann loves him so much especially as he sees himself as worthless and tarnished. But he appears to be cut off at the bottom of page 10. Brian, please let us have page 11.*

Swamp Dog says:
*Shakespeare went surfing? Cos it says he was down and falling in the surf. So it can only mean he was once a beachcomber – probably a pot-head. And he says he sees himself as a fish in a sewer, so he's clearly halluminating.*

Cecelia says:
*@Swamp Dog – you're such a silly sweet pickle! You're so unique!*
*@Passion Fruit: Bit mean to practice your feminine charm on poor Jason! Did it work on the head teacher?*

Brian Jones says:
*Page 11 looks like a gruesome one – I can see something about the 'Oxfordshire cannibals'. Here it is.....*

(William spies the light of a fire in the forest)

Hold and quiet! What villainous light is that? Out here in the depths of nowhere live only the wretched, untameable scraps of humanity; diseased men and women who would hail thee as a friend and then use thy upturned skull as a bowl for their soup. Oft have I heard of the Oxfordshire cannibals, but it's said that all those who have seen them ended their journey as excrement on the forest floor. Rest I wide skirt this beacon of culinary delights and —

— Arrrrg!

(Rough hands pull William to the ground. Struggling and protesting William is dragged towards the fire. Once at the fire he is tied to a stake facing the blaze. His legs are splayed apart and tied down. He is stripped naked except for an open shirt that's left hanging from his shoulders. Before him stand the three Morton brothers.)

Hick Morton : Well William thou cometh like a moff flutterin' to de slaughterin' flame! O fut fuckin' fut! Makes we poor eyes shed tears o' blood for yor it does!

William : Let me go you revengeful cretins!

(Judd Morton draws his sword and points it closely at William's exposed genitals)

Judd Morton : Der's de cause of all our troubles!

William : Thou art the cause of all —

Hick Morton : Chut it! Hold Judd! We ain't prop'ly welcomed our patient! Let me introduce

((

Passion Fruit says:

*You must be joking, he was repulsive! The girls used to joke that he had testicles like shriveled prunes! Anyway, when he arrived – looking as usual like a human ferret – he took one glance at me, and squeaked with his ferrety voice 'Jack Southerland – to my office now'. 'My name is Susanne,' I answered quietly, 'I will go when you call me by my real name.' The ferret glanced with these red, pin-prick eyes at my form teacher, looked around the room at the rows of dumbstruck students, then back at me and said 'This is no time to play games Jack or test my patience.' 'I'm not. I just want you to call me by my real name – that's not a lot to ask.'*

 Moriarty says:

*He sees the light of a fire and immediately assumes that it is the 'untamable scraps of humanity', cannibals who live in the forests of Oxfordshire.*

 Brian Jones says:

*Ah! He's been ambushed by the Morton brothers! This should be interesting!*

 Cecelia says:

*So did the ferret do as you asked? That would have been a sort of victory.*

 Passion Fruit says:

*He did – but I couldn't help slapping him in the face with a sarky comment, because when he said 'Very well, for the sake of peace and co-operation...Susanne Southerland please come to my office immediately and stop this...this charade', I replied 'I can't go with you alone – you know a girl can't be too careful these days.' Shit! I was soooo cheeky! 'Indeed! Indeed!' he shrilled like only a ferret can. Then my friend Kate called out 'I'll go with! Me and Ja- Susanne are mates!' 'Very well! Very well! This is no place for theatrical scenes! To my office now, the both of you!' And with that he vanished.*

Swamp Dog says:

*They're going to burn him alive on stage!? No way! And what does '...me poor eyes shed kars of blood' mean?*

Wrecking Ball says:

*William's got some guts, because even though he's naked, tied up and almost on fire, he still has the chutzpah to call the Morton brothers 'revengeful cretins' to their faces.*

Swamp Dog says:

*And it looks like they've left his tackle swinging in the breeze!*

Molotov says:

*But look at the malicious sarcasm which Hick Morton uses when he says at the bottom of the page 'we ain't prop'ly welcomed our patient'. As though they've captured, stripped and bound William in order to help him!*

Cecelia says:

*@ Molotov: Poor Shakespeare! They're obviously going to kill him – it's three against one – the play will end before it's started! @ Passion Fruit: So did you and your friend Kate go to his office? What did he say?*

Moriarty says:

*@ Cecelia: Again you are falsely assuming that the 'William' in this play is Shakespeare – but there is no evidence that this is an autobiographical play. In fact we still don't have any real concrete facts that this isn't a total fabricated sham. Many on this blog and elsewhere have already noted that the language is too sparse compared to the linguistic and conceptual density that Shakespearean text usually exhibits. Brian, can you upload page 12 please?*

Brian Jones says: *Here we go.*

docktor fudd 'ere, hoo, as thou canst see, is a skilled blood-letter. Onlie 'e dun't use leeches or 'ot suckin' bells — O no! 'e's far too skilled wiv all sorts o' rusty blades. fudd, say hello.

fudd Morton (spitting on William): Ritch-lickin' faggot!

Hick Morton: Little 'ot-'eaded is our fudd. Now der's docktor Skellp 'ere — young to de trade 'e is, but so fuckin' keen! Ain't yer Skell!? 'e wants t'sharpen 'is talents in middlin' faggots like thee o' such interno-hearts as wot infect thair gizzards an' guts. Onlie 'cos 'e's just learnin' an' all, 'e keeps makin' some 'orrific mistakes. Skell, say 'ello to our patient.

Skell Morton: Debauched devil!

Hick Morton: An' den der's me, docktor 'ick — or docktor Grievous — take yer pick. But William thou knowest all about me don't yer? 'Cos it auz me wot iscovered thee an' our Thomas heddled togever wrapped up like two virgin girls.

fudd Morton: You 'ad yer sex-roots up each other like sick bastards! Set me skin all a'crawlin' wiv maggots just f'tinkin' 'bout it! Sticks in me 'ead like a ... a ... like a disgustin' glue. Everytime I closes me eyes I see youze ruttin' away, fartin' an' moanin' like whores at it in the street!

William: We were young and in love.

Hick Morton: Love!? In Love!? Thou callest that nameless, shameless thigh-slappin' love!? Man-on-man filth ain't love! Real men don't love each other — real men hate each other!

fudd Morton: Come on 'ick! Der's too much yappin'! De night's draggin' on, let's get on wiv it!

12.

Passion Fruit says:

*When we were in his office the ferret looked even more like a small, red-eyed rodent sitting behind a vast desk. After we closed the door he said 'Now Jack, Susanne – or whatever you want to call yourself – what's this all about? Do your parents know? You can't come to school with a different identity, a different errr…' He began to stumble for the word, so I helped him, 'Sexuality? Why not? There's nothing in the school rules to say I can't?' I suggested. 'That's not the point!' he squeaked. 'So what is the point?' I demanded. His whiskers twitched and he adjusted some papers on the desk in front of him as though again searching for the right words. 'You…you are being disruptive! Your dress is far too provocative! Far too menacing! You are much too…err'. Again I helped him with the 's' word, 'Sexual?' 'Indeed! It's unacceptable and…and just not right!'*

 Cecelia says:

*He sounds like someone trapped by his own thinking – or rather trapped by his own thoughtless sexuality. Could be he found you attractive? – which is why he said you were too 'menacing'. Maybe you woke in him the Gorgon of his own secret yearning for gay love?*

 Molotov says:

*The lethal sarcasm is almost unbearable because at the top of page 12 Hick Morton introduces his brother as 'Docktor Judd…a skilled blood-letter…' Then he continues, calling his other brother, Skelly, and himself, both 'Docktors'. This sarcasm is supposed to create the sense of looming murder, of mean, giant cats circling their helpless prey before they tear it apart. What exactly they are going to do we don't know. But it appears that he and William have met before – 'Cos it wuz me wot 'scovered thee an' our Thomas bedded togever wrapped up like two virgin girls.'*

 Moriarty says:

*Judd Morton then comes out with a homophobic rant, but William answers innocently that he and Thomas were just young and in love.*

Molotov says:

*But read how Hick Morton replies – he gets so tangled up in his own logic that he finishes by condemning the whole masculine world as something driven only by hatred. He shouts - 'Thou callest that....love!? Man-on-man filth ain't love!? Real men don't love each other! Real men hate each other!' I'm keen to see what happens on the next page! Brian any chance?*

 Passion Fruit says:

*Perhaps. But who knows what tangled up ball of emotional string was inside his head? Anyway he then said 'I'm contacting your parents and sending you home. I'm suspending you for 2 days and unless you can return to school as Jack Harris, further, more severe disciplinary measures – such as permanent exclusion – will have to be considered. A taxi is waiting down in the main car park to take you home. Good day.' 'That's not fair!' Kate objected, 'You can't tell him what sexual orientation to have! It's his choice and none of your business!' 'It is my business,' the Head squeaked back, 'when Jack is in my school dressed like a tart provoking homosexual anarchy!' That made me so angry, so I challenged, 'My name's Susanne and I don't like you calling me a tart!' Then raising his voice he replied, 'You have two days to sort yourself out, now leave!' 'Well if Susanne's a tart, you're a prick!' Kate shouted as we left. 'Two days!', the ferret yelled behind us through the closing door.*

 Brian Jones says:

*Here's page 13. I can see nipples all down the page! I must say this play seems very much about love but this blog seems very much about by sex – good human emotions I guess, but I wonder where it's leading? When I look through the pages still to come I can see the characters of 'First and Second Beggars', of 'Edward', of 'Queen Elizabeth' and 'Walsingham' and of 'Priests and Soldiers'. At a glance Page 13 looks like William is trying to talk his way out of his 'looming murder' as you called it Molotov.*

**Hick Morton:** Alright fudd! Alright! Now, bein' dockter it's onlie right an' proper we've got to cure de patient.

**William:** It's you Mortons that need curing — I'd rather die with my love than live with your hate.

**Hick Morton:** Shut thy mouth! Thou hast no position to give me any 'rather this and rather that.'

**William:** Stop playing with me! kill me if you must! But spare my wife and children — they never harmed the Mortons.

**Hick Morton:** Kill thee!? O gawd no! We ain't no common, shoe-string cut-throats! 'Ow can we cure thee of being a woman one day and a man the next, if we kills thee?

**Judd Morton:** Get on wiv it 'ick! Stop yaffin'. Cut off what we said and let's go 'ome.

**Hick Morton:** Right thou art fudd! So, t'cure thee of bein' an' 'alf woman, we 'as got to cut off thy nips.

**William:** That being so, Hick Morton, thou art too a woman.

**Hick Morton:** Shut it!

**William:** All men have got nipples.

**Hick Morton:** I said shut it!

**Judd Morton:** Wot's 'e sayin'?

**Stelly Morton:** Never thought o'dat. Den...den wot's us men's nips for?

**William:** All men were once women.

**Hick Morton:** Open thy mouth again an' I swear I'll peel de skin from thy skull!

**Judd Morton:** I ain't no breasty tart!

**Stelly Morton:** Saw a monkey at the fair once — a male it wuz — it 'ad nips.

13.

73

Moriarty says:

**William tells them to stop toying with him and kill him but spare his wife and kids. But Hick Morton – still pretending he's a 'docktor' – continues taunting William by saying ' 'ow can we cure thee of being a woman one day an' a man the next, if we kills thee?'**

 Wrecking Ball says:

**O Fuck! They're going to slice his nipples off! On stage!**

 Molotov says:

**Maybe not Wrecking Ball, because William throws an age-old dilemma into their faces – why do men have nipples? And, adding injury to insult, he accuses them of also being women, because they too have nipples! Cleverly Shakespeare allows the Morton's victim – William – to turn the tables and logically confront the very reasons why they should do him harm – why should they cut off his nipples when they too have nipples?**

 Swamp Dog says:

**Did you know we can have three, sometimes four, nipples? Like a bitch dog's got two rows of nipples, it sometimes happens in people. I saw this programme on the telly where this guy had five nipples – two where they should be, but then he had two nipples either side of his belly button and one on his leg!**

Cecelia says:

**They're called ' supernummery nipples'**

The Redeemer says:

**These extra breasts are meant to suckle the devil. They are a perfect sign of possession and whoever has them – man or woman – must be regarded as a witch, as one of Satan's own. At night the Devil latches on to these extra nipples, suckles forbidden juices and inserts his mighty sword into his victim's anus. There is no escape.**

Wrecking Ball says:

*What do you do for fun Redeemer? Stick suppositories up your nose and set fire to your farts?*

 Ezekiel says:

*We are getting closer Brian Jones! Remove this site or suffer the wrath of Our Lord Jesus! What the Lord did to Sodom and Gomorrah will look like a paltry firework display compared to what We will do to you.*

 Cecelia says:

*You people scare me because you threaten the very meaning of liberty – you are trying to cauterise freedom from our souls. @Passion Fruit: What happened when you got home? Were your parents supportive?*

 Passion Fruit says:

*The short answer is 'No they weren't'. But first let me tell what happened after we left the ferret's office. Kate whispered that she had 'got it all!' and for a second I didn't understand what she was on about, until I saw her pat her pocket. When we got to the taxi she kissed me so sweetly on the cheek and told me not to worry. That night she posted the whole conversation online. As I lay under my duvet wondering what I was going to do in the morning, Kate texted me - 'He's going to get homosexual anarchy in the neck!'*

 Molotov says:

*Brian please upload page 14 asap – though I doubt it very much, I want to see if William can indeed use his linguistic gifts to escape his impending mutilation and possibly his certain death.*

 Brian Jones says:

*Just glanced at page 14, Molotov, and it looks quite gruesome, quite sick. Read it with a bucket beside your chair.*

Judd Morton: 'e's sayin' I'm a girlie boy 'cos I got nips!?

Hick Morton: Will you two stop goin' on 'bout nips! Enough yappin'! And thee! No more wise-man, nipple-talk for thee!

(Hick Morton takes hold of one of William's nipples and cuts it off)

William: Arrrg!!

Hick Morton: 'ere Rexy! (Throws William's nipple to his dog who eats it).

Judd Morton: Go on 'ick! Do the other one!

Hick Morton: Can't 'ave thee bein' a one-breasted woman now can we?

(Hick Morton takes hold of William's other nipple, cuts it off and throws it to his dog)

William: Arrrg!!

Hick Morton: Now that thou canst not be a woman, it's time t'cure thee of being a man.

Judd Morton: Go on 'ick! Do it like we said!

Hick Morton: Ye see, Rexy 'ere likes 'is morsels — ain't dat so Rexy? (pretends to talk to his dog) Wot!? Is dat right Rexy? Well I never! (addressing William) says 'e's partial to a bit o' roast! Fetch me a torch!

(Judd pulls a flaming branch from the fire and hands it to Hick Morton)

William: ...Don't!... Don't do this Hick Morton!

Hick Morton: Pleadin' f'mercy won't touch me 'eart — thou bleedin' cross-breed — it wuz me wot cut down our Thomas!

H.

76

Wrecking Ball says:
*O Christ! His nipples are cut off! And the Morton's dog eats them!!!!*

Moriarty says:
*And it looks like that's not the end of William's troubles because Hick Morton tells William that his dog is 'partial to a bit o'roast' and he screams out for a flaming torch from the fire.*

Wrecking Ball says:
*Holy sweet fucking Jesus! I can't read this! They're going to barbecue his balls!*

Molotov says:
*I think you're right Wrecking Ball because after severing both of William's nipples, Hick Morton then says 'now that thou canst not be a woman, it's time t'cure thee of being a man' – which can only mean one thing, they intend to roast his testicles! I doubt if such unprecedented cruelty could ever have made it onto the Elizabethan stage. I'm reminded of Gloucester's eyes being gouged out on stage in King Lear – which is sordid enough – but the public burning of a man's testicles while he is still alive, shows to the audience just how quickly sadistic torture can rise from the murky depths of human nature. This scene, in itself, might have been one reason why Shakespeare chose not take his last play to London, because he knew full well that even the sophisticated audiences of Elizabethan London would not be able to either comprehend or accept the moral depravity the play depicts. I mean just look at what has happened so far in just the first three scenes – an act of suicide, a haunting, a wife that exposes her breasts, the amputation of both of William's nipples and now the roasting of his testicles. Imagine how an Elizabethan audience would have reacted! So instead, he buried it somewhere in Stratford. Just a thought.*

Moriarty says:

*The other reason could be that this play was just too personal. I mean here was Shakespeare writing about his early intimate life and sexuality and putting it up on stage for the whole world to see and scrutinise. Maybe this is why he chose to bury it? And not because he feared the public's moral outrage?*

Wrecking Ball says:

*But that makes no sense at all Moriarty! Because why write it in the first place if it wasn't meant for performance?*

Moriarty says:

*Well maybe Shakespeare was looking to the future for exactly this sort of unearthing – he buries his last play in the hope that one day someone will discover it and, in a more enlightened time, understand it.*

Cecelia says:

*Look, does anyone even know if Shakespeare had nipples? If he was relieved of them as a young man, as is alleged, then surely this would corroborate the story of this play – we would then know that Shakespeare was way-laid by the Morton brothers, had his nipples fed to a dog and his testicles barbecued. Surely there are records?*

Moriarty says:

*I'm not sure the public records office has ever kept an eye on the state of peoples' genitalia!*

Wrecking Ball says:

*I guess with balls the consistency of hamburgers Shakespeare would definitely have been infertile?*

Moriarty says:

*If Shakespeare's testes were – as you put it Wrecking Ball – the 'consistency of hamburgers', the smell would have been revolting! They would have become the site of chronic infection and he would have had flies constantly buzzing around his privates.*

Molotov says:

*Has anyone ever thought that if Shakespeare did have his nipples fed to a dog and his testicles cooked, maybe this was why he wrote so much? He was trying to compensate intellectually for what was missing physically? Just a thought. Anyway Brian, let's have the next page – I'm sure we're all eager to see what happens.*

Flynn says:

*You're all lunatics! You have all convinced yourselves that this is the work of Shakespeare! And the only scrap of dubious evidence is the dating of the wax! You all have wax instead of brains! What would Shakespeare call you - 'You souls of geese that bear the shapes of men...!' You are so eager to have Shakespeare return from the dead that you speculate about his nipples and testicles as though you are holding them in your hands! And through the rosy wax covering your eyes you cannot see the maelstrom of stupefying falsehoods that spins before your nose. You have become so mesmerised by the fake, brown-looking paper and olde-worlde hand writing, by the 'thees' and the 'thous', that you have sacrificed good, healthy skepticism for the blind worship of your new god – Jesus Fucking Shakespeare! You are like the maimed and sick who have bought snake oil from the smooth-talking showman with a curly moustache. Like the desperate cripples who are told by the fat monk to smear his rare and expensive saint's urine over their lifeless limbs if they want to walk again! You cannot be serious! Shakespeare is rolling with laughter in his grave! He's pissing himself silly! Can't you hear him roaring with mirth? Brian Jones is a third class charlatan! A fraudster who even fakes his hand-written text with the wrong tools! Can't you see the script has clearly been penned using a fine, steel nib – something completely unavailable to an Elizabethan, they just didn't have the technical know-how to produce such things – instead they used sharpened goose quills that produced an entirely different style of script. Open your eyes to this nonsense and leave Mr. Brian Jones to become the laughing stock he deserves to be! So bring on the next page – we, who so love being duped!*

Judd Morton: Burn 'im 'ick! Burn 'im Proper!

Hick Morton: Every cook knows dat de quickest way t'bald a pig is wiv fire!

(Hick Morton waves the burning branch below William's genitals singeing his pubic hair.)

William: Arrrg! Please!

Judd Morton: 'ick! it's takin' ages! Hurry up an' cut them off like we said!

Hick Morton: Right. F'dis special surgree I 'specially sharpened me blade!

(Hick Morton throws down the torch and takes out a large knife. With the blade tip he flicks aside William's shirt. He takes aim and is just about to cut William's genitals off, when there is the loud explosion of a musket. Hick Morton claws at his throat which is now gushing with blood and falls dead. The others all run from the scene. Gabriel enters hurriedly from the forest's shadows carrying a musket. He rushes to William and frees him)

Gabriel: William!

William: Gabriel! I owe thee my life now twice over! Arrrg my breasts! they hurt!

Gabriel: We must hurry! Get dressed!

(While William quickly dresses, Gabriel reloads his musket)

William: But how didst thou find me!?

Gabriel: Thou hast thy dear wife Ann to thank — she implored me to find thee and accompany thee to Oxford. So I took our father's horse and musket and here I am — and not before time!

William: And Ann and the children? — Are they safe?

15.

Brian Jones says:

*A fine outburst Flynn – I feel smashed to smithereens, torn to shreds, exposed and tied to the rocks! What can I say to convince you except that I am now as doubtful as you are. I did find these papers just as described but the more I read what people like you are saying I'm becoming more convinced by the day, that I too am the victim of a bad joke. How can these papers be authentic? How can they have survived for over four hundred years in the ground without being eaten by worms and bugs? OK they were surrounded by thick layers of leather tied with cord and the whole bundle had somehow been immersed in a block of tallow wax several inches thick. This wax block was again tightly wrapped in leather and rags and locked inside a metal box. Professor Osborne, who is dating the artefacts, examined the metal box carefully and noticed that along the rim where the lid meets the body of the box there are signs that the lid was deliberately sealed with something molten like sealing wax, and he took a few samples to date them. So whoever buried the box in my back garden was going to a lot of trouble to make sure that the contents would last for a long, long time. I thought at first it was some sort of 'time capsule' like the ones that were buried all over the country by school children at the turn of the last millennium, but there is too much evidence that the ravages of time have been at work. For instance, the metal of the box seems to be lead as it's very heavy but it is badly corroded in many places. Inside, all of the rags have rotted to dust and most of the leather wrappings show signs of decay. Insects have started to burrow into the block of tallow but none have yet reached the interior leather wrapping which is still in quite good condition. Why am I telling you all this? To show you that I am as puzzled as you are why someone should bury this piece of writing in such a careful way, but I am sure it has not been buried in modern times. Maybe it was placed here in the nineteenth century? or the eighteenth? I should be hearing from Professor Osborne soon. Sorry for this long post but I wanted to explain to those like Flynn who are convinced this is all a big joke, that it's not because I'm a Shakespeare fan (I never did like his stuff at school by the way!) but because there are things about this 'find' that do seem convincing. Anyway what do you all make of page 15? What happens?*

Moriarty says:

*From what I've read the barbecued testicles have given way to full castration! And just as it looks like Hick Morton is about to slice off William's complete manhood, Morton is shot through the throat! Exciting stuff!*

 Wrecking Ball says:

*Fancy losing your crown jewels to a sadistic bastard like Hick Morton!*

 Cecelia says:

*Hurrah! William is saved by Gabriel! I think he's kinda cool!*

 Passion Fruit says:

*@ Cecelia: Have you forgotten me?*

 Cecelia says:

*Not at all sweetheart! I just got wrapped up in Shakespeare's testicles. What happened when you got home?*

 Passion Fruit says:

*When the taxi arrived back at my house it was mid-morning. Although my parents were both there, at first they wouldn't let me into the house. My father kept shouting through the letter box that he'd only let me in if I promised to go straight upstairs and 'dress properly'. Some of the elderly neighbours across the street started peeping from behind their curtains to see what was going on, so I turned and waved to them making sure they could see every part of my new identity – including lifting my skirt! As I thought, the front door opened immediately and my father almost dragged me inside shouting that I was a disgraceful exhibitionist and he ordered me to go upstairs and change. This was what I'd wanted to do anyway, so I leapt up the stairs, dived into my bedroom and slammed the door behind me. Finally I was on home ground.*

Brian Jones says:

*Here's the last page of Act 1.*

Gabriel: Have no ~~fear~~ they are safely housed with our father and are protected by ~~dozens~~ of uncles and cousins. Come we can talk later. I needed to be stealthy so my horse is some distance away. Although I have reloaded I don't want the other Mortons to know who shot ~~their dog~~ of a brother. Come, hurry! Lean on me!

(With Gabriel supporting William they both disappear into the dark forest).

 Molotov says:

*Notice the symbolism here – Shakespeare the wounded transvestite is again rescued by the masculine ideal of Gabriel, brother to Ann, the Amazon wife who also rescued William after his public disgrace with Thomas Morton, his first sexual partner. This is again very similar to how the sixteen year old Thomas fell into William's arms - 'as a bird which hath crashed against the glass, thou fell like a soft angel to my pillow...' In some ways all of these situations fall into cliché mode – the weak, feminine youth or transgender person who needs the strong man and the strong tiger-wife to lift them up and set them on the straight and narrow.*

 Moriarty says:

*Then maybe this play was written by a nineteenth or eighteenth century transvestite and buried in Brian Jones's back garden? Is that possible Brian? When was your house built?*

Brian Jones says:

*News just in from Professor Osborne! Two other labs have confirmed the date of the tallow as the end of the sixteenth century! Professor Osborne has sent more samples of the hard, almost black wax used to seal the lead box, to two labs in the USA and one in Germany. He said his first analysis of the wax came in with a date in the second half of the sixteenth century – roughly the same as the tallow. But as Flynn has already pointed out, this doesn't count for much because with a little effort a forger might have got hold of some sealing wax from the sixteenth century along with the tallow. Anyway Prof. Osborne said he's going to run a second test soon and start looking from where to take small samples of the paper and the ink, as he doesn't want to damage the manuscript. This could take several more weeks he said.*

*@ Moriarty: Unfortunately I live on a modern housing estate – but I was once told that the land used to be part of Lord Tewkesbury's estates. It was sold to the Local Council after the war to pay off debts. Another rumour is that there used to be a medieval hamlet somewhere around here with it's own cemetery (and, of course, ghosts!) but where exactly I've no idea.*

*I'm uploading Act 2, scene i. Looks like we are now in a street in London.*

# ACT 2

Act 2.

Scene i

(A street in London, two beggars.)

First Beggar: Canst thou count?

Second Beggar: Och aye! On dis one and I got ten fingers!

First Beggar: Wot!!?

Second Beggar: I is cross-eyed see.

First Beggar: Dat'll do nicely! So listen — Over der see, is wot I calls a vacuous 'ouse — no human soul within — every room a tomb.

Second Beggar: Der tomb of 'annibal!

First Beggar: The very same! Now look you — take an empty sack, an' put in two rabbits. Wot yer got? Two rabbits? Nah! 'cos you opens de sack and two rats crawl out! So, eever de sack weren't empty to start wiv — which just ain't possible — or de two rabbits wot went in, was charmed inta rats! So, wot y'got?

Second Beggar: An 'aunted sack!

First Beggar: Well, it would make de sack exceedin' magical. Now, over yonder, we 'as an exceedin' magical 'ouse wot charms anyone wot goes inside.

Second Beggar: Inta rats?

First Beggar: Dunno wot they is.

Second Beggar: Dat tomb of 'annibal 'ouse?

First Beggar: The very same! Y'see I've bin doin' some 'rithmetics — countin' like — inta dat 'annibal 'ouse. Oft 'ave I seen two womens go in but two mens come out — wot means dat out of two dat's really four. But! But de 'ouse is still empty!

Second Beggar: Dat's 'aunted 'rithmetics dat is! 17.

Moriarty says:

*This looks like some sort of riddle about rabbits and rats, a sack and a 'vacuous 'ouse' – 'vacuous', of course, meaning empty?*

Wrecking Ball says:

*Let me get this straight – there are two beggars, one is cross-eyed and can count, but the other is an 'empty louse' and can't count? I'm confused.*

Swamp Dog says:

*No! One of them is a mutant! Says he's got ten fingers on one hand! On 'dis' could mean 'diseased' and this is why he's a beggar- right? 'On my diseased hand' is what he's trying to say and no one wants him with so many fingers. I read in the papers about this guy who said he masturbated so much he grew an extra finger on each hand. He said he had pregnant hands and there was a picture showing one of his hands with six fingers! There's loads of stuff on Google about this.*

Big Foot says:

*One of them says 'I is cross-sexed see' – is he saying he's a trany? And who's 'Anni Ball'? – another trany!?*

Moriarty says:

*Welcome Big Foot to Act 2, scene (i), blog (i). The hand-writing does take some getting used to I admit, but I don't think we can see transvestites behind every badly written word. I think it reads 'cross-eyed' and not what you suggest – this would also explain why he sees ten fingers on one hand. I also don't think it says 'Anni Ball' – it looks more like ' 'annibal'. The apostrophe before the 'a' means he has dropped his 'h' and he's really saying 'Hannibal'. Though what the 'Tomb of Hannibal' has got to do with the story is a mystery to me.*

Swamp Dog says:

*Hannibal? Didn't he come over the Alps on an elephant? When did he conquer England?*

Big Foot says*:*

*You mean there was elephants in England in Roman times? They never taught us that at school.*

Swamp Dog says:

*The Romans did have circuses so it stands to reason they rode elephants.*

Big Foot says*:*

*So, you saying the Romans rode around London on elephants?*

Swamp Dog says:

*Well think about it – where did the Elephant and Castle come from? The Castle must have been something like an elephant stables in Roman times. No wonder Queen Boutique didn't stand a chance against the Romans.*

Wrecking Ball says:

*Shit man! What are you guys saying with all these loopy ideas? This is beyond confusion! Molotov, can you please sort out this mess and explain where the Tomb of fucking Hannibal comes in?*

Molotov says:

*I admit, this is a really tricky opening to Act 2. I'm just wondering if this 'Tomb of Hannibal' thing isn't some vague allusion to the fact that, over the centuries, there have been many claims by archaeologists of having found Hannibal's tomb. However, when they have excavated, the tomb has always been empty. This would then make some sense with regard to the 'vacuous 'ouse' – the empty house – which the First Beggar is talking about. Just a thought. However, the First Beggar then begins to build an analogy – I think – between an empty sack and the empty house, though I'm not sure why?*

Moriarty says:

*Looks like he wants to say something about the empty house being magical. He compares it to a magic sack that changes two rabbits into two rats. He asks the Second Beggar 'So, wot y'got?' and the answer given is 'An 'aunted sack!'*

Wrecking Ball says:

*Then it's easy – he's saying it's a haunted house – end of story! Why he can't just say this without all the rat-and-rabbit rigmarole I don't know.*

Molotov says:

*Maybe it'll make sense further on, because he says the house 'charms' all those who enter. At the bottom of the page the First Beggar says that he's often seen two women go into the empty house and two men come out, which altogether makes four people – but the house is still empty! So the two women that go in are likened to two rabbits, and the two men that come out are likened to two rats – which, I suppose, is why he thinks the house is magical. But to make sense of this scene we will need to see the complete dialogue. Any chance we can have page 18 Brian?*

Big Foot says

*Shakespeare's sexist – he makes the women as soft, fluffy rabbits and the men as dirty, scruffy rats. Hummmm...maybe he has a point.*

Brian Jones says:
*My pleasure. Here it is.*

First Rogger: Well, eever de 'rithmetic is bewitched or de 'ouse is.

Second Rogger: Dat's mischief beyond de mind! 'Cos if two rabbits goes inta a sack — or an 'ouse — two rabbits 'as got to come out!

First Rogger: 'Xactly! Dat's wot 'rithmetics learns thee! But as thou says der's clear mischief in dis 'rithmetics. But look to thy bottle! 'Ere they comes! Arm-in-arm, wiz smiles fat t'charm birds into crocodiloee! The good ole evenin' to y'majesties!

(Enter William and Edward, arm-in-arm, dressed as women)

William: Well, if I am thy queen be careful I don't ask the Duchess of Southwark here to deprive thee of thy cheeky tongue.

First Rogger: I wouldn't want no duchess runnin' off wiv no tongue your highness — wivout me tongue me life would stoonify!

Edward: With or without the tongue thy life hath already stoonified, Why doest thou live in this filthy gutter?

First Rogger: For de same reason kings live in palaces y'grace — 'cos I was born 'ere. Dis is gutter is me palace. Dis fish-head's a gift from a mighty cookin' queen wot rules the kitchens yonder up de street. An' dis pig's tooth is a tribute from the noble butcher across de way.

William: Here, take this and get thyself and thy friend, the duke here, a banquet fit for a king.

(William gives him some money)

First Rogger: May your majesty's kindness sweep the world!

(William and Edward continue and enter the 'vacuous' house in the street As they talk they slowly change out of their women's clothes and into men's attire).

18.

Molotov says:

*Since he can't make any sense of the numbers going in and out of the 'vacuous' house, the First Beggar says something very apt at the top of the page, he says 'Well, eever de 'rithmetics is bewitched or de 'ouse is.' This little phrase reflects the tussle between the ultra-rational discipline of mathematics and the superstitious mentality which has dogged mankind for thousands of years. And the idea that mathematics can be seen as 'bewitched' I find fascinating.*

 Moriarty says:

*Ah now it's clear – it says that William and 'Edward' appear arm-in-arm dressed as women. Clearly time has moved on and William is has hitched up with someone new.*

 Big Foot says:

*I told you they was all tranies!*

 Molotov says:

*The First Beggar announces their arrival with a sarcastic edge to his voice saying ' 'ere they comes wiv smiles fit t'charm birds into crocodilloes!' He's implying, I think, that just like the 'charmed' house, these two women, with their false smiles, are like witches who have the power to transform animals. He then compounds this two-faced attitude by greeting them effusively as royalty 'the good of the evening to y'majesties!'*

 Swamp Dog says:

*Well they're beggars and William and this new dude are two queens – right? So o' course a beggar would say 'y'majesty'. The fact that these two queens are as bent as the Eifel Tower don't come into it. And I see that as a good thing cos instead of screaming 'faggots!' or 'queers!' – which is what you would expect from street beggars – they hails them as royalty, even if it does sound a bit sarky.*

Moriarty says:

*But William seems to detect the two-faced civility of the First Beggar because he threatens to let Edward – the 'Duchess of Southwark' – 'deprive thee of thy cheeky tongue'. Of course, the First Beggar doesn't want that to happen because 'wivout me tongue me life would stagnify'*

 Passion Fruit says:

*'I'm going to carve your fucking cheek with an 'F' - so everyone'll know what a shit-hole faggot you are!' 'Go on rape him! Rape him!' I was down on my back on the school field. An ugly kid called Chamberlain was sitting on my stomach his knees painfully grinding down on my shoulders. He'd taken out a knife and was flashing it menacingly in front of my face. A gang of baying morons had surrounded us and were waiting for blood - for my blood. I wanted to scream and roar but I was just so terrified I lay there like a stunned animal that knows it cannot win and must submit to death.*

 Cecelia says:

*How awful! You poor, poor thing! I wish I could have been there to help you! But why were you at school again? Weren't you stood down for two days? What happened?*

 Passion Fruit says:

*After two days my father said he would only let me go back to school as Jack and only if I was dressed like a male sixth former. I agreed – just to get out of the house – but on my way to school I went round to Kate's house and changed into Susanne. This time I wore a pair of Kate's black, knee-length stockings and, most deliciously, I pulled on a pair of her red-laced panties. We had such fun! It just felt so 'right', so agreeable, so perfectly me somehow and I felt so overwhelmingly happy at last becoming Susanne for a second time. Kate gave me one of her dark, pleated skirts that came down to just above my knees and one of her bras which we padded out with two old socks! Finally I pulled on a white shirt, the tails of which I tied together just above my belly button leaving my sweet midriff naked. Then arm-in-arm like twin princesses we walked to school. I felt glorious! I felt I was floating off the ground with happiness! Little did I know what would happen at school!*

Molotov says:

*There now comes a very succinct exchange between the First Beggar and Edward who asks the beggar why he lives in a 'filthy gutter'? The beggar immediately replies that he lives there for the same reason kings live in palaces – because he was born there. The luck and lottery of birth! Something that was so true in medieval times because people tended to remain in that strata of society into which they were born. There was very little movement, or even very little opportunity to move, between the social classes. If you were born into a family of beggars you would remain a beggar, if into a family of labourers, you were destined to be a labourer, merchants would remain merchants, nobility nobility, etcetera.*

 Moriarty says:

*Is this so different from today's world? Sure, these days education can help you to transcend social classes, but realistically what chance would you have if you were born into a dysfunctional family of pot-heads or recidivists living in a run-down block of inner-city flats?*

 Wrecking Ball says:

*WTF! I live in some inner-city flats! OK I'm not a fucking brain surgeon, but neither am I a pot-head or a whatsit! You're full of middle class bull shit Moriarty!*

 Moriarty says:

*Maybe – but I bet you drive a red bus just like your dad!*

 Brian Jones says:

*Now gentlemen let's remain civilised! Let's keep the focus on our friend Shakespeare. Wouldn't you say that Shakespeare was truly 'classless and free'?*

Swamp Dog says:

*No way! He was a snot! You can't understand a fucking word he says! He doesn't speak for the working classes! He speaks only for your educated snotty-eyed two-shoes! He can't say things straight! Like he has to go to the moon and back just to say 'Hey love! Fancy a bit o' jiggy-jiggy?' I mean, when you try and read some of the stuff he wrote, it's so tangled up, you'd think he'd been trying to play the flute with his arse.*

Moriarty says:
*Sic transit gloria mundi.......*

Passion Fruit says:

*Chamberlain rammed my chin upwards with the bottom of his fist, closing my mouth so I couldn't scream, and brought the tip of his knife towards my face. With utter terror and panic I began breathing and roaring through my nose and I must have blown some snot onto his hand. 'Ah yuck! You stinking bitch!' he yelled and he moved the glinting blade down towards my forehead. Suddenly there was a commotion and a sickening, loud thwack and Chamberlain rolled off me and lay on his side. I turned and saw his two eyes staring immobile at the grass and a small ribbon of blood trickling from his nose towards his lips. 'Susanne? Are you OK?' Above me – tall, heroic and wonderful – stood Andrew the sixth former who had greeted me in the playground on my first day as Susanne. He held out his hand for me to take and gently helped me to stand up. In his other hand he held a cricket bat. Then he said the most extraordinary thing, he said, 'Come, we have to go.' Instinctively I knew this meant we had to escape and I glanced around at the wide circle of silent morons who stared at us from a safe distance. At our feet lay their leader, a dead alpha male. Andrew took my hand and together we walked across the school field, the spears and arrows of their eyes jabbing at our backs. As we reached the gates Andrew said quietly 'Don't look back', and still holding hands for all the world to see, we walked out into the street.*

Molotov says:

*It's only at the bottom of page 18 that all this 'vacuous' house, and the rabbits-and-rats conundrum makes sense. The stage directions indicate that William and Edward enter the vacuous house and slowly change their women's clothes for men's. My thoughts are that although Shakespeare may have intended them to be just two Elizabethan transvestites, the politics of the time – especially in London – was rife with conspiracy and catholic plots to overthrow the protestant monarchy of Elizabeth. So I'm wondering if the play is going to turn into some sort of political drama with overtones of catholic intrigue. In other words, are these two 'women' simply innocent transvestites, or have these men dressed as women to disguise some evil intent – an attempt on the life of the Queen for example? Let's see how it unfolds on page 19.*

Cecelia says:

*@Passion Fruit: OMG Susanne! It's you the police have been looking for for almost two years!! You are Jack Southerland!! Sorry I mean Susanne Southerland!! OMG! The newspapers said you were a cold blooded killer? There was nothing about this Chamberlain and what he was about to do to you! You poor thing! OMG! It was self-defence all along! Why didn't you give yourself up? Running away only seemed to confirm the vitriol the papers were screaming!*

The Redeemer says:

*No transvestite can be described as innocent! Each time their sin of sex is enacted via the anus, God vomits forth a cloud of flesh-eating locusts to crawl over the entire world. These carnivorous locusts, instead of stripping the leaves from plants, will rip transvestite flesh, piece by piece, from their faces. Such men and such women, instead of tears, shall shed maggots from their eyes and wear, like a crown, their own faeces on their heads.*

Wrecking Ball says:

*O fuck! The Redeemer's back! I thought I could smell something.*

Edward: Thou straineth my heart William.

William: Edward — it's Christmas. I haven't seen my sweet children for six months.

Edward: Thou useth the children to hide the real intent! For six months thou hast not been in thy wife's bed!

William: Edward!

Edward: 'Tis true! The cause is simple — thou lovest her more than me!

William: Truly Edward thou hast the yellow sickness! Its corrosive acid will burn deep holes in thy heart for no good reason. And why? Because thy heart is too blind to see love for what it is.

Edward: O the great William knows the true nature of love! And I, whose acid heart weeps rivers whenever thou leavest me, whose eyes burn like dying candles waiting for thy return, know only the endless, narrow corruption of jealousy! Please William, tell me why I should not be jealous of thy wife?

William: Because thou wouldst have love a prison, whereas I see love as something universal, as —

Edward: What tosh! If love is 'universal' why dost thou not take that beggar in the gutter outside into thy bed? Why doth he not qualify for a piece of thy universal love?

William: Edward, love is not measured out in drops of seed!

Edward: So love hath no gradation? no scale? no size? no immensity?

William: Love is the measure of all things, true, but love cannot measure itself. All we know Edward is that for some brief explosion of time, our anguished, immortal souls do mesh, As fit as a key doth to a lock — My key doth fit perfectly thy lock as doth thy key mine — We open each other. Is this love? Is this how love doth spin its fatal web? I know not.

19.

Molotov says:

*Looks like they are having a lover's tiff. William , it seems, is returning to his children in Stratford for Christmas, and Edward  - who we must assume is his new partner – says that what William really wants is to be back in his wife's bed. William accuses Edward of jealousy and says 'thou wouldst have love a prison'.  I guess this is the notion that some lovers try to possess every aspect of their partner to the point where they must either suffocate them or imprison them with their love? At which point, of course, this so-called 'love' becomes pathological.*

Moriarty says:

*If love is a prison then it's not really love – it's obsession. This is why William accuses Edward of having the 'yellow sickness' – jealousy, and likens its action to that of an acid in the heart. Anyone who's been   the victim or sufferer of jealousy knows just how true this is.*

Swamp Dog says:

*I was jealous once. Tore me apart it did. My best friend had an 8 inch erection and all I could manage was 5 and a half – and that was after a lot of 'stretching'. Those 2-and-a-half inches extra meant so much to me I couldn't sleep at night. I kept dreaming up devices with heavy weights that would stretch my schlonk but all I got was a very painful dick that just wouldn't get any bigger. Stupid, but I felt I was only 'half' a man, not really 'developed', somehow stunted, my John Thomas always on its knees, unable to stick its head above the battlements – if you know what I mean.*

Wrecking Ball says:

*I think it's better for your John Thomas to keep a low profile rather than waving his big, bald head high above the battlements, just in case some big hairy twat blows his head off. My John Thomas – though not as high and mighty as 8 inches – has had to duck and dive a few times in his career to avoid the odd, wild cannon ball I can tell you!*

Olga says:

*@John Thomas: I do not worry about bald head. If you have beard I give special discounts for lickings.*

 Moriarty says:

*But don't you think Edward mocks William when he says, 'O the great William knows the true nature of love!...' whereas he, Edward, is just consumed with jealousy and left longing for William's return?*

 Molotov says:

*True but William then goes on to contrast the 'love-as-a-prison' with the airy-fairy notion of love as something 'universal' – which immediately provokes Edward to declare derisively, 'What tosh! If love is 'universal' then why dost thou not take that beggar in the gutter outside into thy bed!?'*

 Cecelia says:

*@Passion Fruit: Your story has hit hard something in me but because you are wanted by the police I will not ask for any more details. I would only like to know if you are happy in your new life. Are you still with Andrew?*

 Moriarty says:

*But I'm not sure I fully understand what William is getting at when he replies that 'love is not measured out in drops of seed'. Is he trying to make a distinction between the bestial side of 'love' – the physical injection of semen into another person during intercourse – and the notion of love as something universal between people, like a brotherhood or sisterhood of mankind? Or is he trying to equate this 'universal' feeling to 'Platonic' love? I don't understand.*

 Molotov says:

*I think the clue lies in Edward's reply, he asks 'So love hath no gradation? no scale? no size? no immensity?' Remember that Edward*

*is convinced William is returning for Christmas to his wife because William loves his wife 'more' than Edward, and if this is true then that is exactly how Edward thinks of love as something which can be measured on a scale. But, in fact, I think Edward trips himself up with his last question when he asks 'no immensity?' because this, I suspect, is exactly what William is getting at – that universal love has some immense quality which lies beyond humanity, which transcends humanity, a quality which he – William – is trying to render into words.*

Wrecking Ball says:

*That's too fucking intellectual for me Molotov – 'an immense quality beyond humanity'? It feels like you are trying to spray-paint my eyeballs. If you mean the quality of fruit in the supermarket, then I get it, I really do, but 'love' as some 'immense quality' makes as much sense as a chicken with three heads. But then it gets worse! Then you say this three-headed chicken is 'beyond humanity' – well that I would agree with, because it's certainly beyond me.*

Passion Fruit says:

*@Cecelia: I don't mind telling you these things Cecelia because I really feel you listen and somehow it helps me to make sense of everything that happened. Yes, I am blissfully happy and Andrew and I have a baby! I bet you weren't expecting that! Naturally Andrew and I can't have children in the usual way – but we do have a beautiful baby girl – but more about her later! But let me tell you what happened when we left the school field. We walked a little way along the pavement, then, turning a corner, Andrew said quietly 'Just follow me – but we'll have to hurry. Can you run?' So, still holding hands, we ran down several streets full of parked cars and eventually, a little out of breath, we stopped beside a white van with small curtained windows on each side. 'Welcome to my home,' Andrew announced as we climbed in. It was so cool! A mini-sofa , a mini desk, a mini cooker and fridge, a mini-TV, a bookshelf and a mini-loo and shower! Andrew was living in it, finishing his A-levels, while his parents were abroad – his own*

*home-on-wheels! In 30 minutes we were driving through open, green countryside, the windows down, glancing at each other cautiously and smiling.*

Moriarty says:

**William's answer that** *'Love is the measure all things...but love cannot measure itself,'* – **is this Shakespeare or someone else because I'm sure I've hear it before somewhere?**

Molotov says:

*It was the Greek philosopher Protagoras who famously said that 'Man is the measure of all things'. Shakespeare – or whoever – seems to have borrowed this to mean that it's not man, but man's love that defines the world.*

Wrecking Ball says:

*What the hell does 'man's love defines the world' mean? You gotta be joking! Just take a look around and see how much man's 'love' is defining the world! There is nothing but shit going on – and why? because of 'man's love'? Crap! If anything it is man's fucking ignorance which is still defining the world. I think that song said it better than Mr. Protogories, 'The world turns upon a woman's hips' – or better still, by yours truly, the earth spins on the end of the devil's dick.*

Molotov says:

*Listen Wrecking Ball if you don't like what I post don't read it. And if you're so super down-to-earth, you tell me, what is Shakespeare getting at with the statement 'Love is the measure of all things'? Come on, give us your interpretation, open yourself up, let us into your mind, let us wander through your thoughts – if you have any – and test them out.*

Passion Fruit says:

*Both Andrew and I knew what would happen that night and so after supper we found a single track road into a dark wood and parked well away from the road and other people. For several minutes we just sat as though we were both holding our breath at the edge of an enormous canyon that fell away below us into oblivion. Andrew reached out and again taking my hand said softly, 'I'm just as scared as you are.' Then we jumped. The passion was explosive. It was my first time and I whispered to Andrew that he would have to be gentle and help me. He was so sweet and loving, so tender – I couldn't believe it. I had never before known how much one human being could be so caring of another – and now that 'other' was me! Love became sex and sex became love – somehow there just was no difference. We made love four times that night and each time it became slower and more intense. By the morning we were both so exhausted, we made tea and toast and, in the early morning light, went back to bed and slept till about noon.*

 Moriarty says:

*I guess, Molotov, you have to ask the question why was Shakespeare so obsessed with trying to define love? Right from the beginning we have this obsessive theme with Thomas Morton scrutinising his relationship with William. My take on all this 'agonising over love' is that Shakespeare was indeed an Elizabethan transvestite who knew he was somehow different. But he would also have known that his attraction for other men was contrary to all biblical teaching, and yet here he was, repeatedly falling in love with someone of the same gender. So, of course, in almost everything he did, he would obviously be thrashing around in his mind for a way of understanding what love exactly is. On the one hand he talks about love 'spinning its fatal web' – which doesn't make it sound very enticing – but on the other hand he says 'All we know Edward is that for some brief explosion of time, Our anguished, immortal souls do mesh...' and, like keys fitting locks, 'We open each other.' Certainly the sub text I see in this dialogue, is that love is not bound or constrained by gender. Gender is just a biological state, whereas love is an emotion, a feeling without gender.*

Wrecking Ball says:

*OK fruit fly! I may not have the gift of the flabby-gab like you but what Shakespeare was probably on about with 'Love is the measure of all things' is the very opposite – that hate brings chaos to all things. You see, people love measuring don't they – like, how many kilos do I weigh? How many kilometres is it to the moon? How deep is the Atlantic? What's the temperature in Madrid? But if you hate measuring things what you end up with is chaos. Imagine someone walks into a shop and asks 'Can I have some sugar?' and the assistant asks 'How much would you like?' and they reply 'I don't know just some sugar,' and they are never able to say how much they want except 'some sugar', well, as you can see, it's chaos.*

Molotov says:

*That, Wrecking Ball, is a 'sweet' explanation which I will not argue with. @ Moriarty: You may be on to something with this explanation – especially because what we're trying to do with our minds is think like an Elizabethan with their minds – which, let's face it, is impossible.*

Swamp Dog says:

*But time can't explode, it just ticks! Shakespeare doesn't make any sense.*

Wrecking Ball says:

*And the 'key' fitting the 'lock' is pretty clear what that means – Shakespeare must have been one randy bastard. Imagine if you had a bunch of keys that fitted many different locks? Or a skeleton key that fitted all locks? And then I guess there are rusty keys and rusty locks?*

Swamp Dog says:

*What about locks that have never been 'unlocked'? Or keys that have never once opened a lock in their lives? And what about 'bolts' sliding into 'bolt-holes'? But then how would you explain a 'pad-lock'?*

Wrecking Ball says:

*A 'pad-lock' is easy – the bolt fits into itself – it's masturbation pure and simple. Though the key that opens the pad-lock troubles me.*

Molotov says:

*@Swamp Dog: You're wrong, time can explode. Before the Big Bang there was no space and no time. When you think about it, time is only a way of recording change. Just imagine a universe – galaxies, stars, planets and space itself – that never, ever changed, a universe that was completely static, frozen, unmoving. In such a universe time could not exist because there would be no way of observing any change in anything. And here's another idea for you – imagine when you reached 20 years of age you stopped aging, you just never grew old, your skin remained smooth, your eye-sight stayed perfect, your health was always great. And this went on not for decades but for centuries, so that after 500 years you were still the same youthful 20 year old – and you went on and on and on like this for yet another 500, 1000, 1 million years. But not only you have remained unchanged but all those people around you, all the world around you – the rivers, the skies, the clouds, the mountains, the animals – imagine these too had never changed in a billion years, how then could 'time' have any meaning? Before the Big Bang nothing existed, so there could be no alteration, no difference in anything because there was nothing. The Big Bang kick-started change and so time was born. So in some ways, Shakespeare – or whoever wrote this play – is well within their rights to say that 'for some brief explosion of time, Our anguished, immortal souls do mesh...' but then such lines as these lets loose another crocodile infested river – the existence of 'souls' and 'immortality'...but I'm not going there, no way!!*

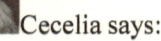

Cecelia says:

*A baby! Wow! That's amazing – I can't wait to find out how you and Andrew managed that! Now I understand what you said about being a fugitive. And all this serious passion sounds exhausting! But tell me more please – I mean, only if you feel like it.*

Passion Fruit says:

*It wasn't all so serious! There were funny moments, many of them. One morning, for instance, not long after our first night together, we woke up all covered with soft spread margarine which we'd used as lube the night before. We decided to wash each other down in the shower but, no matter how hard we tried, our feet were so oily we just couldn't stand up and, laughing hysterically, we both slid out of the cubical onto the floor! But the serious stuff did hit because we knew from the radio that the police were looking for us, so whenever we went for petrol or groceries we went in alone wearing sunglasses and a cap. Andrew had a card that still worked but we knew that every time we used it the police would be able to track us. So the next day we drove into a large city and, over a three day period, withdrew as much cash as we could and headed back into the countryside. The next morning Andrew bought some dark blue paint and a spray gun and we spent the afternoon, hidden away in the woods, changing the colour of our van from white to dark blue. I can tell you all this now because we sold the van ages ago. After we had done quite a professional job changing the van's colour we hit the road with a purpose and a plan. I can't say where we headed but after several weeks of driving we were in a warmer, friendlier place and it was here we found our baby!*

 Moriarty says:

*Brian I think we need to see page 20.*

 Brian Jones says:

*Glad to oblige. Just to let you guys know, Professor Osborne is expecting results from the American labs tomorrow. I'll keep you updated. To my eyes it looks like Page 20 is a goodbye scene between William and Edward. William says his 'coach leaves on the hour' (did they have 'coaches' in Shakespeare's day?) and why he must leave 'my little ones are waiting for their father' – he's going to see his kids for Christmas.*

Some would rather say this is how hate doth germ
itself.
When thou canst define love, they argue, love is dead,
and the death of love is the very seed of hate –
so runs their logic.
Love – a terrified animal worried into the ground
by clarity.
Edward, prey listen; my coach leaves on the hour
– I must hurry to Shoreditch. I will be
away for Christmas as my little ones are
waiting for their father – I cannot break
their hearts for they are like small, unopened
flowers who have not the wisdom to shield
themselves from life's bitter disappointments.
Thou hast a bigger, stronger heart which I shall
– I promise thee – make run wildly when I
return.

Edward : When wilt thou return?
William : After ten or twelve days we will show each other
such passion as will make dogs blush and
mountains sing halleluiah.

(They embrace each other passionately)

Edward : William? Before thou goest, say thou lovest me.
William : I love thee Edward, I love thee to the point of
pain and beyond.
Edward! I almost forgot! My absence
will give thee silence and time to finish
thy essay! Thou hast only the last few pages
to write.

(A clock bell is heard)

Hush! I must make haste! Goodbye my
sweet!
Edward : Goodbye William – keep me in thy heart as I will
keep thee in mine!

20.

Moriarty says:

*It is a farewell scene as you said, but again there's more at the top about love which is quite interesting.*

 Molotov says:

*Yes, but it is the age old philosophical argument which we have touched upon before, that when you can define something – especially like a human emotion – you destroy the very thing you want to define. So when you finally capture the essence of love, you instead, create a situation where 'the death of love is the very seed of hate'. But then Shakespeare finishes by saying something really strange, he tries to predict the consequences of the very thing he himself is battling to do – to understand what love is. He says, 'Love – a terrified animal worried into the ground by clarity.' I'm not sure if this is an astonishing insight by Shakespeare about the limitations of his powers, or a simple admission of defeat. Clarity is what he is striving for, yet this terrifies the animal back underground?*

 Moriarty says:

*But could this be a statement about his own sexuality? So, for instance, could it be read to mean – 'if I am absolutely honest with myself that I, Shakespeare, always fall in love with other men, this truth, this confession, is so terrifying that it frightens me back into the closet underground?' Just a thought?*

 Brian Jones says:

*I like the line where William says that when he returns 'we will show each other such passion as will make dogs blush and mountains sing halleluiah.'*

 Swamp Dog says:

*But dogs can't blush, everyone knows that – they have too much hair. Or did they shave dogs in Shakespeare's time?*

Wrecking Ball says:

*O yeah! And the mountains were singing long before Julie Andrews! Come on Swamp Dog, you can't be such a simpleton – you're pulling the wool? Right?*

 Swamp Dog says:

**Who the fuck is Julie Andrews? I haven't seen her in the play? Is she one of Shakespeare's women? He did get around a bit.**

 Moriarty says:

**Brian! Please upload Page 21 before I go insane!**

 Brian Jones says:

*I agree Moriarty. But before I do that I just want to let you guys know that Professor Osborne emailed me this morning to say the two American labs he sent samples to, have now, each independently, dated the dark, black wax used to seal the box. It's between 400 to 450 years old. This would make it anytime between 1565 and 1615, which matches nicely with what Professor Osborne has already found.*

 Molotov says:

*What's this 'essay' William says Edward can finish while he is away?*

 Brian Jones says:

*One last thing about the dating. Prof. Osborne has decided to take a small sample of the paper from the back sheet of the manuscript and to scrape off some of the dried ink that is thickest where crossings out were done – like the one on Page 6. He's becoming quite excited especially as all the dating so far seems to agree on the end of the sixteenth century. So far, he says, there has been nothing to indicate this is a modern forgery. But who knows, it might be an ancient forgery!*

(They kiss goodbye briefly and William leaves the house
now dressed as a man and disappears in a hurry
down the street)

First Beggar : Seest thou! De first rat's out!

Second Beggar : So onlie one ratty-rabbit left!

(Edward settles down at his writing table and shuffles
some sheets of paper. While he does this we see
the Second Beggar rise up and move into the
shadows where a darkly dressed gentleman is
standing. They exchange a few words and the dark
gentleman clearly gives the Second Beggar some
money. The Beggar returns to his friend and moments
later the dark gentleman, together with several well-
armed men, approach the house Edward is in and
hammer on the door. But before waiting for an answer
they burst the door down, rush in and arrest Edward.
They bind him and drag him away. The dark gentleman
collects Edward's papers, notices the woman's clothes
and wigs, puts what he can into a sack and
                                        leaves.)


                Scene ii.

(The Queen's apartments. The Queen and
        Sir Francis Walsingham.)

Queen Elizabeth (reading some papers) : Good Walsingham.
        these sheets read not of a conspiracy of
        catholics, yet their language has a strange,
        disturbing sharpness that doth much unsettle me.

Walsingham : Tis most true your Majesty, there is no clear
        hatred or challenge to thine own person or
        authority, yet it is sharply writ more as a
        conspiracy against all royal and earthly power.
                                                21.

Moriarty says:

*Looks like the two beggars have been watching the 'vacuous' house. As William leaves dressed as a man, one of them says 'Onlie one ratty-rabbit left!'*

Molotov says:

*Ah har! I thought these beggars were too nice – they're spies! Elizabethan London was full of them – spies and double spies, conspiracies and rumours, plots and counter plots. I think by the time the old Queen died in 1603 there had been well over a dozen foiled plots to assassinate her. It looks as if one of the beggars informs a 'darkly dressed gentleman' about what he's seen. This 'gentleman' then returns with armed men, forces entry into the 'vacuous' house, arrests Edward and takes away his papers and the women's clothes.*

Wrecking Ball says:

*Where I live the police do this all the time.*

Swamp Dog says:

*What do the police want with women's clothes?*

Moriarty says:

*OMG!! Let's look at scene ii before I have to read that all police are cross-dressers! Queen Elizabeth and Sir Francis Walsingham are reading some papers which she finds unsettling because of their 'disturbing sharpness'?*

Molotov says:

*Yes, Walsingham was the Queen's adviser. He controlled a large network of spies whose job was to report on any suspicious activity that might endanger the Queen's life. So my guess is that the 'darkly dressed gentleman' who appears at the end of Act 2 scene i, could be Walsingham.*

Moriarty says:

**What does Walsingham mean when he says that the papers are** *'sharply writ more as a conspiracy against all royal and earthly power'* **?**

 Cecelia says:

**@ Passion Fruit: You can't just 'find' a baby, I mean they don't exactly litter the pavement.**

 Swamp Dog says:

**Babies can litter the pavement – like when they throw stuff out of their buggies. I've seen it happen hundreds of times. Babies are the worst litter-bugs!**

 Passion Fruit says:

*I don't know if we found the baby or the baby found us – by the way, we named her Imi, short for Imogen. It is a story which is so sad and yet so wonderful it pierces my heart just to think back to that day we found her. Andrew and I had been camping for some weeks near the sea (I can't, of course, tell you which sea) and one morning we decided to take a canoe which had been lent to us by a local friend and paddle along the coast to explore some of the other bays. Since we would be away for most of the day I put together a picnic basket with some bread and cheese, a few tomatoes, a little wine and a bottle of water. First though, we had to paddle quite far out into the sea to go around a large headland. This wasn't really a problem because on that morning the surface of the sea was like a smooth sheet of blue glass – it was quite magical. We paddled for about an hour and were just about to change course to go south and hug the coastline, when Andrew said 'What's that?' and, shielding his eyes, he pointed far out towards the horizon. But no matter how hard I squinted I could see nothing. I couldn't even see where the sky met the sea because, in the distance, they both disappeared into the same white, grey blur.*

 Brian Jones says:

**@Moriarty: Here's page 22 to answer your question.**

Nonetheless the author is a catholic — a circumstance it would be most dangerous to ignore, for any such perverted faith must besmirch all thought and action.

Q. Elizabeth (reading aloud): 'A Treatise on Power or The Rights of a Free People To Govern Themselves.'

Walsingham: I have marked some of the more provocative passages your Majesty.

Q. Elizabeth: Here? Ah yes (reading aloud), 'All monarchs, emperors, popes and priests are tyrants stretching from the benign to the murderous. All are, without exception, self-enraptured despots, monsters with their cloven hooves pressed firmly on the throats of their subjects'.
Walsingham! This is vile sedition! This venom could bring ruin to all earthly authority and crown Chaos and Destruction as the ultimate despot of all kings!

Walsingham: Indeed so your Majesty. Those rebellious lines concerning God's own Church are on the next page.

Q. Elizabeth (aloud): 'The Pope is no more than the Devil's executioner on Earth — he never was, nor ever will be God's ambassador. The Catholic See of Rome spreads the tyranny of superstition and ignorance by robbing the poor not only of their money but, more importantly, of their ability to think.'
Well Walsingham, I can find nothing disagreeable in that!

Walsingham: But read on Your Majesty, there is more.

Q. Elizabeth (aloud): 'Not only the Roman Papacy but all churches of whatever creed or doctrine, of whatever sect or soul — even Protestantism — are nothing more than Satanic engines designed to create human suffering and perpetuate intolerance. If a truly righteous, loving God could see as.

Swamp Dog says:

*At the very top in the first line it says 'Nonetheless the cathor is a cathote?' Is a 'cathor' someone who hates cats? I can't find it in the online dictionary. And what's a cathote' – is it something like an Apache?*

 Wrecking Ball says:

**Oh yeah Swamp Dog – the Mohicans overran the Tower of London for a while before being beaten back by the Vikings. And there were running battles with the Huron down Drury Lane. The Sioux of Southgate were also a formidable force especially when they defeated Julius Caesar at the Battle of Waterloo.**

 Molotov says:

**For the record the first line reads** *'Nonetheless the author is a catholic – a circumstance it would be most dangerous to ignore...'* **I'm almost certain Walsingham is referring to Edward, and the papers the Queen is reading are those taken from Edward's desk. But just look at the title the Queen reads aloud** *'.....A Treatise on Power or The Rights of a Free People to Govern Themselves'...***Don't forget this is almost 200 hundred years before the French and American Revolutions! That something like this could have been written at the end of the sixteenth century is astonishing because the whole social and political order was still very medieval in its outlook. They still believed, for instance, that a king ruled because it was ordained by God – the so-called 'Divine Right' of monarchs. Superstition, both divine and demonic, was rife and the notion that a people should be** *'free'* **to** *'govern themselves'* **would have sounded so strange as to be incomprehensible. In Shakespeare's time there wasn't a single country or institution in the entire civilised world that was run as a democracy. If there had been it could have acted as an example to any monarch that the power to rule was not really a divine gift but something which could be organised differently.**

Moriarty says:

**But the Queen is pretty clear about what it means because she exclaims**
*'This is vile sedition! This venom could bring ruin to all earthly authority
and crown Chaos and Destruction as the ultimate despot of all kings!'*

Cecelia says:

*@ Moriarty: I agree with Edward – 'All monarchs are self-enraptured
despots...'*
*@ Passion Fruit: So what did Andrew see? It can't have been a baby?*

Passion Fruit says:

**Well we paddled out a little further in the direction Andrew had pointed
and then I too thought I saw something on the horizon. I turned to see
how far from the land we'd come and I have to say a wave of panic hit
me because the coastline behind us was now looking dangerously faint.
'Andrew, don't you think we should turn back, we're very far out?' I
asked anxiously. 'Don't worry Susanne, Captain Andrew has
everything under control! Let's go see what that is and if it's just a
piece of floating junk we'll turn back I promise.' Well, as we got nearer
it was clearly a boat of some sort but it wasn't going anywhere because
it was just floating on the mirror of water. Then the most extraordinary
thing happened. 'I can hear something,' I said. 'Me too,' Andrew
replied. At first it was very, very faint but as we paddled closer to what
now looked like a very dilapidated, small rowing boat, the noise was the
very distinctive cry of a baby. The moment we recognised the sound for
what it was we started paddling madly towards the boat. And what a
state it was in! It was obviously sinking slowly because it was so far
down in the water. We paddled our canoe alongside and peered over
into the boat and what we saw made my stomach churn. Half
submerged was the bloated corpse of a woman her eyes already eaten
away by the gulls.**

Cecelia says:

**How awful!! But where's the baby!?**

Wrecking Ball says:
*What's this fucking baby got to do with Shakespeare!?*

Moriarty says:
*I think, Wrecking Ball, that will remain one of the mysteries of the universe.*

Passion Fruit says:
*Inside the boat, bobbing around over the dead woman – who was probably the mother – was a wooden box covered with a cloth and it was from inside this box that we could hear the small, pathetic cries of a baby. But the cries now seemed to be shuddering and faltering as though the poor thing inside was running out of life. I cannot tell you how much, at this moment, my heart was screaming with anguish! How much searing pity I felt for those whimpering cries! I leant over and tugged the floating box towards me and removed the covering. There at the bottom, on a bed of rags, was the most gorgeous baby I had ever seen and she was starving! Gently I lifted her into our canoe and immediately she gripped my finger and pulled it to her mouth! She had the biggest, darkest eyes I had ever seen – she looked like she could swallow up all the earth, all of space and all of my heart. But her looks were also somehow tainted with the panic of death.*

Cecelia says:
*Was she dying!!!?*

Wrecking Ball says:
*I'm dying.*

Passion Fruit says:
*Well I had to act quickly. I gave her to Andrew to hold while I rummaged through the picnic basket for the food. I bit off a small piece of bread and cheese and chewed and chewed until it was a fine mush in my mouth. Then I spat it into a picnic cup and added water to make a very liquid slurry of cold bread and cheese soup. The wee mite must*

*have known food was coming because she began kicking and waving her arms. Then, so, so carefully I dripped the liquid food from the tip of my finger into her mouth. I had absolutely no idea what I was doing. I only knew this poor baby had to have food and water and the more liquid this food was the better. So there Andrew and I were, out in the middle of this vast, calm sea, with not the faintest breath of wind, feeding a baby in a canoe.*

Moriarty says:

*Any chance you guys – Cecelia and Passion Fruit – can find another blog? Heartfelt though your story is, it doesn't really fit to understanding this play - possibly by Shakespeare.*

Cecelia says:

*Of course it fits! It fits perfectly! You are putting Suanne and Andrew down because they're a same-sex couple! But don't you see – they are like William and Thomas, like William and now Edward. Theirs is just as much a traumatic love story as Shakespeare's. They belong with us! And another thing – you don't know how the plot is going to play out, maybe there is a baby coming – then you would have egg on your dick! @Passion Fruit: Don't worry about Moriarty he's just a boring, straight and stiff appendage from the masculine world. So, you and Andrew are miles out at sea with a starving baby – what did you do next?*

Passion Fruit says:

*Thanks Cecelia. Andrew and I couldn't take our eyes off her. But just then we heard a bubbling noise and when we looked up we saw the wreck of the rowing boat slipping quietly beneath the water's surface. It disappeared as though being sucked down by death itself. 'I wonder who she was?' I asked as I dripped my cold, homemade soup into the baby's mouth. 'A desperate, pregnant woman trying to reach Europe. Probably when she started to give birth the traffickers cast her adrift in that crappy boat without food or water. Bastards.' While I held the baby – now wrapped in a picnic blanket – and fed her, Andrew turned the canoe around and headed back to dry land. Alone it was a long way, but the hatred I knew he felt for the traffickers seemed to fuel his efforts and about an hour later we reached the shore where our tent was pitched. That night Andrew and I slept with an unbelievably lucky, well-fed baby between us.*

Molotov says:

*If these are Edward's papers the Queen is reading then the uncompromising criticism of the catholic church is somehow to be expected in a society ruled by a protestant monarch, but the further dismissal of all religions as 'Satanic engines designed to create human suffering and perpetuate intolerance,' is absolutely startling. Here is a young man not just rejecting the enemy faith of catholicism, but also rejecting the whole notion that religious faith of any description is a force for good. Indeed he affirms the opposite - all religious faith is fundamentally a celebration of ignorance. This is not even agnosticism, it is an outright declaration that the rational mind is atheist – which is an even more radical opinion than that proposed by Thomas Paine 200 years later in his book The Age of Reason! Whoever Edward was meant to be – some intellectual London luminary, or just another mouthpiece for Shakespeare himself – these ideas, had they been published, would have seemed like the discovery of a fabulous, unknown continent. A bit like if we, in today's world, made contact with an extra-terrestrial intelligence – if this happened, overnight every one of the world's major religions would implode and the entire superstructure of our human identity would slide off the edge of the planet.*

Moriarty says:
*I can't wait! And I can't wait for Page 23! Brian please!*

Brian Jones says:
*This is proving to be exciting stuff alright! From hallucinations to love, from spies to extra-terrestrial intelligence! We're moving around all over the place! Let's see what you make of Page 23 – here it is!*

what the religious nobility enact in His name, He would crush this vast Earth with a fist of fire. But since God doth not, how can we call Him righteous or loving? How can we even call Him God?'

This is not just sedition Walsingham, it is treacherous, open blasphemy! He slanders the church, then he slanders God himself! That there are men like this in my England who can think in this way is monstrous! With thoughts like these all shadows are now but the harbingers of the Great Apocalypse!

(Elizabeth continues reading aloud)

'The divine Right of Kings and Queens to rule is no more than a Tyrant's Right to tyrannise. The Divine Right to rule is invoked simply to excuse any blood-thirsty seizure of power — for it is only those who have snatched power by force-of-arms who do generously wallow in the delusion of their own Divinity. The truth is, it is only their Might which has given them their Right — there is nothing Divine about it. To claim that God has ordained their victory is to say that God has ordained their Right to slaughter.'

Walsingham! Bring this villainous demon before me! There is more than a traitor in such a mind!

Walsingham: I fear your Majesty's sensitive disposition would be far too shocked — he hath been wracked in the Tower these three days for we know he hath an accomplice.

Q. Elizabeth: Do not fret about my disposition Walsingham, I will speak with this impudent cur before you separate his soul from his body. Fetch him!

Walsingham: Very good your Majesty. (exit Walsingham)

Q. Elizabeth (reading more aloud): If the simple truth be told, the power that dynasties wield is only

23.

Molotov says:

*Wow! But what's very noticeable – especially on page 23 – is that although the Queen is openly shocked and outraged by what she's reading, yet somehow she can't stop herself from reading even more of Edward's writing! For all her righteous cries* 'This is not just sedition Walsingham, it is treacherous, open blasphemy!...', *she nonetheless appears totally fixated by the iconoclastic ideas Edward is expressing.*

Moriarty says:

*But you're missing an immensely damming swipe at God himself right at the top of the page, because Edward says, that if God could see what was done in his name he would* '...crush this vast Earth with a fist of fire.' *But because he doesn't do this, because he lets us stumble on from one act of evil to the next, God can't be righteous or loving, so why call him God at all? The Queen was very religious and very loyal to the Protestant faith – maybe she is so shaken by what she's reading it's like she must keep on reading in order to comprehend how anyone could think in such a destructive, irreverent way?*

Passion Fruit says:

*Cecelia – Andrew and I are not a 'same-sex' couple as you said. I know you were only trying to help and that's nice of you, but I'm hermaphrodite. Although I'm sort of in-between I so much lean more towards my girl side. In the last twelve months my breasts have started to develop – needing a proper bra, nipples getting tender, that sort of thing. I have a beautiful, sensitive vagina and for a clitoris I have a normal penis that lies tucked away until its needed! Before I met Andrew, when I used to masturbate, I would begin by playing with my 'clitoris' which soon grew into a fully erect penis. Then I would continue to masturbate as a boy until I ejaculated. And when, eventually, I did come, the strangest thing used to happen – I experienced vaginal contractions and would orgasm like a woman. Andrew finds me 'complicated' but we love each other deeply and I count myself so lucky to have met him, even though the circumstances of our meeting were not pleasant. He is so tolerant and understanding. He has taken to Imi like a real father and since Imi's arrival he has not been able to keep his hands off me! We have been making love twice a day and every night. I think he's trying to make me pregnant. I think I must have a womb and ovaries because I've been having period pains and showing small drops of blood once a month for a few years now, so who knows? But now that you know all about me Cecelia, what about you? What's your story? From a few of the comments you've made, I think you don't have a high opinion of men? Am I right?*

Moriarty says:

*Half way down the page the Queen says something quite interesting. She orders Walsingham to bring the author of these pages to her and says '...There is more than a traitor in such a mind!' What could this remark mean I wonder? Does she mean worse than a traitor or something else besides a traitor?*

Molotov says:

*I think it is just a sign of her abhorrence and fascination for the author. But just look at what she has, presumably, just read – it's something which would have shaken even the most pious monarch's confidence in their so-called 'divine' calling '...- for it is only those who have snatched power by force-of-arms who do generously wallow in the delusion of their own Divinity.'*

Cecelia says:

*My story is nothing special – very boring actually. I've been involved with three men who all turned out to be lying bastards. I lived for 5 years with Bastard 1, we got on well, were happy, had good sex, then one day – just by chance – I found out his daughter from a former marriage was living in the same street just five doors down. He never told me. Lived with Bastard 2 for 3 years until one night, after shagging me, I found him in the early hours of the morning, shagging the dog – a golden retriever! I also discovered he was screwing his friend's wife. Bastard 3 was more promising until I found pictures of very explicit child porn on his computer – which explained why he often wanted me to dress like a schoolgirl in the bedroom – this was after 18 months. And that's it – badly burnt and scarred three times. For me it's been too much of an education into the masculine mind. I just wish there was a way of filtering out all the male dross from this world and dumping it on a faraway island, a safe haven where all the men could shag each other into oblivion – but I guess there wouldn't be an island or rubbish bin big enough for so many pricks! Nowadays, my most loyal, trustworthy and reliable friend is my vibrator. It never forces itself upon me, never moans or complains if I don't feel like sex; it never leaves a mess in the bed; it never orgasms and – just when I need it most – shrinks away into a useless, wrinkled, floppy sausage leaving me high, my whole body aching with disappointment and nowhere to go! No, my vibrator always stays erect and fully present for as long as I wish – it couldn't be more obliging – and I can always position it at the right moment exactly where I want it to be. It's always ready and waiting when I need it – not the other way round. It doesn't snore or fart or smell. I never have to argue with it over stupid things and it never leaves the top off the toothpaste!*

Wrecking Ball says:
*Cecelia! I'm a real man! Loyal, true and lonely! We were meant for each other! Throw away your vibrator!*

Brian Jones says:
*Guys this is not a dating site!*

Moriarty says:
*Brian – unless you can restore your editing functionality, this blog of yours will become – indeed, has already become – something for which it was not intended – a mess!*

Cecelia says:
*So, Wrecking Ball, you want to be lying Bastard number 4? What, sweetie, have you got to offer which can persuade me to give up my vibrator? Even with a 10 inch penis you'd only be in with a slim chance because my vibrator is extendable to any length I desire – can you match that? I thought not. The only thing my vibrator doesn't have is a*

*bank account – it's a complete pauper, not a penny to his name. So, cupcake, what about you? You stand no chance if all you can offer me is take-away pizza every night. You would have to have an income of at least a million dollars a year if you want my vibrator to stay in his box. He has also asked me to point out that, as a piece of advanced technology, he has the latest nickel-cadmium batteries that can withstand 12 hours of continual use – could you match that level of performance? 12 hours of continual intercourse? I doubt it somehow. My vibrator has also asked me to warn you that he goes everywhere. Sometimes, besides working hard in my vagina, he also likes to visit my colon and he would definitely want to explore your colon. Would you be OK with that? No? Oh well, nice try Wrecking Ball, but as you can see you would be a poor alternative to the real thing!*

Molotov says:

*The Queen orders Walsingham to bring the 'villainous demon' who wrote these pages to her, despite the fact he has been 'racked...these three days'. And what does she do the moment Walsingham leaves? She continues reading. However, Page 24 should reveal if Edward is the author. Brian?*

Wrecking Ball says:

*Then I'm on the fucking scrap heap! All men beware! We are destined to become lone wankers! I know of so many couples who've had babies without sex – they went to an AI clinic. They say it's now easier to get pregnant at an AI clinic than it is in bed. Advanced technology is condemning us men to a life of sexual exile! Woe! Remember me! Remember me! But don't forget my fate! Mind you, when I think about it, a vibrator up my bum might feel quite sexy. Holy fuck, what am I saying!*

Big Foot says:

*I put a carrot up my bum once – just to see what it felt like. Shouldn't have taken it out the fridge though.*

truly used to keep a ruling clan or family in its privileged position of wealth and luxury. And to keep itself in power at all costs, the ruling clan must allow incest, murder, rape and regicide to become normal expressions of successful government.' These ideas could spread a multitude of venomous serpents across the land. They fall from these pages like diseased ~~fruit from~~ a diseased mind — nobody must ~~ever~~ think like this!

(reading more) 'And the churches collude in this privileged butchery by making what is truly a crime an act of God, an act which they pretend shines with the legitimacy of Almighty God's Grace and Will — whereas all power stolen like this is fundamentally illegitimate.'

(Enter Walsingham. Edward is dragged in. He cannot walk)

Walsingham: Although we have been extremely strenuous in ~~our efforts~~ Your Majesty, this traitor hath steadfastly ~~refused~~ to give neither his own nor the ~~names~~ of his fellow conspirators.

Q. Elizabeth: So, I am a tyrant?

Edward: My broken body is answer.

Q. Elizabeth: Your body Sir hath been broken to keep England safe.

Edward: Wilt thou be safe only when England is full of broken bodies?

Q. Elizabeth: Walsingham, he threatens me!

Walsingham: Hold thy tongue wretch!

Edward: I am no conspirator.

Walsingham: Then why ~~went~~ thou using the disguise of a woman to plan thy treachery?
24.

Moriarty says:

*It's almost as though these pages are on the point of declaring war against the established monarchy and church.*

Molotov says:

*Indeed Moriarty, it doesn't take a huge leap of imagination to see that if 'successful government' involves the use of 'murder, rape, incest and regicide', then this so-called successful government is morally corrupt and therefore deserves to be brought down by all means available, and if that means outright rebellion against the establishment, then so be it. No wonder the Queen proclaims 'nobody must ever think like this!' There is little doubt that ever since recorded history – from the Egyptians, to the Romans, to the European dynasties – these methods of gaining and holding on to power were the norm. What the Queen is reading therefore is the naked truth about her own position, and so she would see it as something far worse than just some local lunatic spouting seditious nonsense. To her these words would imply the permanent rejection of all divine and dynastic authority.*

Moriarty says:

*She even reads her rule described as 'privileged butchery'. You'd at least think such words would make a monarch stop and reflect about how they got into power and what inhuman cruelty they have sanctioned to stay in power. The last words the Queen reads before Edward is dragged in, are 'all power stolen like this is fundamentally illegitimate' – which would have been an uncomfortable truth for any monarch to read.*

Molotov says:

*But can you imagine the monumental terror this must have produced in someone brought up to believe that they, and they alone, had a 'divine right' to be monarch? How could God give 'The People' the right to govern themselves? Because if this was in any way possible, then it's obvious 'The People' no longer need kings or queens to tell them what to do. Political authority would now lie in the collective will of the people, not in the individual will of a single patriarch or matriarch.*

Moriarty says:

*The queen has obviously been troubled by what she's read, because look at the first question she asks Edward 'So, I am a tyrant?' I think this shows that because of what she's read, she clearly feels accused of being a tyrant, even though in her own mind she no doubt sees herself as a caring mother to her people.*

Molotov says:

*Yes, and look how Edward replies 'My broken body is answer' – thus affirming that she is indeed a tyrant because only tyrants break other people's bodies.*

Moriarty says:

*And for someone for whom this could be their last chance to save their life, Edward is very bold and irreverent. When the Queen replies 'Your body sir hath been broken to keep England safe', he replies with the challenge, 'Wilt thou be safe only when England is full of broken bodies?' The only statement Edward makes in his defence is 'I am no conspirator.'*

Molotov says:

*And look at the confusion that follows – Walsingham, not realising that Edward is a transvestite, declares that only a conspirator, with evil intent towards the Queen, would want to disguise himself as a woman. In Walsingham's view of the world, the only reason why a man would put on women's clothes is to hide his identity for a politically sinister purpose – an assassination attempt?*

Moriarty says:

*Brian we need page 25 to see if Edward manages to save his life – though with a 'broken body' it's difficult to see how he could do this. He would have to openly declare himself as gay, as a man who actually prefers to wear women's clothing, who prefers the feminine world – unfortunately this might give his tormentors even more reason to burn him at the stake, not less. So Brian, any chance of Page 25?*

Vena Cava says:

*I sometimes feel that England is not full of broken bodies but broken minds. Why? Because we have begun wrestling with old, familiar ghosts. Corpses of battles fought and won long ago are beginning to move, are being revived and are starting to rise like zombies from beneath the civilised gardens in our heads. People are still being burnt at the stake of public opinion. Tribalism and sectarianism are becoming stronger. Unbelievably there have even been beheadings and public executions in the shires of England. Not a week goes by without another car bomb shattering this once green and pleasant land. I am not some rabid nationalist who blindly wraps his mind in the country's flag and thinks the rest of the world is contemptuous, but somehow, millimetre by millimetre, we have lost control over our own society – from being seen by the rest of the world as the very model of a civilised country, we have woken up to find ourselves immersed in barbarism. Sorry for the pessimistic rant, it's just that my wife lost both her legs in a suicide attack some months ago while out shopping and sometimes I can't control myself.*

Moriarty says:

*Welcome to the blog Vena Cava and sorry to hear about your wife. But, apart from the modern means of slaughter, your rant sounds like a perfect description of Elizabethan England. Just visit the torture instruments on display at the Tower of London, and you'll see what I mean.*

Molotov says:

*Welcome VC. My sympathies to you and your wife. If you post please try to make your contributions relevant to the discovery of the manuscript we are discussing. Brian's computer has a virus which has blocked his editing function and sometimes the blog gets overloaded with irrelevant (and mind-bogglingly stupid) posts. We are waiting for Brian to upload Page 25.*

Q. Elizabeth: A woman!?

Walsingham: Indeed Your Majesty, we found wigs, costumes and various devices to disguise his manhood at his lodging — all clearly to be used to cloak his true purpose. And we have every reason to believe that his fellow conspirators are using the very same methods.

Q. Elizabeth: Tell us thy name! Who art thou? What art thou?

Edward: I am no more than what I am.

Q. Elizabeth: This word play sir may cost thee thy head if thou dost not answer plainly — Who art thou?

Edward: I am thee, thou art me, I am a Queen of England.

Q. Elizabeth: Walsingham! He hath lost his mind — therefore he hath no need of a head to keep it in! Out of my sight!

(Edward is dragged away)

You say there are others?

Walsingham: Indeed there are Your Majesty.

Q. Elizabeth: I want them found. I cannot have such pestilential corruption abiding in the minds of my people. And burn all these papers. Their heat shall counter the heat of the ideas writ on them — it shall warm the heart of at least one good to naught!

Walsingham: Very good Your Majesty.

25.

Brian Jones says:

*This morning Prof. Osborne cut off a few centimeters of blank paper from the last sheet for dating. He's sending samples to labs in Japan, Canada, the US and France. He also scraped off some of the black ink from a heavy correction. He also wants – so he said – to fire gamma rays (I think that's what he said) at some of the writing to see if he can tell what substances were used to make the ink. In those days he told me, they used to use two things to make ink – one was soot and the other was something from an oak tree, like a wart he said. The soot made a really black ink and the oak tree ink a sort of dark brown ink. Looking at the pages on my desk I think the soot ink was used because it is so black. Prof. Osborne has given me a special container to keep the manuscript in. It has a humidity control on the outside. He said the paper must not be left to dry out, otherwise it might start to crumble. It must be kept at a certain level of humidity and in sterile conditions to prevent mould attacking. Also he told me not to expose the manuscript to sunlight and I'm only allowed to handle it if I wear soft, clean white cloves which have been sterilised. He said I could scan the individual sheets like I've been doing but only once, and then keep them in the dark in the special humidity box. So, Molotov, Moriarty, what do you make of Page 25? It doesn't look good for Edward because I can see half-way down the page, in brackets, it says, 'Edward is dragged away'.*

Molotov says:

*You're right Brian, Edward does nothing to save himself except indulge in word play with the Queen. When she insists he tells her who he is, he replies that he is 'a queen of England'. Of course, we know exactly what he means, but Elizabeth is so frustrated – and possibly insulted – she declares him insane and more or less orders his execution. She says, 'He hath lost his mind – therefore he hath no need of a head to keep it in!'. Edward is then dragged away to his fate. Then she orders Walsingham to burn Edward's papers – which to me seems a little odd given the fact that, a few minutes ago, she couldn't stop reading them. I'm afraid Brian you'll have to upload Page 26. What, I wonder, happens next? I'll take a guess: we see Edward's brutal execution? Or maybe not?*

Q. Elizabeth: Walsingham?

Walsingham: Your Majesty?

Q. Elizabeth: Am I a tyrant? I know thou hast ~~not~~ the ~~buttery~~ tongue of a flatterer, so speak freely and without ~~fear~~, what truly thinkest thou, am I a tyrant?

Walsingham: Your Majesty, it is the inevitable consequence of what thou art that ~~every~~ decision thou taketh becomes an irrefutable ~~fact~~ in history. But the question 'Art thou a tyrannical queen or a tolerant queen ~~of wise governance~~?' is a question with ~~so~~ many different answers, the question itself may be meaningless. To most catholics thou art ~~quite~~ clearly a tyrant. To protestants thou ~~art~~ the ~~protector of~~ their faith, the only bulwark against the Papacy, the only monarch on the globe with the courage and will to say to the Pope and his minions, 'I rule England, not you.' Thou canst only do what thou feelest in thy English bones is right for England, and so thou mayest be the only person who ~~can truly~~ ~~say~~ they are ~~quintessentially~~ English. Thou art a single person, a monarch who hath, in the name of the English people, embraced ~~Protestantism~~ because it may, in ~~vettas~~, be the ~~first~~ step on a long, historic journey to how the English discover for themselves the true significance of freedom. So, art thy decisions those of a tyrant? Or rather the decisions of a determined Queen

26.

Molotov says:

*I think you scored a bullseye Moriarty – the Queen has certainly been 'troubled' by what she read in Edward's papers because right at the top of Page 26 she's now asking Walsingham for his opinion on whether she is a tyrant. Edward has indeed touched a raw nerve.*

Ezekiel says:

*The Grand Council of Ecumenical Law has today proclaimed that this wicked blog transgresses God's Commandments and furthermore that you Brian Jones have been denounced by The Grand Council as a heretic and Antichrist! We have followed closely the many times you have encouraged and promoted on this site the carnal act between man and man, between woman and beast. We have seen with horror the many times the Devil hath spoken with his anus pressed hard against our face, screeching and laughing at Our Lord Jesus. The Lord knows how we have shown the patience of His Son Jesus, how we have turned the other cheek, how we have refused to let Satan push his swollen rod of fire between our lips. Chaste and celibate we have remained throughout, despite all the sweet and sly temptations of the Evil One. But now the time has come, Brian Jones, to strip off thy robes of false modesty and expose thy naked flesh which is covered with the writhing tongues of demons in every direction. You must now submit to God's broad staff! At midnight in the coming days there will be an online exorcism of this site. If this fails to dislodge the demons possessing you and your blog then further action will be taken. You will then be given 48 hours to take down this site or punishment will be enacted by the righteous followers of Our Lord Jesus!   Signed – The Internet Crusaders For The True Christ.*

Moriarty says:

*It would appear that the raw nerves of more than the Queen of England have been touched. Brian, maybe Molotov has a point? You must find a way of restoring your editing function so you can remove all these inappropriate postings – after all the whole purpose of this blog is to discuss an historic manuscript which may turn out to be Shakespeare's last play and written in his own hand. If this blog was just that it would go a long way to placating these religious fruitcakes.*

Brian Jones says:

*Personally I don't really know what they are on about. They know a virus has disabled my editing function – I've said so many times – so I have no control over who posts what. So how can they blame me for what appears on the site? And anyway, as I've said before, my philosophy is live and let live, but theirs seems to be the opposite – die and stay dead. Is it not everyone's duty in a free country to defend our freedom of speech? It is very simple - we are either free to say what we want or we are not. I have discovered a manuscript which may have been written by Shakespeare himself and it has shaken up a lot of people to be outspoken about their sex lives. So what? I see that as a good thing and nothing to do with demons and devils and such nonsense. We are after all living in the twenty first century. We have sent space probes out beyond our solar system and are on the point of curing cancer, yet there are people out there who are still yapping on and on about imaginary creatures such as demons! Thanks Moriarty for your – and Molotov's – concern, but this is far more important than my own personal safety. As I've said before, what's the point in being free to think what we want, if we can't say what we think? If this is allowed to happen then it's like we turn our minds into a prison for our thoughts. I, for one, will not let my mind become a cage.*

 Molotov says:

*Nobly said Brian. In some ways what is happening in this play, written some 400 years ago, reflects on some of the things happening today. Intolerance masquerading as freedom and real freedom being condemned as intolerant and racist. I suppose when all around you is universal deceit, telling the truth becomes a revolutionary act. And it's going to take clear-minded men and women to not fudge or blur the meaning, or the boundaries, of freedom. God knows there are so many obfuscators around as it is. Right! Let's get back to the beginning of the $17^{th}$ century! How does Walsingham answer the Queen? Moriarty, you've had time to read it, what does he say?*

Moriarty says:

*He basically says that her question 'Am I a tyrant?' has no real meaning because it can't have one simple answer. He talks a lot about her being 'quintessentially English', but then, near the bottom of the page, he comes out with something which I find quite interesting. He says that in embracing Protestantism, she – Elizabeth – may have taken the first step to '...how the English discover for themselves the true significance of freedom.'*

 Molotov says:

*Isn't this just Walsingham saying that breaking away from the Catholicism of Rome and, instead, espousing Protestantism, is the first step the English are taking towards intellectual liberty? What else could the 'true significance of freedom' mean? But what I don't understand is Walsingham saying that she has chosen Protestantism because '...it may, in veritas, be the first step....to how the English discover for themselves the true significance of freedom.' He's almost suggesting that the Queen has consciously chosen the Protestant faith because of the quest for freedom it represents. But I'm not sure the Queen would have been capable of making such a far-sighted decision. Maybe the next page will tell us more. Page 27 Brian – please!*

 Brian Jones says:

*From what I can see of page 27, my religious 'friends' should be very happy as it looks like this Walsingham and the Queen are having a deep discussion about God. But there's no sign of Edward. By the way, this page is the end of scene (ii). Oh – before I forget – Prof. Osborne called me this morning. He said he had a quick look under his microscope at the paper and he can definitely say it was made from recycled textiles – by which he means old rags. He said this was how most paper was made in those days, they collected rags and mashed them up in a mill, then squeezed out the water and rolled the resulting pulp out into sheets – something like that. He said he hasn't chemically dated the paper as yet – he'll do that in the coming days – he just wanted to confirm that the stuff the paper is made from is consistent with how paper was manufactured in the 16th century.*

who hath struck a course for her country out
into the unknown waters of freedom?

Q. Elizabeth: But are not facts like these charting
that very freedom?

Walsingham: Perhaps — but not at the root of apocalyptic
anarchy Your Majesty. And, pray, for what
reason should men destroy God?

Q. Elizabeth: But for what reason Walsingham have
we stepped outside the bossom of the
Almighty?

Walsingham: We are all encompassed by the bossom
of God Your Majesty, but God hath
near limited how far we may look beyond
what he holds.

Q. Elizabeth: But why do we always need to step
beyond God? Is it to explore freedom.
But freedom from what? From the See
of Rome, certainly. I sometimes feel,
Walsingham, it is the evil himself who
whispers to me that the freedom we
seek is a freedom from even God
himself.

Walsingham: Sometimes, Your Majesty, thou appeareth
more seditious than many of the traitors
I execute.

Q. Elizabeth: What? Wouldst thou arrest thy Queen
Walsingham?

Walsingham: That, thank God, will never happen as thou
canst not be a traitor to thyself. But
should that day ever arrive, I will call
myself an ape and learn to fish the mighty
seas for elephants.

(exeunt Q. Elizabeth and Walsingham) 27.

Moriarty says:

*Holy cow! Now she's supporting Edward.! Walsingham says she has struck a course* 'out into the unknown waters of freedom', *but she replies with the question* '...are not tracts like these charting that very freedom?' *Yet she has just ordered Edward's 'tract' to be burnt!*

Molotov says:

*Walsingham seems to concede the point but he says it can't be* 'at the cost of apocalyptic anarchy'. *Then he asks a really poignant, delving question* 'And, prey, for what reason should men destroy God?'

Ezekiel says:

*That men could destroy God is laughable! Only God can create and destroy – as you, Brian Jones, shall find out in tonight's online exorcism! In God's eyes you are not even a grain of salt in the ocean, not even a fleck of spittle from a mad dog's mouth! You and your fellow sodomites have less significance in God's creation than a bed bug. And as you roam the world seeking God's innocent children for your anal abominations, He will be watching you ! Yea! Even though ye hide in the wicked abysses of the Earth, drooling and rubbing in the darkness, Our Lord will see all! Tonight you will see God's power over the demons on this site! Domine, dirige nos!*

Wrecking Ball says:

*The last thing I think I said to you Ezekiel was to go and shag a meat grinder – well that clearly hasn't worked. You and lunatics like you have been shitting on people's heads for well over two thousand years and you're still at it! From where do you get this endless supply of garbage? Your holy books? Your holy books are so full of crap you couldn't use them for toilet paper! After reading your posts I always feel I have to disinfect my mind – with a double whiskey! I give up.*

Moriarty says:

**The Queen counters Walsingham's question with one of her own – a question which, I think, stretches our imaginations far beyond the start of the 17<sup>th</sup> century, she asks,** *'...for what reason have we stepped outside the bosom of the Almighty?'*

Molotov says:

**Isn't it like she is tussling with the idea - For mankind to survive, is it man who needs God? Or, for God to survive, is it not God who needs man? Just look at what she asks Walsingham next,** *'But why do we always need to step beyond God? Is it to explore freedom?'*

Moriarty says:

**Just a thought, but I wonder if this has anything to do with her troubled conscience about being called a tyrant?**

Molotov says:

**What do you mean? I don't follow.**

Moriarty says:

**Well she seems to be edging her thoughts towards saying that maybe, once mankind begins to explore real, intellectual freedom, mankind does not need God. If mankind does not need God, then, of course, we can make our own definitions of what is good and bad. Being accused by your fellow men of being a tyrant is 'bad', naturally, but maybe there are some unavoidable circumstances when it is necessary to act like a tyrant – for the greater good, for example? Maybe she's saying that sometimes tyranny is the price we need to pay if and when we widen the boundaries of freedom?**

Molotov says:

**I see what you mean. But all this depends on how you define the 'greater good' and what these 'unavoidable circumstances' are. The religiously inclined would, of course, argue that when you behave like a tyrant, you have indeed stepped outside God's control and have fallen into the hands of the Devil. The Queen herself seems to intimate something like this when she muses** *'...sometimes I feel....it is the Devil himself who whispers to me that the freedom we seek is a freedom from even God himself.'*

Moriarty says:

*After all this heavy theology it is quite nice to see how they end their discussion with a jest – Walsingham says that sometimes she sounds worse than some of the traitors he executes, and the Queen counters with 'What? Wouldst thou rack thy Queen, Walsingham?' He replies that she cannot be a traitor to herself, but if that ever happens, he will call himself an ape and '...learn to fish the mighty seas for elephants'.*

 Swamp Dog says:

*Shakespeare's way off here! Elephants don't swim in the seas! I checked on Google! Nowhere does it say elephants swim in the oceans. So you can't fish for them. Shakespeare's again talking crap!*

 Big Foot says:

*But elephants swim in rivers – says so in Google. So maybe there was elephants in the Thames long ago when Shakespeare was around? Maybe, like we said before, they was brought to England by that Roman guy Hannibal and they spread to the rivers? But since then they've all been fished out? Google says that hippos were called water horses, so maybe it was hippos in the Thames what Shakespeare saw?*

 Wrecking Ball says:

*But don't forget Swamp Dog that in Shakespeare's day people went around London strapped to ostriches – it's true! Google it.*

 Swamp Dog says:

*Nah! Fuck off! You're just pullin' the wool! We already found out they went round on the elephants the Romans left behind. It's not on Google! Just checked. Wanker.*

Big Foot says:

*You is talking bollocks Wrecking Ball – Google says ostriches are 'flightless birds' which means they can't fly, so they wouldn't have been able to fly people around London. Gotcha there!*

Wrecking Ball says:

*'Struth! You caught me with me knickers down! I never said they flew people about did I? – it was their long legs, see! In them days the streets was oozing shit and crap something chronic because there was no sewers and no garbage collection, nothing like that. People just chucked their piss and turds straight out of the bedroom window into the street. Now because ostriches had long legs they could run real fast and step over the crap and so get people about without getting shat on. So you see, ostriches were the first London taxis. And if you can't find it on Google it's cos Google don't know about it either – they're just catching up with history all the time.*

Moriarty says:

*Brian I think it's high time for scene (iii)? Although the recent exchanges above do beg the taxing question about the reliability of online information. These people can't be serious, can they?*

Molotov says:

*I think Moriarty it's a legacy of the old print world. The belief that something written down, whether scratched on rocks, on slates, on wood, on skins or on paper, is somehow the finished truth, has permeated society right back to when people first made marks in the sand. Then, after centuries of scratching our signs on skins and paper, along comes the printing press. Overnight it makes individual hand-writing styles completely redundant and allows millions of people to clearly read and understand what an author is saying. Then, for the next 500 years, authors        bound their printed works into books which could easily be transported and read anywhere from Africa to Alaska. The important point is that once something was printed, it carried authority. And now in the digital age a similar thing is happening – because something appears printed on a device, on a screen, it must carry authority, it must be true. If it's not on Google, therefore it doesn't exist, it never happened.*

Scene iii

(Ty the Barn Street, London. Enter William
carrying bags.)

Young Man (shouting): William!

William: Christopher! Now thou art such a cheery surprise!

Christopher: Indeed! I haven't see thee since before
St. Crispin! But what's with bags and
travel cloak — art thou leaving us?

William: No Christopher! Quite the opposite — I'm
returning from the country! I've been away
for the Holy days.

Christopher: Come! Tell me all over some good London
ale! The Pig and Duck are just here!

William: thou wast always too generous Christopher, but
alas I'm tired from my journey, I must
get home and rest.

Christopher: Be wary of the streets William.

William: Wherefore? Wherefore thy hushed warning?

Christopher: The old, iron Queen sees traitors and
catholic assassins on every corner. She's
been festooning the city with special
Christmas images of gore that do not
bare looking upon.

William: T'was always so Christopher.

Christopher: Indeed, but caution never harmed good
souls. Wilt thou soon be at the theatre?

William: Of course! Come tomorrow and see my new
play!

Christopher: What title hast thou given it?

28.

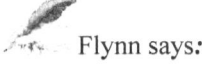 Flynn says:

*But that's exactly what you're doing Molotov – giving credence to this forged piece of shite! The more you talk about it, the more you drop the name 'Shakespeare' here and there, the more you quote bits from the play, the more people will think this adolescent drivel is genuine! I've been reading up a little about the statistics. The real Shakespeare wrote just under 900,000 words in all his plays and poems – yet not a single, original manuscript has survived; not a single paragraph, line, or word – not even so much as a full stop – in his own hand writing, from any play, exists. And here this Brian Jones pops up claiming to have found Shakespeare's last, lost play in his back garden – with all 120 or so pages conveniently written in Shakespeare's own hand! You're worshiping moonbeams! Every one of you who believes this is authentic has swallowed pixie dust! You are blindly perpetuating one of the most absurd hoaxes of all time! Open your eyes!!*

 Molotov says:

*You know Flynn, because of your gut-wrenching vehemence in denouncing this play it makes me somewhat suspicious that you must have had a hand in its creation – maybe you are the forger and you are stoking up the flames of controversy online as a way of increasing the play's profile? I'm sure this sort of reverse publicity has been done before. You say I – and others – are giving credence to a 'forged piece of shite'? But not all shite is forged Flynn. So far – if Brian Jones is to be believed – the dating is coming through as consistent with the end of the 16th century. So if the paper and the ink confirm this then someone in the 16th century must have penned this 'piece of shite' as you call it. And as for it being 'shite' the play is turning out to be quite surprising, as many of the themes it explores clearly run parallel to similar themes in our own world. Does this not indicate that for all our glitzy modernity, emotionally we haven't travelled very far since the 16th century? So I don't think you or I or anyone should condemn it as rubbish just yet - especially as we are only on page 28. There are, apparently, over 120 pages and if it is some sort of sophisticated forgery it might turn out to be quite a good, sophisticated forgery – let's wait and see. If the play does indeed appear to be from the end of the 16th century but not written by 'you-know-who', then it still might stand as a maverick icon of late Elizabethan culture. I remain sceptical but still willing to give the play a chance.*

Moriarty says:

*I for one don't care what Flynn thinks we're doing. Whether it's authentic or not, I'm more intrigued with where this play is going. What I think the opening of scene iii) is really about is the warning this young man, Christopher, gives to William. He tells William to '...be wary of the streets.' And when pressed to say why, he replies, 'The old, iron Queen sees traitors and assassins on every corner. She's been festooning the city with special Christmas images of gore that do not bear looking upon.' And almost nonchalantly William answers ' 'Twas always so Christopher.'*

Molotov says:

*Looks like William has written a new play?*

Moriarty says:

*Yes, but we need page 29 to see what it's called. Brian?*

Brian Jones says:

*Page 29 is on its way. Couldn't help reading Flynn's post with sadness. All what he says might be true about Shakespeare's manuscripts being lost, but I'm convinced this manuscript is from the end of the 16th century. Whether it's by Shakespeare or not I can't tell – how can you tell such a thing? – but someone wrote it, someone immersed it in hot wax, wrapped it in rags, placed it in an iron box and sealed it with sealing wax, and long ago, probably that same someone buried it. Why? I don't know. Then this housing estate and my garden were built. I understand it is an extraordinary archaeological find but, once the dust has settled, I will be talking with the British Museum about giving it to the nation. From what I can see on Page 29 things turn a bit unsavoury – looks like William's about to be murdered?*

Molotov says:

*Christopher thinks William's new play must be 'another smelly comedy!' but are Shakespeare's comedies 'smelly'? Strange thing to say. So where's this murder? Maybe Brian you could upload both Pages 29 and 30, then we'll have more to chew over?*

William: The title will come when I lie in my next bath.

Christofler: Then for sure it must be another smelly comedy!

William: Then I'll write thee the part of a cheeky maid! Look Christofler, I must get home. Come to the theatre tomorrow after rehearsals and tell me thy thoughts.

Christofler: I will with pleasure.

William: Adieu good Christofler!

Christofler: Adieu William and although my greetings come late — Happy Christmas and embrace Edward from me!

William: I will indeed — adieu!

(exit Christofler)

(William continues walking. He turns into a street which has the bloody heads of those executed, spiked at various intervals down the street. Although he tries not to look, his attention is suddenly caught by one head — it is Edward's.)

Ahhhh!.....please!.....let it....not be!

(He stops aghast at Edward's head. Immediately four men violently pounce on William from the shadows, pull a sack over his head and carry him off screaming.)

First Man: Shut it! Thou squealin' rascal!

Second Man: Slit 'is neck!

Third Man: Shred out 'is tongue!

First Man: First gouge 'is eyes!

29.

Fourth Man: Can I 'ave de liver?

(They each take out a knife, look about and carry William still struggling into a dark alleyway.)

First Man : William! Ssssssh! Be quiet! Thou art with friends! Sssssh now!

William (still sacked): I... I know that voice!

First Man : And so thou shouldst!

William : Jonesie! Is that you?

Jonesie : Aye! Me an' me beatin' 'eart!

(They remove the sack).

William : And Hans! Such welcome faces! What!? I thought you would all be dining on me! But why? Wherefore this mock-violent abduction? Wouldst thou frighten me to death for some merciless wit?

Hans : Ve iz saving thy lifes Villiam!

Jonesie : Thou hast seen Edward's fate? Walsingham and his spies are everywhere seeking thy head to spike alongside poor Edward. This house and all the nearby streets are being watched day and night.

Hans : Thou iz luck ve gets to thee first Villiam!

Jonesie : Hans is right — t'is now much safer for thee if Walsingham and his spies should think thou art dead — hence this murderous charade.

William : But why should that be so? I saw no spies watching thy blood-thirsty play?

30.

Moriarty says:

*William says goodbye to Christopher, goes down a street lined with severed heads, spots Edward's on a spike and is immediately set on by a gang of cut-throats who carry him away screaming! Great to be back!*

 Molotov says:

*Yes, but look at the following page – he's been abducted by his friends! It looks like Edward's head is a decoy set up to trap William. The character 'Jonesie' says, 'Walsingham and his spies are everywhere seeking thy head to spike alongside poor Edward.' And the character 'Hans' says William is lucky they found him first because now they can fake his murder. If they do this it should be on Page 31. Brian?*

 Ezekiel says:

*Exorcizamus te, omnis immunde spiritus, omni satanica potestas, omnis incursioinfernalis adversarii, omnis legio, omnis congregatio et secta diabolica, in nomini etvirtute Domini nostri Jesu Christi, eradicare et effugare a Dei Ecclesia, ab animabusad imaginem Dei conditis ac pretioso divini Agni sanguini redemptis. You have been warned Brian Jones!*

 Wrecking Ball says:

*What a way to order a pizza! Extra peperoni! Extra olivi! Extra artichoki! Extra Jesu Christi!*

 Vena Cava says:

*I'm a retired civil servant, nothing flash, but I worked for 35 years doing my civic duties and in my own pedestrian way I kept the wheels of local government oiled and turning. How has all this so easily crumbled away? This site for instance, this Shakespeare thing – you are raving on and on about some old papers found in a box buried in someone's garden, while above ground ancient oppressions are piling down on our shoulders every day with increasing force and wiping away generations of civil structures we all thought were built for an eternity.*

Jonesie : Jost thou think they stuck Edward's severed
neck out there by chance? It's a lure. They've
been waiting and watching to see who'd scream
most at his dead face. They saw thee and
our lovely murder and no mistake. So now,
for thine own good William, thou must die!

William : Jonesie!

Hans : Don'y vorry Villiam! Thou makest nice dead
pig.

Jonesie : Hans hurry! Splash him — 'specially over 'is head.
William, now thou hast to do the best acting of
thy life — let thy death be thy life's guide.

(They splash lots of pig's blood over William)

William : But where, what safe place is there for me
Jonesie?

Hans : A platz vere everyvon and noven can be hidings.
Come!

Jonesie : Let the face of death be that which preserves
thy life! Let's away!

(They carry a limp, blood-soaked William
back out into the street. They again carry
him passed Edward's head, pretend to stumble
with the weight of a dead body, and disappear.)

31.

Wrecking Ball says:

*I've heard stuff on the news and I know you must be mad because of what happened to your wife, but you sound depressed to me. You seem stuck in a black hole?*

Vena Cava says:

*I just don't see how knowing if Shakespeare was gay or not can reverse society's drift into savagery? When I was a young man we had hope, we had a vision that we were building a better world. How naive that sounds today. Today, vast numbers of young people are spending the best, youthful years of their lives playing online computer games, totally disconnected from the real world. They know nothing – and care even less – about how their society works, about who is responsible for what, about crime and justice, about policing and the rule of law. And why should they? They are immersed in a virtual reality which is far more dramatic and exciting than the actual reality. I guess this wouldn't be so bad if it wasn't for the social vacuum it has created which has been filled by all kinds of conceivable warring factions.*

Wrecking Ball says:

*Well, on the estate where I live, it's definitely safer to stay at home and watch Star Wars or some gooey romance, than go out and get mugged. But it dosen't leave me depressed – life's always been like this round here  – is it any different anywhere else?*

Vena Cava says:

*Yes, yes it used to be very different. People did look out for each other. People did care – even for strangers. But what you describe as a choice between staying home or getting mugged, is paradise compared to what is now happening. Let me give you an example. Last week I needed to take my wife into our nearby town to the clinic for her check-up. It's a drive that usually takes about twenty minutes. Since losing her legs I am the only way she can get around. We drove out of our village and almost immediately came to a group of well-armed men wearing black balaclavas who had blocked the road with razor wire. 'Please get out of the car in the name of Our Creator!' one of them barked. I got out as they asked and, trying to sound friendly, I asked what was going on? 'It's a FARB' one said through his balaclava. 'A FARB?' I asked. 'Yes, a Faith Affirming Road Block.' I nodded as though I knew what they were talking about and four of them put a firm hand on each of my shoulders, closed their eyes and began loudly praying in unison. When they'd finished I thanked them and asked if I could continue on into town. That wasn't possible. I would have to take a much longer route because, they told me emphatically, up ahead was another road block manned by 'a load of shit-crazy jihadists who'll throw acid in your face.' Realising I had no choice, I took their advice, again thanked them, and turned the car around. As I did so my wife gave a muffled scream and covered her eyes. On a metal spike beside the road was a woman's severed head. I drove back the way we'd come feeling as though an ice-cold fist was reluctantly loosening its hold around my throat.*

Moriarty says:
*Looks like that's the end of scene (iii) and you're right Molotov they dowse William in pig's blood and fake his murder for the benefit of Walsingham and his spies. I guess if they believe William is dead they will stop searching for him, as the character Jonesie says at the end, 'Let the pose of death be that which preserves thy life!'.*

Wrecking Ball says:
*How come we've not heard of stuff like this happening? How do I know you ain't making all this stuff up? If things like this were happening it'd be all over the news? I don't get it. I think you're pullin' the wool.*

Vena Cava says:
*I've asked myself the very same question Wrecking Ball. There seems to be a reluctance to admit that such things are happening, or can happen here in the heart of England. One problem I've noticed is that if you criticise these people – of whatever sectarian colour they belong – you are immediately accused of being a racist, and no one wants to be called that as it is still the one word capable of destroying your own feeling of self-esteem. But it's being used as a catch-all adjective to*

*stifle any criticism of even criminal behaviour. I heard a man on TV only last week who accused the police of being racist – why? Because they had caught him red-handed stealing a car!*

Moriarty says:
*Brian any chance we can have scene (iv) on the next page? Also, do you have any updates from Prof. Osborne?*

Brian Jones says:
*Nothing much seems to be spoken in scene (iv). It looks like there's an old woman begging and something to do with a kid being chased? No Moriarty, sorry no updates. The Prof said these next dating tests on the ink and paper might take longer because the instruments take a long time to set up. And he won't do just one experiment but probably four or five to make sure the results are sensible. He said the same is true for the other labs in Japan and the US. Did you know that the paper and ink samples he took were flown in a private jet with two security guards to these overseas labs? Pretty crazy really. Some billionaire film actor supplied his private jet. I've now received offers for the first performance from ten countries around the world, but I think – if the manuscript turns out to be genuine – that it's only right and proper the first performance is given in Stratford, mine and Shakespeare's home town. Anyway here's scene (iv) on Page 32.*

Wrecking Ball says:
*But why are you posting all this stuff on this Shakespeare site? I don't get it?*

 Molotov says:
*I think I might know why Wrecking Ball. Vena Cava thinks that what we are doing is a complete waste of time. He thinks we are like children playing noughts and crosses while the house is burning down around us. That academics in universities, colleges and schools are all playing at civilised behaviour, while beyond the class-room walls untold savagery is stalking the land. Am I correct VC?*

Scene iv)

(A crowded street near to a bridge over the Thames.
Blind, old woman sitting begging from
passers-by.)

Old Woman: A crust t'a blind, old maid wot never did
no 'arm t'man or mouse! A spoonful o'gruel!
A little porridge t'warm me olwin' 'eart! Please!

(Suddenly a young teenager, carrying a bulky sack,
dashes here and there between the people. When he
reaches the Old Woman, he quickly gives her the
sack, receives some money in return, and snatches
up another heavy sack the Old Woman gives him.
Now shouts of 'There he is!' are heard. Several
men appear, they are clearly chasing the youth. The
boy runs out across the bridge and throws the heavy
sack over the side into the river. He runs off
pursued by the men. When the commotion is over
the Old Woman gets up slowly, conceals the
sack beneath her copious garments, and waddles
off 'feeling' her way along the walls and through
the crowd.)

32.

Vena Cava says:

*Yes Molotov, something like that. What I'm saying is that while you are arguing about Shakespeare, real, meaningless evil is etching its way through our society. When the division between sanity and insanity is now so blurred, how can understanding Shakespeare restore a clear sense of humanity into people's lives? My wife is a very simple, very kind person, who has always tried her best to be sincere and genuine in her dealings with other people. She is without any trace of prejudice, bigotry or hatred, a thoroughly decent person. Naive perhaps, but she always has tried to be scrupulously fair. When we were younger, and before we had children, I used to tease her that she would either end up the mother of my children or a nun in a cloister. Now she is a maimed cripple I have to lift on and off the toilet. How can understanding Shakespeare explain this? I mean no disrespect to the LBGT community – who I supported for many years – but how can knowing if Shakespeare was gay or not restore my wife's legs?*

Molotov says:

*You must love your wife very much VC and what she has gone through is truly heart breaking. But I want to try and explain why I think understanding Shakespeare is important. By the way it's not just understanding Shakespeare, what you are really asking is why understanding any literature or music, any picture or film, any piece of artistic expression – even a piece of science – is important. In a nut shell, I think the more we understand ourselves and each other the less barbaric we become. And all of art and all of science is our way of trying to understand what we are doing floating through space on an insignificant lump of rock. If we can come to terms with this reality, the more we can appreciate the bonds that unite us all as a species. But we have to be careful, because civilised norms are no guarantee of safety – as the Jewish people found out to their cost in Nazi Germany – the cultured society of Mozart, Beethoven, Goethe and Schiller, was no protection against institutionalised barbarism. What you have told us VC is very disturbing and I hope it enrages all decent people into action. But now I want to see what happens to William and what it can tell me about my own humanity. Moriarty, what's happening in scene (iv)?*

Moriarty says:

*Not too sure. It looks like a swop. An old, blind woman is begging. Then the stage instructions say a youth, carrying a large sack, runs through a crowd. He gives the sack to the begging woman and receives some money. Then he picks up a different, heavy sack and runs off across a bridge pursued by 'several men'. The youth throws the sack over the bridge into the river. When everything's died down the old woman 'conceals the sack beneath her copious garments' and leaves 'feeling' her way along the walls. You know what's in the sack don't you? I think it's Edward's head. Can this get any more gruesome!*

Molotov says:

*You're not getting squeamish Moriarty surely? Who was it who told another blogger on this site to go visit the torture rooms at the Tower? If this is a swop, I bet the 'blind, old woman' is William in disguise and he's now taking Edward's head home – wouldn't you do that if you loved someone so much?*

Moriarty says:

*I'm not sure having my wife's severed head on the mantelpiece would show how much I loved her! For one thing she wouldn't blend with the décor and for another she'd attract too many flies. She'd have to be kept in the freezer – though I'm running short of space, what with my mother's frozen head and the dog's. So Molotov, no chance of my becoming squeamish just yet. Now let's see if you're right about the old, blind woman. Brian can we please have scene (v), Page 33? Thanks.*

Brian Jones says:

*Looks like another long solo from William. And you're right he's put Edward's head on a table and he's talking to it! It's becoming the House of Horrors!*

Scene v)

(At night. We see the blind Old Woman going into a large, dark building — it is back-stage in a theatre. Around the walls is a multitude of costumes. Once inside she places the sack ~~carefully~~ on a table. She divests herself of her garments ~~and we see~~ 'she' is really William. Slowly William lifts Edward's severed head ~~from~~ the sack and places it before him on the table.)

William: O dear, dear friend, thou hast ~~taken~~ my ~~heart~~, and more than thou couldst ever have known, deep into thy living grave.
For thee only shall I pluck out mine eyes and softly kiss them into thy vacant sockets.
For thee only shall I tear out my tongue and stitch it to thy pretty mouth.
For ~~thee only~~ I shall turn my heart to be thy grave so that we may ~~still~~ laugh and lie ~~together~~ in this all so living-dying world.
For thee I did return full with such promises ~~of love~~ they ached my being and ~~tore free~~ such desires as would consume the seas with ~~tumultuous~~, virgin fire,
And yet, here do I find thee butchered and dressed like some clod of stinking meat.
Thy purposeless agony and death is ~~but~~ a savage testament ~~writ~~ by those whose own monumental thirst for life has given this crazed madness all the colours of diseased, contagious tyranny.

33.

Swamp Dog says:

*What's a 'living grave' mean? No one lives in a grave, it makes no sense! Doesn't Shakespeare mean a 'dying grave'? I think he got his words mixed up because a grave is where you put dead people – right? And another thing – he's only got the head, he doesn't know where the rest of Ed's body is, so there can't be a grave – living or dead!*

Wrecking Ball says:

*OMG what a plonker! William is talking to his butchered lover whose eyeballs are probably hanging out, so he's bound to be upset. What it means is that in William's mind Eddie is still alive, so maybe that's why Shakespeare says 'living grave'? Use y'noggin!*

Molotov says:

*In this first line isn't William declaring that he too has died, that Edward has taken William's heart and 'more than thou couldst ever have known', with him to whatever is beyond the grave? It is an emotion very often found between lovers – when one dies the other feels the loss so acutely, so tragically that a part of them also dies and their existence suddenly becomes robbed of all meaning?*

Moriarty says:

*And just look at what William offers to do for his dead friend in order to bring him back, he wants to 'pluck out mine eyes and softly kiss them into thy vacant sockets.'*

Wrecking Ball says:

*O shit! I feel sick! You're sayin' he wants to pull out his own eyes, put them in his own mouth and with his tongue push them into the eyeless head of Edward? That's just so gross!*

Molotov says:

*Not only that Wrecking Ball, William wants to tear out his own tongue and stitch it to Edward's 'pretty mouth'. Wouldn't you do that for someone you loved very much?*

Swamp Dog says:
*You mean be an organ donor?*

Wrecking Ball says:
*Chopping off bits and pieces of my body for love just ain't my cup o'tea Molotov.*

Swamp Dog says:
*I'm pretty sure they didn't donate organs in Shakespeare's times?*

Moriarty says:
*For once Swamp Dog that is a very astute observation.*
*@Molotov: For me I think the most telling lines occur at the bottom of the page. After saying all these heart-rendering things about what he was hoping to do with Edward and yet here Edward is* 'dressed like some clod of stinking meat', **William says,** 'Thy purposeless agony and death is but a savage testament writ by those whose own monumental thirst for life has given this crazed madness all the colours of diseased, contagious tyranny.' *What do you make of this? I know what I think it means but I'd like to know your opinion and see if it matches mine.*

Molotov says:
*It's one of those far-reaching statements Shakespeare is so famous for where he seems to 'wrap-up' a vast philosophical idea into a few words. What I read here is that Edward's suffering and murder are symbols not just of the state's tyranny, but are the unavoidable consequences of other people's selfish pursuit of power. And he calls this pursuit a* 'monumental thirst for life' *as though equating the quest for political power with how life itself seems to be something irrepressible. But I have to say, that these words come dangerously close to excusing those who commit murder in the name of the state or ruling monarch, because it's almost like saying, 'We can't help killing people because our 'thirst for life' is just so strong.'*

Moriarty says:

*But isn't that the real motive of every tyrant – 'My thirst for power, is my thirst for life'? It reminds me of what alpha males do in pack animals and bulls do in herds – each is genetically programmed to fight to become the top procreator and will, if necessary, harry all its rivals to death in mortal combat, until one day it too is toppled by a younger, more virile procreator.*

Molotov says:

*Not sure it's that simple Moriarty, because what your argument implies is that all tyranny is the ascent of testosterone.*

Moriarty says:

*But it is like this! All tyranny is the expression of testosterone and all testosterone is the hormonal tyranny to procreate. It's inescapable!*

Wrecking Ball says:

*Hang on! Hang on! Testosterone is in our balls – right? And to 'procreate' really means to fuck? So what you're sayin' is, all tyrants are cruel bastards because they are driven by the pressure in their balls to fuck their way to the top – right? But did Shakespeare really mean this? Because if he did, then – wow! – I'll hang my hat on his erection!*

Swamp Dog says:

*You can't, Shakespeare's dead.*

Wrecking Ball says:

*OMG Swamp Dog! I swear you have the insight of a dead frog!*

Moriarty says:

*Brian! We are in desperate need of page 34 before we are attacked by legions of dead frogs!*

Brian Jones says:

*Here goes! Looks like William is still going strong.*

O dear, dear Edward define for me, speak,
what is this world that can do such things
to such people?
Do men still need to cannibalise themselves?
Do we still need to devour the flash and
substance of our own humanity?
Tell me! Speak my love! Can'st thou not hear me?
Prey, open thy lips and tell me just one thing — is
there any pleasure, any sensuality in death?
If thou answereth 'yes', then safely can I understand
men's obsession and generosity in spreading
death so freely.
But if thy reply is 'no', then I am left without
reason why men do, so joyfully and with such
begging prediction, let loose thee oceans of
blood?
No, my love, thou hast no need to answer.
There is no pleasure in death, only in the violence
of death,
And of that, thou art wholly innocent.


(William carries Edward's head and places it on a
bedside chair/table. He slowly undresses, puts on a night-
-shirt and climbs into bed.)


So how am I now to love thee?
Should I now pretend to surpass the infinite
grief that now doth sit like a crucible
at the centre of my life?

34.

Molotov says:

*He's asking Edward a desperate, rhetorical question about the world they live in. It seems he wants Edward to tell him why it is that men still seem to consume themselves with hate and violence? He asks Edward's lifeless head -* 'Do we still need to devour the flesh and substance of our own humanity?'

 Moriarty says:

*But in asking a lifeless head such questions isn't William really asking the audience to give an answer? Isn't he really asking the audience to question the quality of their own humanity? Also I think by posing these questions – which, of course, cannot be answered by a lifeless head – what William is really betraying are his own thoughts about human cruelty. And you can see this a little further on, when – in the same vein – he asks his dead friend to tell him if* 'there is any pleasure, any sensuality in death?'

 Wrecking Ball says:

*So what you two are sayin' is that Shakespeare sees Eddie's dead head as the audience? Then Shakespeare didn't like people very much.*

 Molotov says:

*Not a bad conclusion Wrecking Ball. I too sometimes feel that Shakespeare has little faith in humanity's goodness, but sees rather the meaningless urge to inflict its rage on everything around it – including itself. But, Moriarty, this last question about the 'pleasure' or 'sensuality' in death is quite stunning, because, if you read on, you can see that William has already exempted Edward from giving a response. The question only has two possible answers – either 'Yes' or 'No'. If there is pleasure and sensuality in death then he, William, can understand, can make sense of why men spread death about so generously, but if there is no pleasure, no sensuality in death, then he is* – '...left without reason why men do, so joyfully and with such begging prediction, let loose these oceans of blood.' *William then tells Edward he*

*doesn't need to answer because the only pleasure, the only sensuality in death comes from inflicting it on others –'...only in the violence of death', and of this Edward is emphatically not guilty.*

Moriarty says:
*Have you read the instructions near the bottom of the page? I'm beginning to get a little uneasy about where William is going with this grizzly conversation with Edward's severed head. I mean, after changing into a night gown and getting into bed, he asks the head 'So how am I now to love thee?'*

Wrecking Ball says:
*OMG! I don't believe this! He's getting into bed with a corpse!*

Moriarty says:
*A severed head is hardly a corpse Wrecking Ball. But I agree, it is getting rather suggestive of 'you-know-what' on stage. But I can't believe Shakespeare would go that far, not in Elizabethan times, he could never have got away with it. Maybe this is why he had to bury it in a box?*

Molotov says:
*I'm sure your 'grizzly' suspicions are ill-founded. If you look at what he asks himself, I think it's clear he's talking about platonic love not physical love. He wants to know if he should just 'pretend' to conquer his feelings of grief, but we can't know his answer as William's soliloquy seems to continue on to page 35. So Brian, we need to know if Shakespeare really had the gall to expose his audience to the outrageous spectacle of necrophilia on stage, or whether there is a more benign development that doesn't involve 'you-know-what'. I'm 'dying' to know!*

Brian Jones says:
*Page 35 is the end of scene (v). I hope your suspicions are wrong – I'd hate to have to put William back in a box!*

What if I were to spontaneously melt into a
black fire and blister this world with yet
more outrage?
Or should I instead, turn to sarcastic
bitterness to mock the monstrous, inhuman
filth that men do ever make?
Neither — for I will not betray and waste
myself in betraying and wasting others.
That way lies the self-consuming dragon
who already doth hold our suffering
hearts between his teeth.
Then how to love thee?
I shall have thee for one day more,
And it shall be a day that will stretch so
far onwards some will say eternity
was but yesterday.
Let then this kiss warm thy stony lips,
But let then thy kiss, in return, unravel the
anguished density of my mind.

(William kiss Edward and places Edward's
head on the pillow beside him.)

Tomorrow I promise thou shalt speak and
laugh again,

Tomorrow I promise together we shall banish
all sorrow and all pain.

(lights out).

35.

Swamp Dog says:

*What's going on? Why are you guys in such a flap? What's this 'you-know-what', neckrofiller thing?*

 Wrecking Ball says:

*In simple words Swamp Dog, it looks like William is so randy he's about to screw his friend's head – now do you get it?*

 Swamp Dog says:

*No way! Shakespeare was one sick bastard!*

 Moriarty says:

*However it looks like William is simply considering his options for revenge. He asks, does he become like a* 'black fire and blister this world with yet more outrage'? *Or does he bitterly mock the* 'inhuman filth that men do ever make?'

 Molotov says:

*Neither it seems. And the reason he gives for not pursuing retribution I think I understand, but then he adds on something quite enigmatic. What do you make of the line,* 'That way lies the self-consuming dragon who already doth hold our suffering hearts between his teeth,' ?

 Moriarty says:

*Not sure. But I once heard a very telling expression that says when you fight too long against the dragon, you become the dragon. Whether William is alluding to this it's hard to tell. If he is he could be trying to say that he won't indulge in revenge –* 'betraying and wasting others' *– because he would simply end up between the jaws of the dragon of self-betrayal? This is what the* 'self-consuming dragon' *might possibly refer to. What do you think?*

Molotov says:

*It's a plausible enough interpretation – revenge, once it takes hold, is like a monster eating itself. But look at how magnanimously William has answered his own question to Edward, 'So how am I now to love thee?'. In all likelihood another person would have chosen to show their love for a murdered friend by swearing to hunt down and kill the murderer, or to seek retribution for the crime in some other manner – public humiliation, a money payment etc. Also don't forget that 'taking matters into your own hands' was probably the most common way justice was enacted in Elizabethan times because there was no legal system as we understand it, no police force whatsoever – people were left to their own ways of seeking revenge. But William turns his back on all of this 'self-consuming' justice, and again asks Edward the question 'Then how to love thee?'*

Swamp Dog says:

*Awwwww Christ! I'm going to throw up! He kisses Edward!!! And puts his head on the pillow!!!! I bet he's going to do neckrofiller!!*

Moriarty says:

*We may never know Swamp Dog, because the scene ends with the words 'Lights out'.*

Molotov says:

*Not so fast! It looks like William is promising Edward that tomorrow Edward will 'speak and laugh again' – so there is clearly a plan brewing in his mind. However, I too feel a bit squeamish at the thought of kissing a dead person – even if it is just the head. But don't forget, even today in some parts of the world, it is still common practice to say a last farewell to a deceased loved-one by giving them a final kiss. So maybe this is all that William intends. But the line that, for me, really betrays how much William is suffering is, 'But let thy kiss, in return, unravel the anguished density of my mind.' Even though he has lost Edward for ever, he still hopes that Edward's 'dead kiss' can bring back some peace to his mind.*

Moriarty says:

*Although, let's be honest Molotov, it's hard to see how a kiss from a dead person could restore tranquillity to someone's mind – personally it would freak me out!*

 Molotov says:

*Even if it was from someone you loved very much?*

 Swamp Dog says:

*Zombies kiss.*

 Wrecking Ball says:

*I'm guessing you're speaking from experience Swamp Dog?*

 Moriarty says:

*Actually I'd probably be more freaked out if it was someone I loved. My kissing them is one thing, but the idea they might respond to my kiss with one of their own, is so ghoulish it's beyond creepy! Anyway, William promises to make Edward laugh and speak again 'Tomorrow'; so Brian, can we see how this miracle is supposed to work in scene (vi) page 36?*

 Brian Jones says:

*I have to say I was a bit worried about what was going to happen with this head-in-the-bed scene, but 'Lights out' seems to leave it up to the audience's imagination as to what happens in the dark! Now I have something troubling to report. There's been an unnerving development – I have begun to receive emails from some group calling themselves the Internet Crusaders, warning me to take down this blog or 'action' (unspecified) will be taken. What is worrying me is how these people found my private email address? I know there must be many men called*

*Brian Jones, but I guess there can't be that many who live in Stratford. So by an easy process of elimination they've found my email address. What is crazy is that they say they are loving and forgiving Christians but they back up their sham tolerance with the most obscene threats. We've heard some of them on this site. I know what I should do – my whole instinct is to keep publishing, to keep upholding my right to freedom of speech, to show to the world this wonderful discovery which may possibly have been written by Shakespeare himself. This is what I should do, and – if I am honest with myself – I know I must and will do, but still, I have to admit to being a little uneasy by their bullying threats. It's like they are now invading my own private space.*

Molotov says:

*Intimidation and threats have always been the tools of extremists, fascists and extortionists and gangsters the world over and these Internet Crusaders are no different. They are religious fascists pure and simple and you must not allow them to win – not just for your sake but for all our sakes. My advice Brian is, contact your local police and ask for protection. If these so-called Internet Crusaders have made threats then I think they may already have broken the law and are liable to prosecution – the police will know.*

Moriarty says:

*Or you could delete your email account and open another - I've got three. Some people I know have got 10! The moment anything dodgy happens on one they just delete it and open another. But I certainly agree with Molotov – besides deleting your email account, ask for police protection.*

Brian Jones says:

*I've talked with an old friend who used to be a lawyer before he retired and he said that the problem is their threats are of a religious nature and so beyond the reach of the law – I'm going to be boiled alive in a living hell, or god is going to bless me with testicular cancer, or I'm on the devil's hit list, etc., etc. He said that as long as their threats are of this nature then probably they are just the idle rhetoric of religious fanatics, who can't be prosecuted for being zealots. Anyway, for everyone's sake, here's page 36.*

Scene vi)

(A crowded square. Enter William ~~royally~~ dressed as a
woman, carrying a sack. At a raised, prominent
position he stops and places a golden crown upon
his head.)

A Woman: O look! It's a queen!

A Man : Wi' a good ~~foot~~ an' two onions between's legs

A Woman : ~~Come~~ Sirrah! wager! My flower pot's in sore need of
a good ~~footin'~~!

A Man : Thy ~~flower~~ pot's so full o'dead ~~kitters~~ Nancy,
cats ~~faint~~ as thou walks the streets!

William : Good people o London! My friends! Let
me ~~present~~ myself! I am Queen of
ᴧengland! — a country ~~not~~ too far from
~~your own.~~ In my country my people are of
the happiest in the world because of the love
and ~~respect~~ I bear them. And in this sack,
especially for you, I have brought some of that
love. In this sack ~~there~~ is even the smile of
my God. In this sack is someone who knew
you — but who you never knew. Someone
shadowy shy! Hush! Sssssssh...... Please
~~meet~~ King Walsie!

(William reveals Edward's head — which also
wears a golden crown)

Now Walsie, tell the good people here what
thou doest in ᴧengland?

36.

Moriarty says:

*I see William is back in his favourite costume.*

Molotov says:

**But notice how Shakespeare uses the crowd to show that they are not fooled. I wonder when the word 'transvestite' entered the English language?**

Swamp Dog says:

**I think he's so shook up after doing neckrofiller, he's gone and split his jelly – I mean he's dressed as a tart wearing a crown and he's dragging a roof and onions between his legs!! He's gotta be a fruitcake!**

Wrecking Ball says:

**For once I have to agree with you – the hand writing is shocking. But because they're talking about flower pots I don't think it's a 'roof' but a 'root' between his legs – in other words, his Moby Dick.**

Moriarty says:

**My OED tells me it was 1911 in some journal. Anyway, William is introducing himself to the crowd as the 'Queen of Dengland' and says, *'my people are of the happiest in the world because of the love and respect I bear them.'***

Molotov says:

**This is beginning to sound like a speech laden with irony – one might even say it's beginning to sound like a sarcastic parody of royalty. We know, for example, he must have Edward's head in the sack and yet he tells the crowd it contains some of that 'love' and '*... even the smile of my God'*. How he can equate the ghoulish smile of a severed head with the smile of his God, can only mean there is a deep sense of blasphemy in his words. And who can blame him? Edward is now the second love of his life who has been viciously taken from him. And look how he introduces Edward as King Walsie! He names his dead lover after the very person who contrived Edward's capture and beheading – Walsingham! Please Brian – let's have the next page! I have to see where this is going!**

(William now 'throws' his voice like a ventriloquist into Edward's head. The crowd gasps not only at the first sight of the head but more especially when it appears to talk)

Walsie (William) : I protect my Queen.

A Woman : Bless the saints! It speaks! 'Tis witchery!

A Man : 'Tis the black tongue o' death!

Walsie : I speak to you as one who once lived amongst you.

William : So Walsie, tell these good folk how thou protectest thy Queen?

Walsie : I taketh every man, woman and child and....

William : .... And dost thou give them breads?

Walsie : No, of course not — I chop off their heads.

William : But how doth that show thy love?

Walsie : Because then you and I will have all of England to ourselves.

William : O sweet Walsie! Dost thou mean thou wouldst love me like a man loveth a woman?

Walsie : 'Tis true I love thee, but like the man who begs,
I follow only God's law between my legs.
And alas my root is far too weenie
To fit thy sweeter, bigger queenie.
So with God's commandments between my legs
I am left a King possessing dregs.

37.

Moriarty says:

*And we now have the answer to the 'miracle' of making Edward 'speak and laugh again' - the stage instructions at the very top of the page say William uses his voice 'like a ventriloquist' and makes Edward's head appear to talk! No wonder some in the crowd are disturbed and lean towards a supernatural explanation! Can you imagine the effect it would have had on a crowd of superstitious Elizabethans to hear a severed head begin to talk!? I'm surprised they don't riot! After King Walsie/Walsingham answers that what he does in Dengland is '... protect my Queen', Queen William prompts him to tell the people just how this protection works? And without any shame or hesitation Walsie/Walsingham answers, by the use of mass decapitation! 'I taketh every man, woman and child and... chop off their heads!'*

Molotov says:

*What is amazing is that the crowd doesn't seem to see the connection between this make-belief King and Queen of Dengland and their own country! You would have thought it was painfully obvious? However, Shakespeare – or whoever – seems more interested in delving into the personal relationship between Walsie and his Queen, because Walsie reveals his carnal desires for the Queen despite the fact he sees his man-sex as inadequate for the job '...alas my root is too weenie/To fit thy sweeter, bigger queenie.' And then he continues his blatant sacrilege by saying he only has, 'God's commandments between my legs'. Not too sure what this is supposed to imply – any ideas?*

Moriarty says:

*When I first read it what echoed through my mind was the irresistible drive to procreate. Maybe what he's trying to say is that the overwhelming urge to sexually orgasm dominates all male cognition. As a consequence having a small penis unable to 'fit thy...queenie' leaves him with the 'dregs' – other women who are not as worthy as the Queen perhaps? Brian, can we have Page 38?*

Brian Jones says:

*No problem. You guys have got some great ideas! There are just two more pages to this scene. Here's the next one.*

To protect and love thee
I need heads to count,
To root and kiss thee
All roots must out.
Then with no other roots to challenge my own,
I'll have thee all to myself, alone!

A Woman : A saucy stem indeed!

A Man : Walsie should try a smaller flower pot!

A Man : 'Tis a strange way to love one's people!

William : To show to love a wasp stings everyone she
meets —

Walsie : — But her poison is so strong —

William : — everyone she stings dies —

Walsie : — And when no one is left —

William : — she is all alone —

Walsie : — and cannot bear the heavy —

William : — accusing silence —

Walsie : — so she stings herself —

William : — and dies.

A Man : I understand not thy meaning Your Majesty!

William : Why to show you that a queen who stings
even out of love —

Walsie : — must one day be stung by the loneliness and
savage hatred of her own conscience.

A Man : Methinks Dongland is a place I wouldn't
like to be.

A Woman : Who was this gentleman thou callest Walsie?

38.

165

Wrecking Ball says:

*If you guys are right about this 'root' business, then the real reason he's chopping people's heads off left, right and centre, is because he's trying to castrate the rest of mankind – so he confusing men's heads with what dangles between their legs? Is that right? And only when he's the last one standing with any balls, will he hop on the Queen's butt and shag her – tiny weenie or no?*

Moriarty says:

*Yes, this is the selfish gene syndrome – by first eliminating all other sperm producers but himself, Walsie is guaranteeing the survival of his own offspring.*

Molotov says:

*The crowd are clearly troubled as one woman comments that chopping off people's heads is an odd way for a monarch to 'love' his or her people. So this little tale has indeed sown the seed of doubt about how those in power will use any method they can get away with to stay in power – a theme, I'm sure, which is quite relevant in today's world. Now comes a gruesome dialogue between Walsie and his Queen in which they share each line in what looks like a parable about a wasp, who, after she has killed everyone around her, kills herself. And why? Because if a queen – or anyone – kills out of love she will one day be killed by the 'loneliness and savage hatred of her own conscience.' But what is again noticeable is that, despite the play-acting between William and Edward's head, the crowd does not seem able to make any connection between this wasp parable and their own Queen Elizabeth who regularly festoons the city with severed heads – people whom she and Walsingham arbitrarily decide are traitors.*

Moriarty says:

*But look at the very last line where a woman seems to cut through the charade and asks 'Who was this gentleman thou callest Walsie?' Doesn't this mean she merely sees William for what he is – a man dressed as a woman nursing the dead remains of his executed lover? I find it quite pitiful in some way. But again we are down on our knees begging Brian for the next and last page in this scene. Brian help!*

William: My light and my love, a man and a woman ~~whose~~ thoughts would oft stop the spinning earth and leave me hovering o'er mountains.

Woman: Didst thou truly love him?

William: Madam, he gave to my existence the full meaning of love, and he gave to love the full meaning of existence. Yes, I loved him dearly ~~and truly.~~

Woman: I wish my husband spoke like that.

A Man: Thy husband's too busy crackin' flower pots — big an' small!

(Several men appear to arrest William and try to push through the crowd. However, the crowd ~~obstruct their~~ progress and William escapes with Edward's head.)

Moriarty says:

*And just look how William, in his answer, now sheds all pretence and answers the woman straight from the heart. The woman clearly does not identify Edward's head as Walsingham, but instead knows it was a 'gentleman' whom 'Queen' William loved. We know this because she asks him directly 'Didst thou truly love him?'*

Molotov says:

*Which is, when you think about it, quite open-minded for the times. Homosexuality was a capital offense and was vehemently denounced regularly in every pulpit in the land, so there was clear potential for 'Queen' William to have been confronted by a crowd of religious bigots baying for his blood. Therefore, to ask William if he 'truly loved' Edward shows an extraordinary amount of tolerance, and, if we bear in mind that William is holding Edward's severed head in his hands, the excruciating honesty in his reply, 'Madam, he [Edward] gave to my existence the full meaning of love, and he gave to love the full meaning of existence,' is probably one of the most tragic things any actor has ever said on stage.*

Moriarty says:

*What is also obvious is that the crowd are sympathetic to William, because when the Elizabethan Gestapo appear to arrest him, the people in the crowd block their progress long enough for William to escape. So, Brian let's have scene (vii).*

Brian Jones says:

*Sorry, that's the end of Act 2. Act 3 starts, it says, with Queen Elizabeth watching a play at the theatre. She is dressed as a nobleman! And William is on stage playing – guess what – a wife! Looks like there's going to be an execution – more death! This play requires a strong stomach that's for sure.*

# Act 3
## Scene (i)

(The Queen, dressed as a nobleman, is watching a play at the theatre. On the stage is a bound man, about to be executed and an executioner with an axe. A king stands close by accompanied by royal counsellors and attendants. Also present on stage are the condemned man's children and his tearful wife, played by William.)

**Bound man:** Mercy Your Majesty!

**King:** Why shouldst I show thee mercy? Didst thou, in the public market, show me mercy? No! With loud, open ostentation thou freely abused me with burning jokes, with comical songs, with lampooning dances and mimicry that wouldst have enraged the cruel Devil himself! No sir, thou dost not merit lenient mercy!

**Wife:** Good sir, let not thy power have all the hues of hapless revenge, which some will doubtless re-construe as murderous intent, but rather show the other hopeful side of thy authority — of mercy, forgiveness and love, despite the wrong done to thee. Such action would show a stronger, more magnanimous king than one who rages like a cruel, embittered Devil and lets fall the axe at every slight and whimsical trespass. There is a certain nobility in rising above ridicule and buffoonery.

**A royal counsellor:** If thou couldst, my Lord but ride the waves and misfortunes of snapping satire,

# ACT 3

Wrecking Ball says:

*So what's the 'Bound Man' gone and done? Is he another RC assassin? Or another one of those Jesus-shits – ooops! – I mean Jesuits? Though I don't see how this hangs together with castration and Walsingham being the last man standing with an erection?*

Moriarty says:

*I think you've climbed into the wrong tree Wrecking Ball. The 'Bound Man', according to the King, has been caught making fun of him – the King – in a public place. It looks like he's about to be executed for abusing the King with* 'burning jokes, comical songs, lampooning dances and mimicry that wouldst have enraged the cruel Devil himself'.

Wrecking Ball says:

*So he's losing his head just for taking the piss?*

Moriarty says:

*Seems so. And he's begging the King to show him mercy.*

Wrecking Ball says:

*Then it's the King who needs to be castrated. It's just like rival males – instead of ramming their horns together on the mountain side, these two are slapping each other across the face with their dicks until one of them submits. The winner then yodels his victory, brings down the axe and goes off to shag all the women – that's how I see it.*

Moriarty says:

*If only life was that simple!*

Molotov says:

*If life was that simple, Moriarty, we'd all be walking around with weapons of mass destruction between our legs – which, in some ways, I think we are. The will to subdue and dominate, as Wrecking Ball has so sharply described, stretches so far back into the fog of our evolutionary past that we can no longer see it for what it is. Having said that, look at how the Bound Man's wife (played by William!) is appealing to the more noble traits of kingship – mercy, forgiveness, love. She even says* 'there is a certain nobility in rising above ridicule and buffoonery'. **Then a Counsellor tries to reinforce this by saying the King needs to** 'rise above the waves and misfortunes of snapping satire' **– but I think there's a comma here at the bottom of the page so there's more to come – any chance Brian?**

Brian Jones says:

*No problem. Before I uploaded this page I had a little read and from what I can understand the King must be standing there biting his tongue as his Royal Counsellor and the Bound Man's wife are pouring arguments into his ears; but it doesn't seem to wash, because I can see at the bottom of the page, the King shouting* 'Enough! Enough!', *and that his decision if final. So it looks like the guy's for the chop! But when I first read this – crazy though it may sound – it reminded me of my own situation. How? Well because, here's this Bound Man who has had the courage to criticise the King in a public place, being shut up by execution. I mean I know in those days there was no idea that people had a fundamental right to freely speak their mind, but today we do have that right. So now, here I am, over four centuries later, having to think of my own safety just because I want to exercise my freedom to tell the world about my amazing find. You see what I mean?*

Molotov says:

*Of course Brian, you are absolutely right. But don't be discouraged – the important thing is not to give in to fanatics and their threats because this would only further encourage them and confirm in their eyes the validity of their ideas. So, can we see what arguments, as you said, are being poured into the King's ears?*

Thou wouldst soon out-grow thy inner-self and
like the cicada who sheds her outer-skin to
become larger and ever more beautiful—
Thou wouldst emerge a monarch so radiant
and increased, so safe in thine own identity.
All other kings and Queens would need shield their
eyes before thy brilliance.

Wife: To laugh with the mockery of thyself brings
wisdom and tolerance to thyself.
But to hate, kill and expunge the mockery
of thyself, will bring only more, much more
savage mockery upon thy head until thy world
is surfeit with gangs of obsequious,
deceitful flatterers each too afeard to
allow even the smallest grain of truth a
place in their hearts.

Royal Counsellor: It is a powerful argument Sire — killing
laughter of invites double score. Let such
satire rather give thee another window into
thyself.

King: Enough! Enough! I have already heard
too much! My decision is fixed! Proceed with
the execution lest we drown in the muntry
vexation of so many cowards! Proceed I say!

Wife: No!

(The condemned man is blindfolded and his head
placed on a block. The executioner takes aim by placing
the axe blade at the man's neck, swings the axe above
his head, brings it down hard and embeds the blade
into the wooden floor an inch from the condemned man's
nose. The King walks over to him and kneels down)

42

Molotov says:

*Ah now I can see where the Royal Counsellor is going, he wants the King to tolerate satire because then he – the King – would 'out-grow' his 'inner-self'. But, for me, the really clinching line is when the Counsellor explains to the King that after out-growing his inner-self he would be 'so safe in thine own identity'. Look at those words 'safe in thine own identity' – isn't this exactly what a tolerance of mockery brings? When you are criticised, when you are satirised, your inner-self feels shaken, jeopardised, fragile, at risk. But, if you can 'out-grow' these feelings, move beyond the threat, then you must emerge with a broader, stronger hold on your identity.*

Moriarty says:

*Now the wife has a go (well she is pleading for her husband's life!) and basically tells the King that if he wants to be seen as tolerant and wise, he has to learn to laugh along at the mockery of himself. But isn't this a repeat of what the Counsellor has just said? However, she then goes on to describe what will happen to the King if he should give in to his feelings of outrage and execute his critics – he will, she predicts, become locked into a spiral of ever-increasing satire and slander while those around him become ever more fearful of their own skins. These people will either desert him or they will descend into fawning flatterers unable to express the truth even to themselves. The poor King, he must feel he is on a sixteenth century psychiatrist's couch! No wonder he explodes when, after the condemned man's wife, his own Counsellor adds 'Let such satire rather give thee another window into thyself.'*

Molotov says:

*Yes, it's as though he explodes because he can't stand another grain of truth about himself – even though he calls it a 'murky vexation'. And so, not wanting to look like an indecisive monarch, he sticks rigidly to his plan to execute his satirical tormentor and cries 'Enough!...Proceed with the execution...!'*

Moriarty says:

*But look what happens! It's a mock execution! In the last three lines it says the executioner embeds the axe in the wooden floor of the stage just inches from the condemned man's nose! Brian! Next page! Next page!*

King: You see, even merciless kings like me can make wicked jokes. Thou owest thy life to thy wife. But know this — thou art banished from my realm you ever and shoudst thou be found, even with the smallest of thy toes, inside my kingdom again, the next axe will fall true and fair. Take him away!

Chorus.

Can mockery subdue a mighty king?
Can the biting refrainment of satire
bring a queen down on her knees?
Is not then the comedian the true Lord of all,
A mortal who maketh lesser lords from power fall?
A jester whose pitiless wit
Can toss all kings and queens into the king pit?
Can lift the blindness of the man of power
Whose arrogance is sometimes sweet but oftimes sour?
We hope our play tonight has brought thee ease
To laugh at kings who dance with fleas.
But alas the hour-glass sand has run right through,
'Tis time to say goodnight, and adieu.

(The audience applauds and disperses. William, who is still on stage and costumed, is approached by an attendant of the Queen).

Attendant: Art thou the author of tonight's play?

William: I am.

Attendant: My lord the Earl of Sussex sends his compliments and would like to make thy acquaintance.

43.

174

Molotov says:

*You're right! The King banishes him then a Chorus summarises how satire can supposedly bring down monarchs. The only problem I have with this is that throughout all of recorded history there has never been a single example of a king or queen being toppled by a joker.*

Moriarty says:

*But perhaps this is not what the Chorus is saying? When it asks, 'Is not then the comedian the true Lord of all...?', maybe what's implied here is that Kings and Queens can remain what they are, but, unless they learn to laugh at themselves, to see themselves as mere mortals who sometimes trip over the dog or drop hot eggs, or who say stupid, thoughtless things, then they will always be 'lesser lords'. Shakespeare even writes that the jester 'can lift the blindness of the man of power,' – the 'blindness', of course, being a reference to the old adage 'all power corrupts'.*

Wrecking Ball says:

*Even though he spares the guy's life, that King is one snidey shit! If it was me I'd go raise an army, come back, defeat the King and make drum skins out of his scrotum.*

Molotov says:

*I suppose, as this is the end of the play-within-a-play, we will never know just how this particular King was corrupted into a 'snidey shit'. But, by conducting this phoney execution and then banishment, this King has ignored all the advice given to him and has started on that ever-increasing spiral of mockery. His decision has sealed his fate – his only protection will be to add on yet another layer of self-delusion.*

Moriarty says:

*Looks like the Queen is calling herself the 'Earl of Sussex' – one of her attendants is on stage to compliment William and to ask if the 'Earl' can make William's acquaintance. The Queen on stage dressed as a man  with William dressed as a woman! Now there again is this theme of flexible gender which is at the core of this play! Brian, can we see what  happens please! This encounter should be fascinating!*

175

William: Please let him come.

(The Queen dressed as a nobleman walks onto the stage.)

Earl (The Queen): William of Stratford?

William: Welcome my lord! We are honoured by your Grace's presence. Thy servant hath said thou wast pleased with tonight's performance?

Earl: With every scene Sir, my interest hath grown more than thou canst imagine. But thy play hath emboldened me to ask thee a question.

William: Prithee, please ask!

Earl: Thou hast implied with avid, forceful clarity that the joker, the witty satirist is the lord of all lords — is that not so?

William: I suppose it is my own fanciful interpretation of humour.

Earl: But how couldst mockery ever win a war? How couldst a jester ever hope to seize victory in an ugly conflagration between nations?

William: But Sir, my play is not about losing or winning wars, it's about losing or winning the war of self-knowledge — Satire breaks the veil of personal pretension. War is the folly of competing obsessions.

Earl: Obsessions? Meaning what prey?

William: Meaning all the reasons people slaughter each other — for territory, for riches, for power, for religion. Irony and satire are but
44.

Molotov says:

*This is really creepy – I could almost chew my fingernails with anxiety! Because, here is William on stage with the Queen, the very person for whom Edward, his lover, was beheaded. Neither William knows the true identity of the 'Earl', nor does the 'Earl' know the true identity of William as Edward's 'co-conspirator'. Will they or won't they discover who each one really is? The Queen says she has a question, which is* '...how couldst mockery ever win a war?' *And what a great response from William,* 'my play is not about losing or winning wars. It's about losing or winning the war of self-knowledge. Satire breaks the veil of personal pretention. War is the folly of competing obsessions.'

Moriarty says:

*Yes, but the Queen fights back and asks William to explain what he means, so he lists all those* 'obsessions' *that drive men to slaughter each other. Then he starts to explain something about* 'Irony and satire' *but the rest is on the next page. O Brian! We are again like hungry kids begging for more!*

Brian Jones says:

*Sure – you 'kids' are reading it faster than I can upload it and making more sense than I ever could. Great job! Another page is on its way.*

Molotov says:

*What I find somewhat touching is the sort of exasperated humility in William's response to the Queen's opening remark. When she asks him if he really believes that the satirist is the* 'lord of all lords', *he replies,* 'I suppose it is my own fanciful interpretation of humour'. *What I ask myself is, if his belief is* 'fanciful' *does he sincerely and truly believe in what he has written about the power of humour? In his play, the King – who conducts the mock execution – certainly walks away the same despotic King as before. His tormentor's humour has certainly not transformed him. So maybe William believes only half-heartedly in these ideas?*

marks of an understanding of what lies within the strong statue of power. A king who thinks he can command the Sun when to shine is deluded and ignorant of his own ignorance. Satire traces, before the king's own face, the flattering mirages and patterns of his absurdity — patterns which everyone else can see, but he.

Earl : True. But may there not come a time in a nation's history — when confronted by a dire enemy intent only on cruel dominance, torture and blood-letting — when a king or Queen must stand, fight and kill? Look Sir at the Spanish Fleet — The Armada. Had our good Queen simply stood on the Dover cliffs and hurled satirical incantations at the Spanish ships, you and I would be speaking Spanish and kneeling to a Catholic God. No amount of sarcasm, wit or irony, Sir, can send an enemy running from the field of battle. Thou canst not stand before someone about to disembowel thee and thy children and tell jokes — surely that is the reserve of weaklings and cowards who thus deserve to be brushed aside by despotic power?

William : In peace and war the rules of humour do change. But thou speaketh as one who understands power and kingly authority? Art thou perhaps a spy for Elizabeth?

Earl : We should all be spies for Elizabeth. Only vigilance will stem a resurgence of catholic power. Dost thou not love our Queen?

45

Moriarty says:

*Thanks Brian. William, it appears, is still clarifying to the 'Earl' what satire is capable of. The Queen concedes the point but almost immediately blasts William out of the water with the down-to-earth example of the Spanish Armada. 'Had our good Queen simply stood on the Dover cliffs and hurled satirical incantations at the Spanish ships, you and I would be speaking Spanish and kneeling to a Catholic god.' And there is more – relentlessly she describes how telling jokes to your enemy means you will, quite rightly in her mind, be swept aside as an irrelevance. And guess what? William smells a rat! He says the Earl speaks like someone who 'understands power and kingly authority,' and adds provocatively, 'Art thou perhaps a spy for Elizabeth?' – he asks the Queen if she is a spy! But what a feisty reply he gets, 'We should all be spies for Elizabeth'! Then she finishes with a question right between William's eyes, 'Dost thou not love our Queen?' O Brian! Another page! Another page please!*

Molotov says:

*For once the Queen might get the ungarnished truth about herself – a rarity for any monarch! Though I guess William has to be careful how he replies because if, as he says, 'In peace and war the rules of humour do change', it is the ruling élite, those who wield political power, who make these rules, not the comedian or satirist. And so if he says the wrong thing – which means if he's far too candid with the Queen – he might quickly find himself in the Tower.*

Moriarty says:

*But when they used the word 'love' in Elizabethan times wasn't it usually taken to mean something like 'support'? So here, 'Dost thou not love our Queen?' could really suggest 'Don't you support our Queen?' – in other words support what she is doing?*

Molotov says:

*Possibly, although I think they used the word 'love' for a monarch as a sort of generic word for loyalty, obedience, reverence, support, deference – these sorts of things. Anyway let's find out how diplomatic William is. Brian we are at your mercy – the next page please!*

William: I hate her!

Earl: Thou shouldst, Sir, be wary-wise about who thou hatest. But prithee, wherefore hatest thou our Queen?

William: It is a personal matter — no more.

Earl: Dost thou think if she knew of this matter she would think differently?

William: Who knows? Who cares? She hath too cruelly betrayed her people!

Earl: How so Sir!? I take vast objection to thy words!

William: Earl — Queen Elizabeth is England's worst traitor!

Earl: Thou art a Papist with allegiance to Rome!

William: I have allegiance to no-one but the people of England!

Earl: But so doth the Queen! How then canst thou call her a traitor?

William: Because she denies them the right to think!

Earl: To think?

William: Aye Sir — to think! Not long ago a dear friend of mine was savagely beheaded by Elizabeth for daring to think and put down his thoughts in a manuscript.

Earl: How was the tract entitled?

William: I forget — something to do with the earthly power of Kings and Queens. He had such wonderful, new ideas and just for this

4b.

Moriarty says:

*A very diplomatic way to the executioner's block!! Why does William do this? He must know the 'Earl' is a loyal supporter of Elizabeth! And he compounds his treasonous words by declaring 'Elizabeth is England's worst traitor'! But why is he provoking the 'Earl' like this? Ah look, he says it's a 'private matter' – now it makes sense – he's still bitter about what happened to Edward, which explains why he's lashing out at any mention of the Queen.*

 Molotov says:

*The 'Earl', of course, immediately accuses William of being a militant Roman Catholic. Then they discover they both have the same allegiance – to the people of England! The puzzled 'Earl' asks why, in that case, does William insist the Queen is England's worst a traitor? Behind all this, of course, is Edward's ghost. William is clearly still distraught about Edward and he relates how 'a dear friend of mine was savagely beheaded by Elizabeth for daring to think and put down his thoughts...' And it is this suppression of thought which, in William's eyes, makes Elizabeth England's worst enemy.*

 Moriarty says:

*But now it's the Queen's turn to smell a rat because she wants to know if William can remember what his 'dear friend's' manuscript was called, because if he can, then the rat's been caught. They are like a lion and a lioness circling around each other, each sensing treachery in the other's words, each waiting for the other to blink first so they can pounce! But William can't remember. Unfortunately he goes on to say it was something to do with the '...earthly power of Kings and Queens' which might just be enough for Elizabeth to close the net. Let's see.*

 Molotov says:

*I don't know why but I get the feeling that nothing will stop William from convicting himself – he's just too honest and outspoken. In the last line he's describing Edward's attributes. If one or the other pounces we'll find out on the next page. Brian help us!*

he lost his life and I lost a dear love. And our Queen — our so-named Protector — is doing this everyday. She has become so scared of catholic assassination, every mouse that squeaks in her presence is crushed as a conspirator. This witch is stifling — nay — suffocating her people with terror and this is what makes her England's worst traitor.

Earl: But —

William: But nothing! Dost thou not know that England could be a Paradice of ideas and invention if only her people's imaginations were allowed free reign — ideas feed off ideas — thoughts on thoughts. Elizabeth hath such an opportunity in history to let the English imagination loose across the globe. But what instead, does she do? She hides in her castles, behind rows and rows of frivolous saints, reading sickly love poems — protected by the grey shadow of Count Walsingham and his web of spies!

(The 'Earl of Sussex' slowly reveals himself as The Queen).

Earl (Queen): The Queen 'hides in castles'? Behind 'frivolous saints'? 'Reading love poems'? Your friend's tract — William of Stratford — was called 'A Treatise on power'! Walsingham! Here's our conspirator! Arrest him!

William: You!!?

(Walsingham and his men rush William and subdue him.)

Queen: Yes! On your knees!
(William is forced to kneel).
I am one Queen who will not genuflect before a bad and witless jester!

47.

Molotov says:

*Thanks Brian. Well this does look like it's curtains for William. He basically accuses the Queen of morbid paranoia, of crushing even mice as would-be Catholic assassins. He calls her a witch who is suffocating people with her own fear. If only he knew who he was talking to!*

Moriarty says:

*And look at how William interrupts the Queen! This would have been something so outrageous, so insulting to the Queen, you wonder why she doesn't reveal herself and order his summary execution! In her entire life she had probably never before been interrupted by anyone, let alone by a lowly playwright – someone who, in Elizabethan times, was just one rung up from a vagabond.*

Molotov says:

*But what's all this guff about letting loose the English imagination across the globe? Is William advocating intellectual totalitarianism?*

Moriarty says:

*And to make matters worse look at how William lays into the common image of the Queen as someone who* 'hides in her castles, behind rows and rows of frivolous skirts, reading sickly love poems – protected by the grey shadow of Count Walsingham and his web of spies'! *After this tirade I guess William is now well qualified for instant crucifixion!*

Molotov says:

*The Queen throws back into William's face all of his slanderous accusations against her while simultaneously revealing who 'he' really is – even taunting William with the title of Edward's manuscript. She orders Walsingham to arrest William and force him to kneel. Then, standing over him the Queen almost revels in her position of power and declares triumphantly* 'I am one Queen who will not genuflect before a bad and witless jester!' *How is William going to talk his way out of this disaster? Brian, could we have the next page please!*

Moriarty says:

*Please Brian – our fate is in your hands! Any chance for the next page?*

Molotov says:

*Brian? Technical issues?*

Moriarty says:

*Brian's never been this slow before Molotov?*

Molotov says:

*Brian? Are you still with us? It would be great if you could upload Page 48 because we're at a very critical moment – William has just been captured by Walsingham and will, in all likelihood, soon be executed.*

Moriarty says:

*But we're only on page 47! I think the newspaper article at the start said there were about 120 pages altogether, so we're not even half-way through! If William is executed now what amazing and grizzly things must the other 70 odd pages hold? Brian! Where are you? We need you! Come back!*

Molotov says:

*Brian? It's been over 24 hours since his last upload Moriarty – maybe he's taking a break?*

Moriarty says:

*But he would have told us – he was a reliable type of guy. He wouldn't just disappear without a word. And anyway this is just too dam important to take a break! BRIAN! Where are you?*

# GUARDIAN POST

It is with immense trepidation, disbelief and sadness that we announce the death of Mr. Brian Jones of Stratford.

Some eight or nine weeks ago Mr. Jones astonished the literary world by announcing he had discovered what he claimed was the last play written by Shakespeare – some 120 pages of hand-written text entitled '*The Tragedy Of Life's Cruel Wisdom By William Of Stratford 1615*'. Leaving aside the volcano of justified scepticism and cynicism which erupted immediately after the manuscript's 'discovery', nothing warrants the brutal and callous homicide of Mr. Jones. For let us not mix our words – Brian Jones was murdered. Why he was targeted and killed is still open to conjecture, but it seems his blog, on which he began publishing his manuscript, offended a religious minority who eventually took matters into their own hands.

According to eye-witness reports, at about midnight yesterday a group calling itself 'Commandos for Christ' broke into Mr. Jones's Stratford home and ran amok with petrol bombs and machetes, screaming 'The blood of the true Christ is rising!' and 'Death to all sodomites!'. They broke into Mr. Jones's study and murdered him in cold blood before fire-bombing his computer and destroying the famous 'Shakespeare' manuscript about which Mr. Jones was so proud. Not content with this heinous crime they set fire to every room in the house shouting slogans in

Latin under the bogus pretence they were performing an exorcism. Within two hours the entire property was reduced to ashes. Fire-fighting crews and other emergency services were prevented from reaching the blaze with yet more petrol bombs thrown by the fanatics who had anticipated their arrival and felled trees to block roads. By the time the police arrived the Commandos for Christ had fled into the night.

As these bare facts illustrate this attack was well-planed and co-ordinated and carried out with ruthless precision – the one objective being the murder of Mr. Jones and the complete destruction of his property. At first light this morning Mr. Jones's remains were found beside a molten mass of metal assumed to be the box in which he kept his precious manuscript. What makes Mr. Jones's passing particularly poignant is that on the very day he was so senselessly killed, the Guardian Post has learnt from Professor Osborne of Oxford University, that the carbon dating results from the many laboratories around the world, all unequivocally confirm the date of the paper and ink of the manuscript to be from the end of the 16th century. This, together with all the other dating evidence, confirms the possibility that the work was penned when Shakespeare was alive. Whether it was written by The Bard himself is still open to debate and controversy. But certainly a great archaeological find has now been lost to posterity.

Mr. Jones joins a whole list of people who, over the years, have paid the ultimate price for daring to exercise their right to freedom of expression. Like many men and women before him who have been imprisoned and flogged, raped and executed, Brian Jones was a brave man murdered because he was guilty of nothing more than honesty and integrity. These are virtues that fundamentalists and fanatics hate. They should, however, inspire us. The struggle for free speech, for free inquiry and for the liberty to believe or not believe, need not be a fight against religion, unless religion is opposed to human dignity. And this struggle has become just that – a struggle against all those forces that are opposed to human dignity and freedom. The struggle is against cowardice and conformism, and against everyone who would crush both truth and imagination into the airless coffin of orthodoxy. For we cannot have human dignity without the freedom to discover what it means. We cannot attain human dignity with duct tape across our minds. The liberty to express our thoughts, however controversial, is at the very core of our human identity.

In the shadow of these tragic circumstances the Guardian Post is privileged to reveal that soon after Mr. Jones announced the discovery of his manuscript, we approached him and – refusing a substantial financial offer – we obtained his permission to make a copy of the complete manuscript on the strict understanding that it was not to be published in our newspaper or related outlets or transmitted electronically in digital form. It was agreed between us that the copy would be kept permanently under lock and key as a safeguard against theft or fire. However, should there arise any unforeseen eventuality, it was agreed the Guardian Post would retain the right to publish but only after consultation with Mr. Jones and with his express permission. Because of the tragedy which has occurred, this is now impossible. By virtue of Mr. Jones's murder and the complete destruction of the original manuscript, we feel it is now our duty to honour his legacy and to publish the copy in our possession in its entirety. Had he still been with us Mr. Jones would, we are convinced, have wanted the Guardian Post to do this. We have therefore attached the complete and unabridged copy of Brian Jones's now famous manuscript to this obituary. We have used an antique font in an attempt to retain the original style of writing, but we leave it to our readers to decide on the manuscript's merits and demerits.

# The Tragedy Of Life's Cruel Wisdom

## By

## William Of Stratford,

## 1615

# The Tragedy Of Life's Cruel Wisdom

## by William Of Stratford, 1615.

### DRAMATIS PERSONAE

William - citizen of Stratford

Ann - wife to William

Thomas Morton - friend of William

Celine Morton - sister to Thomas Morton

Hick Morton, Judd Morton, Skelly Morton - all brothers to

Thomas Morton

Queen Elizabeth 1

Sir Francis Walsingham - advisor to the Queen

Edward , Christopher - friends of William

Jonesie, Hans, Robert, Alex - William's fellow actors/friends at
the theatre

Robert Cecil (Earl of Salisbury) - later advisor to the Queen

Jackie - brothel friend of William

Attendants to the Queen

Henrietta - Lady-in-waiting to the Queen

Priest, Prelate, Bishop of Westminster

Two murderers, Guards, Prison Guards, Spies and Messengers

Sundry actors in street scenes and at theatre

# ACT 1

## Scene i

[At night, in a tree. Thomas Morton sits, a noose around his neck]

Thomas: Unasked, this world hath spun me of silk

Yet I shall, in bitter revenge, unspin this flesh

And cut my tattered existence free of all its tarnished
innocence.

At sixteen a love beyond love was released into my veins

Yet at eighteen doth this same agony

Now throw my raw heart beneath the dancing crowd

To be mocked and spat on.

But why should I care, the multitudes have only ever

Seen their own blindness as the pinnacle of their own

truth, and I, so close to death, have no patience to

stand on their pin-headed mountains to mock at ants

and sparrows.

I, instead, see nothing but the true abyss of my William.

For two malicious years of unfettered, blind confinement,

My thoughts, my cries have so blanketed my mind with their

Encrypted passions that every heartbeat hath blurred the

night into conscious day and each day into sickening

night.

Yet, as I impenitent lay in my cell, thou, William, hast

wived and fathered and thrown

An infinite distance between us,

And it hangs like a colossal dagger in the sky

Not knowing if to point at ecstasy or at the outpourings

of tumultuous imbeciles.

But all this while, my love, thou hast said nothing.

Thy silence hath cast and seeded the worst of all dreams,

For it and it alone hath spawned the termination of my

world,

A cruelty for which there are no trite exonerations, no

sweet-gilded excuses, no flower-wrapped verses,

For it is a cruelty far beyond the infinite malice of all

the stars.

With love's consuming pain I fell to my knees

And swallowed the flames of thy vast, unbridled sex,

And for this celebration, this bright triumph of existence,

I have been murdered many times over.

But no more.

No more shall these trite deaths cheat me of death's final

release.

And so I kiss the rope that soon will swing

My heavy soul across the gaping thresholds of hell.

O William, my heart is in my heart.

Your touch came and disintegrated my soul so much

That I became invisible to even myself,

A secret within a secret.

And now I know more than I know,

With words unable to be words.

And 'though, as I sit poised before the infinite

I still feel your eyes passing through my blood,

I know thou hast escaped the dark, final bond between
    us.

So William, may this egress, this bleak and selfish
    farewell of mine, last forever.

                                        [he leaps]

## Scene ii

[A bedroom, William and Ann asleep. William suddenly springs up

terrified, clutching his throat]

Will: Arrrg! Away! Get me more breath! Arrrg!

Ann: William! What is wrong!? Speak!

W: Arrg! The devil is standing on my throat! Away! Arrrg!

A: There is nothing there William! Thy throat is free!

W: His pointed tail is whipped and wrapped upon my neck!

Let me go!

[William tears off his nightshirt]

A: William stop!

W: He's choking me Ann! Arrrg!

A: For pity's sake William cease! This is just another false twist in

the wretched, false darkness of thy mind! Stop!

[William falls from the bed]

W: Arrg! Ann help! He draggeth me unto the edge of the pit!

A: William! Thou art abed! Come, get up! Stop this!

It is just the frail bubble of your mind which

hath so burst and swamped thine eyes with

poisonous, visionary madness that thou seest

belching vulcanes where there are only bed-sheets!

W: He holds me still Ann! Away!

A: Get up William! There is no god-sent devil about thy neck!

196

[Ann pulls William back onto the bed]

W: Away! Strangle someone other than J! Arrg!

A: William look at me! The devil hath gone! J bit at his slimy tail and
he ran!

W: Jf not the devil, then whose evil, swift cunning doth tighten about my
throat!?

[The ghost of Thomas Morton, a noose around his neck, appears
at the foot of the bed]

Ye gods! He grins and beckons! Ann! Look! Look! His face is
set to shatter my soul! He hath come to strip my bones of their flesh!
Hence!

A: Will look at me! Only J am before thine eyes! Look! Here are my
naked breasts! They and they alone William are the only
reality in this all-tangible world!

W: J see him still – white-grinning between thy breasts!

A: Thou seest thine own inverted mind! Awake J say!

[She strikes William across the face. The apparition vanishes]

W: The...the pit hath...closed...J live...my children?...do J have children?

A: Yes! All three such sweet babes!

[William takes Ann by both shoulders and stares into her face]

W: Thomas...Thomas, J can't.

[Ann shrieks and strikes William hard. She sits on his chest and
beats him]

A: You man-bitch! You counterfeit queen! How dare thee! Thou flimsy-
penised whore!

Why dost thou mouth thy steamy madness at me like this!?

Art thou trying to turn snakes into giraffes! men into stones! and
rainclouds into wild, fierce-dancing women!?

Again and again how dare thee! How canst thou vent that cursed,
disease-driven name into my face!

Less than a name – a bawd, a wretch, a nothing who
magicked thy wholesome, virgin seed from my bed!

What!? Dost thou want thy loins forever to crawl with the
antichrist!?

Wilt thou always pine and scream and eat the very earth this
spineless, empty 'Tom' hath defiled!?

Even though I have lain here in our bed,

My body stained with thy babe's very blood,

Yet you, in this dream-madness, you let this 'thing', this abstract
speck of nothing,

To everyday gut the enthroned love from my heart!

The more thou lovest this dubious 'him', the more thou despiseth me
as a woman!

But be thou doubly secured William, if thou dost not

Sever this wretch from thy soul,

Thou wilt forever drain the whole firmament of my mind

Of all its love and life for thee!

W:  But why Ann dost thou rage so at a mere ghost? Art thou jealous?

A:  Ha! J jealous!? No, J am not jealous! J shall tear my flesh into pieces of sulphurous fire before J bend to jealousy!

W: O Ann hold! Thou wast made to terrify humanity!

To shake men's blinded hearts!

To stab the darkness and strike at their mistakes!

Sweet Ann forgive me!

A: If J do rage Will it is because J have gained an almost-colossus of a man,

The vastness of my fury doth show but the vastness of my love for thee. Do not Will cast it aside on ghosts.

W: Heaven touch me! Methought J was betrothed to the night yet, in truth, J was wedded to the sun.

A: Then let my light stretch out beyond the opaque stench of this grave thou diggest for thyself.

Use not, William, thyself to see, but rip out thine eyes and, between thy teeth, burst their apparitions and falsehoods,

For with this grievous distemper thou canst not see ought but the tantalising chaos of despair!

W: Spare me Ann – say no more!

A: Will J...[she stops aghast]... Will thy neck!

W: Ann do not terrify me! What is it!?

A: Thy reddened skin shows a bruised circle of violence! Was I so

rough with thee?

W: Nay sweet Ann, not thee. Then it must be true, I have been

swung from a gibbet!

A: Only from the gibbet of thy mind William.

W: Bring me a glass! I must see!

[There is loud knocking at the house door. Ann goes to the window and

calls down into the street]

A: Who is it darest wake the living with the dead!? Gabriel! Wherefore

comest thou at this dread hour?

Gabriel: Ann! Let me in quickly! The Morton's will have their claws

into William's face! Hurry!

[William and Ann both descend and let Gabriel inside]

W: Your voice speaks of bloody revenge, what dreadful matter has

happened Gabriel?

Gab: The Youngest Morton, Thomas, the one thou hadst befriended

William, was found hanging in the wood by his sister Celine.

The Morton father, spitting blood and fire, is even now on

his way here, strong-armed with brothers and clan all blind in

anger, to rid the family of its ill-perceived shame! William

you must this very instant fly!

W: I cannot! I cannot leave Ann and my children to bare their throats to mass, ungodly slaughter!

A: William! Do as Gabriel says! Gabriel go with all speed and wake

our father and the family. Tell them what has occurred and

raise them here with haste, well-armed and prepared to save

their daughter's and grand-children's lives. Hurry!

Gab: William fear not, I will use the shield of my soul and body to

protect Ann and thy little ones – that I promise thee. But do

not take the main road. Use the forest tracks thou knowest so

well and go only afoot at night until Oxford. Adieu!

[Exit Gabriel]

A: William! Come dress quickly! I'll prepare a sack!

[William dresses hastily with heavy coat and boots etc., while Ann takes a large sack into the kitchen and throws provender inside for the journey.

When he is ready they embrace.]

W: I will aim for London and lose myself in the multitudes. I will find

employment and send thee what I can, and when all this

tearful chaos has past I promise I will return. Kiss my

children everyday with my love, let them not forget me.

Ann, thou art the certainty of the Sun with its axis

deep embedded in my heart. Without thee and without my love

for thee, I would but cruise and tumble through the

impenetrable obscurity of space like some meaningless

fragment of death.

A: Tush William! Such wild flatteries will delay your life! You must

hurry! Go across those dark fields yonder! Go! Go!

W: One flesh and again one flesh is love's tender price,

One flesh and again one flesh is man's game of dice.

[Exit William]

A: O Will! In the threat of night thou must turn from thy loving wife,

In the threat of night to find thyself and save thy life.

[at night, a forest track]

William:    How far have J come?

But is not the more yielding question – how far with love

have J come?

Or should J not say 'How far 'in' love have J come?'

Or how far 'to' love? Or 'from' love? Or' for' love?

Perhaps 'towards' love would cut better?

Strange how each tiny preposition gives to each 'love' its

own new, oblique understanding, as though mere words, just

by using here and there a tricky prefix, suffix or crude

conjugation of epithets, can push so many meanings in so many

directions. But can love have a language built from utterance?

What words then can enshrine poor, sweet Thomas, my first

ever love? What canst thou, Thomas, now be but someone

else's breath?

O Thomas, as a bird which hath crashed against the glass,

thou fell like a soft angel to my pillow and lay stunned and shy

in my arms, thy tiny heart racing with love's all-honeyed pain.

Wherever thou art Thomas, know J loved thee so truly that,

had not the world despised us, J would have gladly wedded

with thee into whatever dark bliss exists beyond eternity.

And Ann and our sweet babes, my second love.

When first we met J was an almost-dead fish,

a bony youth, down and falling apart in the surf,

yearning for air, gasping for just one breathless atom of

meaning in this chaotic, murky sewer called life!

So why Ann didst thou love me so? J was nothing,

J brought nothing and J remain nothing, so why –

[William spies the light of a fire in the forest]

Hold and quiet! What villainous light is that!    Out here in the depths of

nowhere live only the wretched, untameable scraps of humanity,

diseased men and women who would hail thee as friend and

then use thy upturned skull as a bowl for their soup.

Oft have J heard of the Oxfordshire cannibals, but it's said

that all those who have seen them ended their journey

as excrement on the forest floor. Best J wide skirt this

beacon of culinary delights and..........Arrrg!

[Rough hands pull William to the ground. Struggling and protesting William is dragged towards the fire. Once at the fire he is tied to a stake facing the blaze. His legs are splayed apart and tied down. He is stripped naked except for an open shirt that's left hanging from his shoulders. Before him stand the three Morton brothers.]

Hick Morton: Well William thou cameth like a moff flutterin' to de

        slaughterin' flame! O tut fuckin' tut! Makes me poor eyes

        shed tears o'blood for yer it does!

W: Let me go you revengeful cretins!

[Judd Morton draws his sword and points it closely at William's exposed

genitals]

Judd Morton: Der's de cause of all our troubles!

W: Thou art the cause of all –

Hick: Shut it! Hold Judd! We ain't prop'ly welcomed our patient! Let

        me introduce docktor Judd 'ere, hoo, as thou canst see, is a

        skilled blood-letter. Onlie 'e don't use leechees or 'ot suckin'

        bells – o no! 'e's far too skilled wiv all sorts o' rusty blades.

        Judd, say hello.

Judd [spitting on William]: Bitch-lickin' faggot!

Hick: Little 'ot-'eaded is our Judd. Now der's docktor Skelly 'ere –

        young to de trade 'e is, but so fuckin' keen! Ain't yer Skell!?

        'e wants t'sharpen 'is talents in riddin' faggots like thee o'

        such inferno-beasts as wot infect their gizzards an' guts.

        Onlie 'cos 'e's just learnin' an' all, 'e keeps makin' some

        'orrofik mistakes. Skell, say 'ello to our patient.

Skelly: Debauched devil!

Hick: An' den der's me, docktor 'ick – or docktor Grievous – take yer

        pick. But William thou knowest all 'bout me don't yer? 'Cos

it wuz me wot 'scovered thee an' our Thomas bedded togever wrapped up like two virgin girls!

Judd: You 'ad your sex-rods up each other like sick bastards! Sets me skin all a'crawlin' wiv maggots just finkin' 'bout it! Sticks in me 'ead like a...like a disgustin' glue. Every time J closes me eyes J see youze ruttin' away, pantin' and' moanin' like whores at it in the street!

W: We were young and in love.

Hick: Love!? Jn love!? Thou callest that nameless, shameless thigh-slappin' love!? Man-on-man filth ain't love! Real men don't love each other — real men hate each other!

Judd: Come on 'ick! Der's too much yappin! De night's draggin' on, let's get on wiv it!

Hick : Alright Judd! Alright! Now, bein' docktors it's onlie right an' proper we've got t'cure the patient.

W: Jt's you Mortons that need curing — J'd rather die with my love than live with your hate.

Hick: Shut thy mouth! Thou hast no position to give me any 'rather this and rather that.'

W: Stop playing with me! Kill me if you must! But spare my wife and children — they never harmed the Mortons!

Hick: Kill thee!? O gawd no! We ain't no commom, shoe-string cut-throats! 'ow can we cure thee of being a woman one day and a

206

man the next, if we kills thee?

Judd: Get on wiv it 'ick! Stop yappin'. Cut wot we said and let's go
'ome.

Hick: Right thou art Judd! So, t'cure thee of bein' an 'alf woman, we 'as
got to cut off thy nips.

W: That being so, Hick Morton, thou art too a woman.

Hick: Shut it!

W: All men have got nipples.

Hick: J said shut it!

Judd: Wot's 'e sayin'?

Skelly: Never thought o'dat. Den...den wot's us men's nips for?

W: All men were once women.

Hick! Open thy mowff again an' J swear J'll peel de skin from thy
skull!

Judd: J ain't no breasty tart!

Skelly: Saw a monkey at de fair once – a male it wuz – it 'ad nips.

Judd: 'e's sayin' J'm a girlie boy 'cos J got nips!

Hick: Will you two stop goin' on 'bout nips! Enough yappin'! And thee!
No more wise-man nipple-talk for thee!

[Hick takes hold of one of William's nipples and cuts it off]

W: Arrrrg!

Hick: 'Ere! Rexy!     [Throws William's nipple to his dog who eats it]

Judd: Go on 'ick! Do de other one!

Hick: Can't 'ave thee bein' a one-breasted woman now can we?

[Hick takes hold of William's other nipple, cuts it off and throws it to his dog]

W: Arrrrg!!!

Hick: Now that thou canst not be a woman, it's time to cure thee of bein' a man.

Judd: Go on 'ick! Do it like we said!

Hick: Ye see, Rexy 'ere likes 'is morsels – ain't dat so Rexy!? [pretends to talk to his dog] Wot!? Js dat right Rexy!? Well J never! [addressing William] Says 'e's partial to a bit o' roast! Fetch me a torch!

[Judd pulls a flaming branch from the fire and hands it to Hick]

W: ...Don't!...Don't do this Hick Morton!

Hick: Pleadin' f'mercy won't touch me 'eart – thou bleedin' cross-breed – it wuz me wot cut down our Thomas!

Judd: Burn 'im 'ick! Burn 'im proper!

Hick: Every cook knows dat de quickest way t'bald a pig is wiv fire!

[Hick waves the burning branch below Will's genitals singeing his pubic hair]

W: Arrrrg! Please!

Judd: 'Jck! it's takin' ages! Hurry up an' cut them off like we said!

Hick: Right. F dis special surgree J 'specially sharpened me blade!

[Hick throws down the torch and takes out a large knife. With the blade tip he flicks aside William's shirt. He takes aim and is just about to cut William's genitals off, when there is the loud explosion of a musket. Hick claws at his throat which is now gushing with blood and falls dead. The others all run from

208

the scene. Gabriel enters hurriedly from the forest's shadows carrying a musket. He rushes to William and frees him.]

Gabriel: William!

William: Gabriel! I owe thee my life now twice over! Arrrg my breasts

hurt!

Gab: We must hurry! Get dressed!

[While William quickly dresses, Gabriel reloads his musket]

Will: But how didst thou find me?

Gab: Thou hast thy dear wife Ann to thank – she implored me to find

thee and accompany thee till Oxford. So I took our father's

horse and musket and here I am – and not before time!

Will: And Ann and the children – are they safe?

Gab: Have no fear they are safely housed with our father and are protected

by dozens of uncles and cousins. Come we can talk later. I

needed to be stealthy so my horse is some distance away.

Although I have reloaded I don't want the other Mortons

to know who shot their dog of a brother. Come, hurry! Lean

on me!

[With Gabriel supporting William they both disappear into the dark forest]

# ACT 2

## Scene i

[a street in London, two beggars]

First beggar: Canst thou count?

Second beggar: Och aye! On dis one 'and J got ten fingers!

First: Wot!?

Second: J is cross-eyed see.

First: Dat'll do nicely! So listen. Over der see, is wot J calls a
vacuous 'ouse – no human soul within – every room a tomb.

Second: Der tomb of 'annibal !

First: The very same! Now look you – take an empty sack, and put in
two rabbits. Wot y'got? Two rabbits? Nah! 'Cos you opens
de sack and two rats crawl out! So, eever de sack wern't
empty to start wiv – which just ain't possible – or de two
rabbits wot went in, was charmed inta rats! So wot y'got?

Second: An 'aunted sack!

First: Well, it would make de sack exceedin' magical. Now, over
yonder, we 'as an exceedin' magical 'ouse wot charms anyone
wot goes inside.

Second: Inta rats?

First: Dunno wot they is.

Second: Dat tomb of 'annibal 'ouse?

First: The very same! Y'see J've bin doin' some 'rithmetics – countin' like – inta dat 'annibal 'ouse. Oft 'ave J seen two womens go in but two mens come out – wot means dat out of two der's really four. But! But de 'ouse is still empty!

Second: Dat's 'aunted 'rithmetics dat is!

First: Well, eever de 'rithmetics is bewitched or de 'ouse is.

Second: Dat's mischief beyond de mind! 'Cos if two rabbits goes inta a sack or an 'ouse, two rabbits 'as got to come out!

First: 'Xactly! Dat's wot 'rithmetics learns thee! But as thou says der's clear mischief in dis 'rithmetics. But look to thy bottle! 'Ere they comes! Arm-in-arm, wiv smiles fit to charm birds into crocodilloes! The good o'de evenin' to your majesties!

[Enter William and Edward, arm-in-arm, dressed as women]

William: Well, if J am thy queen be careful J don't ask the Duchess of Southwark here to deprive thee of thy cheeky tongue.

First: J wouldn't want no duchess runnin' off wiv me tongue your highness – without me tongue me life would stagnify!

Edward: With or without thy tongue thy life hath already stagnified. Why dost thou live in this filthy gutter?

First: For de same reason kings live in palaces y'grace – 'cos J was born 'ere. Dis gutter is me palace. Dis fish-head's a gift from a mighty cookin' queen wot rules the kitchens yonder up de street. And dis pig's tooth is a tribute from the noble butcher across de way.

211

William: Here take this and get thyself and thy

friend, the duke here, a banquet fit for a king.

[giving some money]

First: May your majesty's kindness sweep de world!

[William and Edward continue and enter the 'vacuous' house in the street. As they talk they slowly change out of their women's clothes and into men's attire.]

Edward: Thou straineth my heart William.

William: Edward – it's Christmas. J haven't seen my sweet children for

six months.

Ed: Thou useth thy children to hide thy real intent! For six months thou

hast not been in thy wife's bed!

Will: Edward!

Ed: Tis true! The cause is simple – thou lovest her more than me.

Will: Truly Edward thou hast the yellow sickness! Jt's corrosive acid

will burn deep holes in thy heart for no good reason. And

why? Because thy heart is too blind to see love for what it is.

Ed: O the great William knows the true nature of love! And J, whose

acid heart weeps rivers whenever thou leavest me, whose eyes

burn like dying candles waiting for thy return, know only the

endless, narrow corruption of jealousy! Please, William, tell

me why J should not be jealous of thy wife?

Will: Because thou wouldst have love a prison, whereas J see love as

something universal, as –

212

Ed: What tosh! If love is 'universal' why dost thou not take that beggar

in the gutter outside into thy bed!? Why doth he not qualify

for a piece of thy universal love!?

Will: Edward, love is not measured out in drops of seed!

Ed: So love hath no gradation? no scale? no size? no immensity?

Will: Love is the measure of all things, true, but love cannot measure

itself.

All we can know Edward is that for some brief explosion of

time,

Our anguished, immaterial souls do mesh,

Do fit as a key doth to a lock —

My key doth fit perfectly thy lock as doth thy key mine —

We open each other. Is this love? Is this how love doth spin

its fatal web? I know not.

Some would rather say this is how hate doth germ itself.

When thou canst define love, they argue, love is dead, and the

death of love is the very seed of hate — so runs their logic.

Love — a terrified animal worried into the ground by clarity.

Edward, prey listen. My coach leaves on the hour — I must

hurry to Shoreditch. I will be away for Christmas as my

little ones are waiting for their father — I cannot break their

hearts for they are like small, unopened flowers who have not

the wisdom to shield themselves from life's bitter

213

disappointments. Thou hast a bigger, stronger heart which I

shall - I promise thee – make run wildly when I return.

Ed: When wilt thou return?

Will: After ten or twelve days – then we will show each other such
        passion as will make dogs blush and mountains sing
        halleluiah.

[They embrace each other passionately]

Ed: William? Before thou goest say thou lovest me.

Will: I love thee Edward, I love thee to the point of pain and beyond.

        Edward! I almost forgot! My absence will give thee silence

        and time to finish thy essay! Thou hast only the last few

        pages to write.

[a clock bell is heard]

Hush! I must make haste! Goodbye my sweet!

'Ed: Goodbye William – keep me in thy heart as I will keep thee in mine!

[They kiss goodbye briefly and William leaves the house now dressed as a man
and disappears in a hurry down the street]

First beggar: Seest thou! De first rat's out!

Second beggar: So only one ratty-rabbit left!


[Edward settles down at his writing table and shuffles some sheets of paper.
While he does this we see the Second Beggar rise up and move into the
shadows where a darkly dressed gentleman is standing. They exchange a few

214

words and the dark gentleman clearly gives the Second Beggar some money. The beggar returns to his friend and moments later the dark gentleman, together with several well-armed men, approach the house Edward is in and hammer on the door. But before waiting for an answer they burst the door down, rush in and arrest Edward. They bind him and drag him away. The dark gentleman collects Edward's papers, notices the women's clothes and wigs, puts what he can into a sack and leaves.]

### Scene ii

[The Queen's apartments. The Queen and Sir Francis Walsingham]

Queen Elizabeth [reading some papers]: Good Walsingham, these sheets read not of a conspiracy of catholics, yet their language has a strange, disturbing sharpness that doth much unsettle me.

Walsingham: Tis most true, Your Majesty, there is no clear hatred or challenge to thine own person or authority, yet it is sharply writ more as a conspiracy against all royal and earthly power. Nonetheless the author is a catholic— a circumstance it would be most dangerous to ignore, for any such perverted faith must heavily blemish all thought and action.

Q.Eliz [reading aloud]: 'A Treatise on Power or The Rights of a Free People To Govern Themselves.'

Wals: I have marked some of the more provocative passages Your Majesty.

Q. Eliz: Here? Ah yes [reading aloud] 'All monarchs, emperors, popes and priests are tyrants stretching from the benign to the murderous. All are, without exception, self-enraptured despots, monsters with their cloven hooves pressed firmly on the throats of their subjects.' **Walsingham! This is vile sedition! This venom could bring ruin to all earthly authority and crown Chaos and Destruction as the ultimate despot of all kings!**

**Wals:** **Indeed so Your Majesty. Those rebellious lines concerning God's own Church are on the next page.**

**Q.Eliz** [reading aloud]: 'The Pope is no more than the Devil's executioner on Earth – he never was, nor ever will be God's ambassador. The catholic See of Rome spreads the tyranny of superstition and ignorance by robbing the poor not only of their money but, more importantly, of their ability to think.'

**Well Walsingham I can find nothing disagreeable in that!**

**Wals:** **But read on Your Majesty, there is more.**

**Q.Eliz:** 'Not only the Roman Papacy but all churches of whatever creed or doctrine, of whatever sect or soul – even Protestantism – are nothing more than Satanic engines designed to create human suffering and perpetuate intolerance. If a truly righteous, loving God could see what the religious nobility enact in his name, He would crush this vast Earth with a fist of fire. But since God doth not, how can we call Him righteous or loving? How can we even call Him God?'

**This is not just sedition Walsingham, it is treacherous, open blasphemy! He slanders the Church, then he slanders God**

**himself! That there are men like this in my England who can think in this way is monstrous! With thoughts like these all shadows are now but the harbingers of the Great Apocalypse!** [Elizabeth continues reading aloud] 'The Divine Right of Kings and Queens to rule is no more than a Tyrant's Right to tyrannise. The Divine Right to rule is invoked simply to excuse any blood-thirsty seizure of power – for it is only those who have snatched power by force-of-arms who do generously wallow in the delusion of their own Divinity. The truth is, it is only their Might which has given them their Right – there is nothing Divine about it. To claim that God has ordained their victory is to say that God has ordained their Right to slaughter.' **Walsingham! Bring this villainous demon before me! There is more than a traitor in such a mind!**

**Wals: I fear Your Majesty's sensitive disposition would be far too shocked – he hath been racked in the Tower these three days for we know he hath an accomplice.**

**Q.Eliz: Do not fret about my disposition Walsingham, I will speak with this impudent cur before you separate his soul from his body. Fetch him!**

**Wals: Very good Your Majesty.**                    [exit Walsingham]

**Q. Eliz** [reading more aloud]: 'If the simple truth be told, the power that dynasties wield is only truly used to keep a ruling clan or

217

family in its privileged position of wealth and luxury. And to keep itself in power at all costs, the ruling clan must allow incest, murder, rape and regicide to become normal expressions of successful government.' **These ideas could spread a multitude of venomous serpents across the land. They fall from these pages like diseased fruit from a diseased mind – nobody must ever think like this!** [reading more]

'And the Churches collude in this privileged butchery by making what is truly a crime an act of God, an act which they pretend shines with the legitimacy of Almighty God's Grace and Will– whereas all power stolen like this is fundamentally illegitimate.'

[Enter Walsingham. Edward is dragged in. He cannot walk]

**Wals:** **Although we have been extremely strenuous in our efforts Your Majesty, this traitor hath steadfastly refused to give neither his own name nor the names of his fellow conspirators.**

**Q.Eliz:** **So, I am a tyrant?**

**Edw:** **My broken body is answer.**

**Q.Eliz:** **Your body Sir hath been broken to keep England safe!**

**Edw:** **Wilt thou be safe only when England is full of broken bodies?**

**Q.Eliz:** **Walsingham, he threatens me!**

**Wals:** **Hold thy tongue wretch!**

**Edw:** **I am no conspirator.**

**Wals:** **Then why wert thou using the disguise of a woman to plan thy**

218

treachery?

Q. Eliz: A woman!?

Wals: Indeed Your Majesty, we found wigs, costumes and various

devices to disguise his manhood at his lodging – all clearly to

be used to cloak his true purpose. And we have every reason

to believe that his fellow conspirators are using the very same

methods.

Q.Eliz: Tell us thy name! Who art thou? What art thou?

Edw: I am no more than what I am.

Q.Eliz: This word play Sir may cost thee thy head if thou dost not

answer plainly – Who art thou?

Edw: I am thee, thou art me, I am a queen of England.

Q.Eliz: Walsingham! He hath lost his mind – therefore he hath no need of

a head to keep it in! Out of my sight!

[Edward is dragged away]

You say there are others?

Wals: Indeed there are Your Majesty.

Q.Eliz: I want them found. I cannot have such pestilential corruption

abiding in the minds of my people. And burn all these papers.

Their heat shall counter the heat of the ideas writ on them – it

shall warm the heart of at least one good tyrant!

Wals: Very good Your Majesty.

Q.Eliz: Walsingham?

Wals: Your Majesty?

Q.Eliz: Am I a tyrant? I know thou hast not the buttery tongue of a
flatterer, so speak openly and without fear, what truly thinkest
thou, am I a tyrant?

Wals: Your Majesty, it is the inevitable consequence of what thou art
that every decision thou taketh becomes an irrefutable fact in
history. But the question 'Art thou a tyrannical queen or a
tolerant queen of wise governance?' is a question with so many
different answers, the question itself may be meaningless. To
most catholics thou art quite clearly a tyrant. To Protestants
thou art the protector of their faith, the only bulwark against
the Papacy, the only monarch on the globe with the courage and
will to say to the Pope and his minions 'I rule England, not
you.' Thou canst only do what thou feelest in thy English
bones is right for England, and so thou mayest be the only
person who can truly say they are quintessentially English.
Thou art a single person, a monarch who hath, in the name
of the English people, embraced Protestantism because it may,
in veritas, be the first step on a long, historic journey to how
the English discover for themselves the true significance of
freedom. So, art thy decisions those of a tyrant? Or rather
the decisions of a determined Queen who hath struck a course
for her country out into the unknown waters of freedom?

Q.Eliz: But are not tracts like these charting that very freedom?

Wals: Perhaps – but not at the cost of apocalyptic anarchy Your Majesty. And, prey, for what reason should men destroy God?

Q.Eliz: But for what reason Walsingham have we stepped outside the bossom of the Almighty?

Wals: We are all encompassed by the bossom of God Your Majesty, but God hath never limited how far we may look beyond what He holds.

Q.Eliz: But why do we always need to step beyond God? Is it to explore freedom? But freedom from what? From the See of Rome certainly. I sometimes feel, Walsingham, it is the Devil himself who whispers to me that the freedom we seek is a freedom from even God himself.

Wals: Sometimes, Your Majesty, thou appeareth more seditious than many of the traitors I execute.

Q.Eliz: What!? Wouldst thou rack thy queen Walsingham?

Wals: That, thank God, will never happen as thou canst not be a traitor to thyself. But should that day ever arrive, I will call myself an ape and learn to fish the mighty seas for elephants.

[exeunt  Queen Elizabeth and Walsingham]

## Scene iii

[Tythe Barn Street, London. Enter William carrying bags]

**Young man**[shouting]: *William!*

**William:** *Christopher! Now thou art such a cheery surprise!*

**Christopher:** *Indeed! I haven't seen thee since before St. Crispins! But what's with these bags and travel cloak — art thou leaving us!?*

**Will:** *No Christopher! Quite the opposite — I'm returning from the country! I've been away for the Holy Days.*

**Chris:** *Come! Tell me all over some bad London ale! The Pig & Duck is just here!*

**Will:** *Thou wast always too generous Christopher, but alas I'm tired from my journey, I must get home and rest.*

**Chris:** *Be wary of the streets William.*

**Will:** *Wherefore? Wherefore thy hushed warning?*

**Chris:** *The old, iron Queen sees traitors and catholic assassins on every corner. She's been festooning the city with special Christmas images of gore that do not bare looking upon.*

**Will:** *'Twas always so Christopher.*

**Chris:** *Indeed, but caution never harmed good souls. Wilt thou soon be at the theatre?*

**Will:** *Of course! Come tomorrow and see my new play!*

**Chris:** *What title hast thou given it?*

Will: The title will come when I lie in my next bath.

Chris: Then for sure it must be another smelly comedy!

Will: Then I'll write thee the part of a cheeky maid! Look Christopher,

I must get home. Come to the theatre tomorrow after

rehearsals and tell me thy thoughts.

Chris: I will with pleasure.

Will: Adieu good Christopher!

Chris: Adieu William and although my greetings come late – Happy

Christmas and embrace Edward from me!

Will: I will indeed – adieu!                                    [exit Christopher]

[William continues walking. He turns into a street which has the bloody heads of those executed, spiked at various intervals down the street. Although he tries not to look, his attention is suddenly caught by one head – it is Edward's]

Ahhhh!...please!...let..it...not be!

[He stops aghast at Edward's head. Immediately four men violently pounce on William from the shadows, pull a sack over his head and carry him off screaming]

First man: Shut it! Thou squealin' rascal!

Second man: Slit 'is neck!

Third man: Shred out 'is tongue!

First man: First gouge 'is eyes!

Fourth man: Can I 'ave de liver!?

[They each take out a knife, look about and carry William still struggling into a dark alleyway]

First man: William! Sssshh! Be quiet! Thou art with friends! Sssh now!

Will[still sacked]: J...J know that voice!

First man: And so thou shouldst!

Will: Jonesie! Js that you!?

Jonesie: Aye! Me an' me beatin' 'eart!          [They remove the sack]

Will: And Hans! Such welcome faces! What!? J thought you would all be dining on me! But why? Wherefore this mock-violent abduction? Wouldst thou frighten me to death for some merciless wit?

Hans: Ve iz saving thy lifes Villiam!

Jonesie: Thou hast seen Edward's fate? Walsingham and his spies are everywhere seeking thy head to spike alongside poor Edward. Thy house and all the nearby streets are being watched day and night.

Hans: Thou iz luck ve getz to thee first Villiam!

Jonesie: Hans is right – t'is now much safer for thee if Walsingham and his spies should think thou art dead – hence this murderous charade.

Will: But why should that be so? J saw no spies watching thy blood-thirsty play?

Jonesie: Dost thou think they stuck Edward's severed neck out there by chance? Jt's a lure. They've been waiting and watching to see

224

who'd scream most at his dead face. They saw thee and our lovely murder and no mistake. So now, for thine own good William, thou must die!

Will: Jonesie!

Hans: Don'y vorry Villiam! Thou makest nice dead pig.

Jonesie: Hans hurry! Splash him – 'specially over 'is head. William, now thou hast to do the best acting of thy life – let thy death be thy life's guide.

[They splash lots of pig's blood over William]

Will: But where, what safe place is there for me Jonesie?

Hans: A platz vere everyvon and novon can be hidings. Come!

Jonesie: Let the pose of death be that which preserves thy life! Let's away!

[They carry a limp, blood-soaked William back out into the street. They again carry him passed Edward's head, pretend to stumble with the weight of a dead body, and disappear.]

## Scene iv

[A crowded street near to a bridge over the Thames. Blind, old woman

sitting begging from passers-by]

**Old woman:** *A crust f'a blind, old maid wot never did no 'arm t'man or*

*mouse! A spoonful o'gruel! A little porridge t'warm me*

*dyin' 'eart! Please!*

[Suddenly a young teenager, carrying a bulky sack, dashes here and there between the people. When he reaches the Old Woman, he quickly gives her the sack, receives some money in return, and snatches up another heavy sack the Old Woman gives him. Now shouts of 'There he his!' are heard. Several men appear, they are clearly chasing the youth. The boy runs out across the bridge and throws the heavy sack over the side into the river. He runs off pursued by the men. When the commotion is over the Old Woman gets up slowly, conceals the sack beneath her copious garments, and waddles off 'feeling' her way along the walls and through the crowd.]

## Scene v

[At night. We see the blind Old Woman going into a large, dark building – it is back-stage in a theatre. Around the walls is a multitude of costumes. Once inside she places the sack carefully on a table. She divests herself of her garments and we see 'she' is really William. Slowly William lifts Edward's severed head from the sack and places it before him on the table.]

William: O dear, dear friend, thou hast taken my heart, and more than

thou couldst ever have known, deep into thy living grave.

For thee only shall I pluck out mine eyes and softly kiss

them into thy vacant sockets.

For thee only shall I tear out my tongue and stitch it to thy

pretty mouth.

For thee only I shall turn my heart to be thy grave so that

we may still laugh and lie together in this all so living-

dying world.

For thee I did return full with such promises of love they

ached my being and tore free such desires as would

consume the seas with tumultuous, virgin fire.

And yet, here do I find thee butchered and dressed like some

clod of stinking meat.

Thy purposeless agony and death is but a savage testament

writ by those whose own monumental thirst for life has

given this crazed madness all the colours of diseased,

contagious tyranny.

O dear, dear Edward, define for me, speak, what is this world

that can do such things to such people?

Do men still need to cannibalise themselves?

Do we still need to devour the flesh and substance of our

own humanity?

Tell me! Speak my love! Canst thou not hear me?

Prey, open thy lips and tell me just one thing – is there any

pleasure, any sensuality in death?

If thou answereth 'yes', then safely can I understand men's

obsession and generosity in spreading death so freely.

But if thy reply is 'no', then I am left without reason why

men do, so joyfully and with such begging prediction,

let loose these oceans of blood?

No, my love, thou hast no need to answer.

There is no pleasure in death, only in the violence of death,

And of that, thou art wholly innocent.

[William carries Edward's head and places it on a bedside chair/table. He slowly undresses, puts on a night-shirt and climbs into bed.]

So how am I now to love thee?

Should I now pretend to surpass the infinite grief that now

doth sit like a crucible at the centre of my life?

What if I were to spontaneously melt into a black fire and

blister this world with yet more outrage?

Or should I instead, turn to sarcastic bitterness to mock the monstrous, inhuman filth that men do ever make?

Neither – for I will not betray and waste myself in betraying and wasting others.

That way lies the self-consuming dragon who already doth hold our suffering hearts between his teeth.

Then how to love thee?

I shall have thee for one day more,

And it shall be a day that will stretch so far onwards some will say eternity was but yesterday.

Let then this kiss warm thy stony lips,

But let then thy kiss, in return, unravel the anguished density of my mind.                    [William kisses Edward and places Edward's head on the pillow beside him]

Tomorrow I promise thou shalt speak and laugh again,

Tomorrow I promise together we shall banish all sorrow and all pain.                    [Lights out]

## Scene vi

[A crowded square. Enter William royally dressed as a woman, carrying a sack. At a raised, prominent position he stops and places a golden crown upon his head.]

A Woman: O look! It's a queen!

A Man: Wiv a good root an' two onions between's legs I'll wager!

A Woman: Come sirrah! My flower pot's in sore need of a good rootin'!

A Man: Thy flower pot is so full o'dead kippers Nancy, cats faint as thou walks the streets!

William: Good people of London! My friends! Let me present myself! I am the Queen of Dengland! – a country not too far from your own! In my country my people are of the happiest in the world because of the love and respect I bear them. And in this sack, especially for you, I have brought some of that love. In this sack there is even the smile of my God. In this sack is someone who knew you– but who you never knew. Someone shadowy shy! Hush! Sssshh....Please meet King Walsie.

[William reveals Edward's head – which also wears a golden crown]

Now Walsie, tell the good people here what thou doest in Dengland?

[William now 'throws' his voice like a ventriloquist into Edward's head. The crowd gasps not only at the first sight of the head but more especially when it appears to talk]

Walsie[William]: I protect my Queen.

A woman: Bless the saints! It speaks! 'Tis witchery!

A man: 'Tis the black tongue o'death!

Walsie: I speak to you as one who once lived amongst you.

William: So Walsie, tell these good folk how thou protectest thy

       Queen?

Walsie: I taketh every man, woman and child and...

William:...And dost thou give them breads?

Walsie: No, of course not – I chop off their heads.

William: But how doth that show thy love?

Walsie: Because then you and I will have all of Dengland to ourselves.

William: O sweet Walsie! Dost thou mean thou wouldst love me like a

       man loveth a woman?

Walsie:   'Tis true I love thee, but like the man who begs,

       I follow only God's law between my legs.

       And alas my root is far too weenie

       To fit thy sweeter, bigger queenie.

       So with God's commandments between my legs

       I am left a king possessing dregs.

To protect and love thee

I need heads to count,

To root and kiss thee

All roots must out.

Then with no other roots to challenge my own,

I'll have thee all to myself, alone!

A Woman: A saucy story indeed!

A Man: Walsie should try a smaller flower pot!

A man: 'Tis a strange way to love one's people!

William: To show her love a wasp stings everyone she meets –

Walsie: – but her poison is so strong –

William: –everyone she stings dies –

Walsi: And when no one is left –

William – she is all alone –

Walsie: – and cannot bear the heavy –

William: – accusing silence –

Walsie: – so she stings herself –

William: – and dies.

A man: I understand not thy meaning Your Majesty!

William: Why to show you that a queen who stings even out of love –

Walsie: – must one day be stung by the loneliness and savage hatred of her own conscience.

A Man: Methinks Dengland is a place I wouldn't like to be.

A Woman: Who was this gentleman thou callest Walsie?

William: My light and my love, a man and a woman whose thoughts

would oft stop the spinning earth and leave me hovering o'er

mountains.

Woman: Didst thou truly love him?

William: Madam, he gave to my existence the full meaning of love, and he

gave to love the full meaning of existence. Yes, I loved him

dearly and truly.

Woman: I wish my husband spoke like that.

A man: Thy husband's too busy crackin' flower pots – big an' small!

[Several men appear to arrest William and try to push through the crowd. However, the crowd obstruct their progress and William escapes with Edward's head.]

# ACT 3

## Scene i

[The Queen, dressed as a nobleman, is watching a play at the theatre. On the stage is a bound man, about to be executed and an executioner with an axe. A King stands close by accompanied by royal counsellors and attendants. Also present on stage are the condemned man's children and tearful wife, played by William.]

**Bound man:** Mercy Your Majesty!

**King:** Why shouldst I show thee mercy? Didst thou, in the public market, show me mercy? No! With loud, open ostentation thou freely abused me with burning jokes, with comical songs, with lampooning dances and mimicry that wouldst have enraged the cruel Devil himself! No sir, thou dost not merit lenient mercy!

**Wife:** Good sir – let not thy power have all the hues of hopeless revenge, which some will doubtless re-construe as murderous intent, but rather show the other hopeful side of thy authority – of mercy, forgiveness and love, despite the wrong done to thee. Such action would show a stronger, more magnanimous King than one who rages like a cruel, embittered Devil and lets fall the axe at every slight and whimsical trespass. There is a certain nobility in rising above ridicule and buffoonery.

A Royal Counsellor: If thou couldst, my Lord, but ride the waves and

misfortunes of snapping satire,

Thou wouldst soon out-grow thy inner-self and —

Like the cicada who sheds her outer-skin to become larger

and even more beautiful —

Thou wouldst emerge a monarch so radiant and increased,

so safe in thine own identity,

All other Kings and Queens would need shield their eyes

before thy brilliance.

Wife: To laugh *with* the mockery of thyself brings wisdom and tolerance

*to* thyself.

But to hate, kill and expunge the mockery of thyself, will bring only

more, much more savage mockery upon thy head until thy world

is surfeit with gangs of obsequious, deceitful flatterers each

too afeard to allow even the smallest grain of truth a place in

their hearts.

Royal Counsellor: It is a powerful argument Sire — killing laughter oft

invites double scorn. Let such satire rather give thee another

window into thyself.

King: Enough! Enough! I have already heard too much! My decision is

fixed! Proceed with the execution lest we drown in the murky

vexation of so many words! Proceed I say!

Wife: No!!

[The condemned man is blindfolded and his head placed on a block. The executioner takes aim by placing the axe blade at the man's neck, swings the axe above his head, brings it down hard and embeds the blade into the wooden floor an inch from the condemned man's nose. The King walks over to him and kneels down]

King: You see, even merciless Kings like me can make wicked jokes.

Thou owest thy life to thy wife. But know this – thou art

banished from my realm for ever and shouldst thou be found,

even with thy smallest of toes, inside my kingdom again, the

next axe will fall true and fair. Take him away!

Chorus.

Can mockery subdue a mighty king?

Can the biting reprimand of satire

bring a queen down on her knees?

Is not then the comedian the true Lord of all,

A mortal who maketh lesser lords from power

fall?

A jester whose pitiless wit

Can toss all kings and queens into the fiery pit?

Can lift the blindness of the man of power

Whose arrogance is sometimes sweet but ofttimes sour?

We hope our play tonight has brought thee ease

To laugh at kings who dance with fleas.

But alas the hour-glass sand has run right through,

'Tis time to say goodnight, and adieu.

[The audience applauds and disperses. William, who is still on stage and costumed, is approached by an attendant of the Queen]

Attendant: Art thou the author of tonight's play?

William: J am.

Attendant: My lord the Earl of Sussex sends his compliments and
would like to make thy acquaintance.

Will: Please let him come.

[The Queen dressed as a nobleman walks onto the stage]

Earl [The Queen]: William of Stratford?

Will: Welcome my lord! We are honoured by your Grace's presence. Thy
servant hath said thou wast pleased with tonight's performance?

Earl: With every scene, Sir, my interest hath grown more
than thou canst imagine. But thy play hath emboldened me
to ask thee a question.

Will: Prithee, please ask!

Earl: Thou hast implied with avid, forceful clarity that the joker, the witty
satirist is the lord of all lords – is that not so?

Will: J suppose it is my own fanciful interpretation of humour.

Earl: But how couldst mockery ever win a war? How couldst a jester
ever hope to seize victory in an ugly conflagration between
nations?

Will: But Sir, my play is not about losing or winning wars, it's about losing or winning the war of self-knowledge. Satire breaks the veil of personal pretention. War is the folly of competing obsessions.

Earl: Obsessions? Meaning what prey?

Will: Meaning all the reasons people slaughter each other – for territory, for riches, for power, for religion. Irony and satire are but marks of an understanding of what lies within the stony statue of power. A king who thinks he can command the sun when to shine is deluded and ignorant of his own ignorance. Satire traces, before the King's own face, the flattering mirages and patterns of his absurdity - patterns which everyone else can see, but he.

Earl: True. But may there not come a time in a nation's history – when confronted by a dire enemy intent only on cruel dominance, torture and blood-letting – when a King or Queen must stand, fight and kill? Look Sir at the Spanish fleet – The Armada. Had our good Queen simply stood on the Dover cliffs and hurled satirical incantations at the Spanish ships, you and I would be speaking Spanish and kneeling to a Catholic god . No amount of sarcasm, wit or irony, Sir, can send an enemy running from the field of battle. Thou canst not stand before someone about to disembowel thee and thy children and tell jokes – surely that is the reserve of weaklings and cowards who thus deserve to be brushed aside by despotic power?

Will: In peace and war the rules of humour do change. But thou speaketh as one who understands power and kingly authority? Art thou perhaps a spy for Elizabeth?

Earl: We should all be spies for Elizabeth. Only vigilance will stem a resurgence of catholic power. Dost thou not love our Queen?

Will: I hate her!

Earl: Thou shouldst, Sir, be wary-wise about who thou hatest. But, prithee, wherefore hatest thou our Queen?

Will: It is a personal matter – no more.

Earl: Dost thou think if she knew of this 'matter' she would think differently?

Will: Who knows? Who cares? She hath too cruelly betrayed her people!

Earl: How so Sir!? I take vast objection to thy words!

Will: Earl – Queen Elizabeth is England's worst traitor!

Earl: Thou art a Papist with allegiance to Rome!

Will: I have allegiance to no-one but the people of England!

Earl: But so doth the Queen! How then canst thou call her a traitor!?

Will: Because she denies them the right to think!

Earl: To think!?

Will: Aye Sir – to think! Not long ago a dear friend of mine was savagely beheaded by Elizabeth for daring to think and put down his thoughts in a manuscript.

Earl: How was the tract entitled?

Will: I forget – something to do with the earthly power of Kings and Queens. He had such wonderful, new ideas and just for this he lost his life and I lost a dear love. And our Queen – our so-named Protector – is doing this every day. She has become so scared of catholic assassination, every mouse that squeaks in her presence is crushed as a conspirator. This witch is stifling, nay, suffocating her people with her fear and this is what makes her England's worst traitor.

Earl: But –

Will: But nothing! Dost thou not know that England could be a paradise of ideas and invention if only her people's imaginations were allowed free reign – ideas feed off ideas – thoughts on thoughts. Elizabeth hath such an opportunity in history to let the English imagination loose across the globe. But what, instead, does she do? She hides in her castles, behind rows and rows of frivolous skirts, reading sickly love poems – protected by the grey shadow of Count Walsingham and his web of spies!

[The 'Earl of Sussex' slowly reveals himself as The Queen]

Earl – Queen: The Queen 'hides in castles'? 'Behind frivolous skirts'?

'Reading love poems'? Your friend's tract – William of

Stratford – was called 'A Treatise on Power'!

Walsingham! Here's our conspirator! Arrest him!

Will: You!!!?

[Walsingham and his men rush William and subdue him]

Queen: Yes! On your knees!

[William is forced to kneel]

I am one Queen who will not genuflect before a bad and

witless jester!

Will: Thou mayest have power but thou art a tyrannical babe in the

exercise of power!

Wals: Hold thy tongue!

Queen: Nay but let him speak Walsingham – every word he utters will

the more stretch his catholic neck.

Will: I am no recusant! Dost thou not understand – I have no god!

Wals: A godless conspirator!? Ha! There're none on this earth Sir!

Thou art a Jesuite I'll be bound!

Will: Thy vision is as limited as thine enemy's! You ask me to see thy

god – any god – in all this cruelty and malice? Pah!

Queen: Thou hast such a blaspheming tongue Sir!

Will: And thou, Madam, hast such a crucified heart! Thou hast become

nailed to the arms of a circling windmill of murder – in the name of thy god thou wouldst kill those who would kill thee in the name of their god – and so round and round god's murder-mill goes! Thy loyalty to death is as sightless as thine enemy's! Thou art about as different from them as a rat is from a rat!

Queen: Enough! Walsingham! Only when he hath confessed canst thou pull out his tongue – but be sure, at the same time, to extract his heart - rats do love fresh heart!    [William stops speaking]

Wals: Take him to the Tower! If he won't use his tongue to extend his neck, there are other ways to stretch the truth out of him!

[William is taken away]

Queen: Do not rack him yet Walsingham – leave him for a while. For a week or more let fear be his only companion.

Wals: Doest thou think we can bring him to our cause?

Queen: I'm not sure. He is intelligent and can see beyond men's eyes. I do not think 'we' can turn him, but maybe I can. I will think on it.

[exeunt the Queen and Walsingham]

## Scene ii

[At night. We see William chained to several other prisoners being led by four or five guards towards a castle door. One of the guards knocks]

Guard: We bring some of Lord Walsing's specials! Come on open up!

Guard inside [through window]: You gotta take 'em on to the naval prison

        at Dartford by order of Walsingham 'isself, on account that

        we is full t'bustin!

Guard: Dartford!? Sweet Jones! That'll take all night!

Guard inside: Go via the Pig's 'ead Tavern! Nancy's workin' tonight!

[We see the guards leave and lead their prisoners away down some dark lane. Here they are suddenly set upon by a group of wild men. Some of the guards are killed and, completely outnumbered, the rest flee leaving their prisoners in the hands of the attackers]

A Man: We have saved ye! In the name of Our Sovereign Lord

        Jesus ye are free! But come! We must away – the Devil's

        hot gospellers are even now stealing through the night! Away

        – for the Blood of the True Christ is rising!

[Together with their new captors, the prisoners – terrified and still chained – run from the scene and disappear into the night]

## Scene iii

[Walsingham is at his desk in his study. Enter servant in haste]

Servant: My Lord!

Wals: What is it!? Why art thou so breathless!?

Servant: My Lord the prisoners you directed to the Tower tonight were
sent on to Dartford prison as you ordered, but the guards
were attacked on the road by a zealous mob of odd-Christian
men shouting the 'blood of Christ is rising'!

Wals: But what of the prisoners!?

Servant: These crazed men have taken them!

Wals: Tell me – did the prisoners go willingly or with dire coercion?

Servant: Most clearly my Lord they were kept bound and went as
terrified as if the sky and earth were closing over their heads!

Wals: But how knowest thou this?

Servant: I spoke with the sergeant-at-arms who, outnumbered by the wild
affray of slashing iron, fled for his life, but who turned to
watch the fate of the prisoners. With his own eyes he saw
them, still chained and wailing at their plight, being marched,
as he said, straight into the jaws of the beast!

Wals: Go! Muster men and horse! Find every spoor of their escape! I
have had too much of this over-blown catholic Christ! Find
them! Go!                                    [exit Walsingham with servant]

## Scene iv

[A secret catholic church. A flamboyantly dressed priest is conducting mass at an altar. The prisoners – still chained together – stand in a row to one side of the altar. Another ostentatiously robbed priest enters carrying a large gold, jewel-studded crucifix which he kisses from time to time. He also flicks holy water on the prisoners. He stops and addresses them.]

**Priest:** Be blessed! Be purified! May all the plagues of the anti-Christ be driven from the chalice of thy souls! But before thou canst receive the flesh and blood of Our Lord and Sweet Saviour Jesus, each of thy souls must be as pure as the virgin snow and thy bleeding heart open and ready to receive the Holy Spirit of Jesus's Love and Mercy! Repent thy sins! Forgive these corrupt sinners O Lord! First you – woman! Come hither! Be not afeared. What is thy name?

**Woman:** Mary, so please your Grace.

**Priest:** A good catholic name! Wast thou thus baptised?

**Woman:** J don't know what 'thus' be?

**Priest:** Art thou a Catholic!?

**Woman:** J was forced into the Protestant faith your Grace.

**Priest:** How forced?

**Woman:** They laid a sword on the throat of my child and said if J didn't throw down my Catholic belief, they would draw the blade.

**Priest:** So what didst thou?

**Woman:** Forgive me your Grace – J still have my child but not my faith.

Priest: So oft like a drooping flag thy weak sex turns easily in the wind. And!?...And you smell!?

Woman: 'Tis my monthly time your Grace.

Priest: Ugggh! Thou art unclean! Thou canst not receive the True Christ if thou art stained with the oozing filth of thy sex-blood! Thou art wholly unfit to lie with Christ! Dispatch her to the afterlife!

Woman: No! Please! My child hath no one but I! I promise I will be a good Catholic!

Priest: Aye! Thou canst practice thy Hail Mary's in Hell!

[She is approached by an armed man and put to the sword]

Now thee!

[The priest points at a male prisoner who staggers forward and kneels]

Tell me thy worst sin! Speak up! Ah!? What!? Thou didst the carnal act with a dog!? Tush! If that is thy worst sin thou art indeed blessed! Thou art forgiven! I absolve thee! Thou art ready! Here eat of the flesh of Christ.

[The Priest takes a piece of raw meat from a plate and places it on the kneeling man's tongue. He chews and swallows]

And now drink of Christ's Holy Blood!

[The priest takes a chalice and places it against the man's lips. The man tries to drink but gags and vomits blood over the floor]

He is possessed! He hath rejected the True Christ! He is full of Protestant poison! J have seen Lucifer in his eyes!

Cleave op' his head and let out the anti-Christ !

[An armed man hacks the man's head with a sword. He falls dead and is dragged away]

Now it is thy turn!

[The priest points at William who is pushed forward and forced to kneel]

William: J am no protestant!

Priest: A good beginning.

William: But neither am J catholic.

Priest: A bad ending!

William: J have no church!

Priest: What then art thou? Mohammedan?

William: No! J follow no prophet – J wish to be godless.

Priest: Godlessness is the Devil's work.

William: No, it is my choice.

Priest: No one can choose to be without God – you may as well say 'J

am he who was never fathered, who was never pulled from  a

mother's womb'. Jt is not possible to be exterior to God's

grace. But have no fear my son – thou art saved!

William: Saved!? From what?

Priest: From the evil which hath clearly stripped thee of thy soul – now

let us purify what is left! Tell me, what is thy worst sin?

William: My worst sin?.....is that J have never sinned.

**Priest:** *Never sinned! Then thou art indeed more pure than I! Come,*

**time is short, eat of Christ's flesh.**

[The priest takes a piece of raw meat and tries to place it on William's tongue]

**William:** *I...*

**Priest:** *Eat!*

**William:** *What is that slaughtered pig behind the altar?*

**Priest:** *Eat!*

[William is threatened by the armed man. He opens his mouth and allows the priest to place the raw meat on his tongue. He eats and swallows with disgust]

**Priest:** *And now Christ's Holy Blood – drink!*

[The priest approaches William's mouth with the chalice. William tries to drink but, like the man before him, he too gags and vomits – but this time all over the priest]

**Priest:** *A man of no church shalt thou be! And a man with no life! Kill*

**him!**

[The armed man raises his sword and approaches William. But William takes him by surprise and hurls himself upon the man and wraps his chain around the man's neck. At this point there are loud shouts from outside the church, a window is smashed and Walsingham's men burst through the church door and rescue the prisoners]

## Scene v

[A large, palatial room. William is sitting, clean and well-dressed, at a grand table, at the other end of which sits the Queen. In the beginning there is a frosty silence between them]

Queen: Six years before thou wast born William, I was crowned thy

Queen. In the thirty summers and winters that have since

passed, there have been six attempts at my assassination,

uncountable plots and conspiracies to dethrone me, boats full

of Jesuit priests landing by night on our shores, and of late,

a vast Armada sent by the catholic Phillip of Spain to

invade England and drag me to the gallows. I may be old

William, and to thee I may seem a tyrant, but my heart, like

thine, is of a new age. Certain my father broke from Rome to

bed the wives of his own choosing, but the seed he really

planted grew outside the womb. It was my father who really

gave birth. After centuries of frozen catholic

winters, there was, here in England, suddenly a spring. But

this spring, this awakening of independence was and still is

seen by Rome as the most fractious defiance in its history.

Thou hast, William, just seen what we, as Church of

England Protestants, have freed ourselves from –

from a perverse Christianity drenched in the superstition of

blood and brutality; a Christianity corrupted by the wealth and

privilege of a priesthood that must, in every way, glorify

ignorance. It pretends to be an unblemished, pristine faith full of miracles and rituals which are – as you have witnessed – extreme and grotesque. It is a type of Christianity against which, I believe, Christ himself would turn his back. I do not want England – my England, my people – to suffer the re-enthronement of Papal Rule. Had the Armada invaded and their cause succeeded, I am certain that as each town and village was beaten into submission, England's rivers would have coloured the seas around our island with such English blood as would have stained the oceans beyond, black with rage. Had we been defeated the vast tentacle of the Papacy would have dragged our minds back to the Catholic darkness that reigned before Luther. Our courageous new awakening would have been drowned beneath the blood of its own people.

William: But why, Your Majesty, are you telling this?

Queen: Because we need – I need – thy help.

William: But I am an actor! My pen and words are the only sword I have! I know nothing of the world of intrigue and plots!

Queen: But thou knowest of the world of taverns, bawd houses and brothels.

William: In truth, Your Majesty, I have visited such places, but only because I like to glean from the rough speech of the people their odd words and expressions. I like to listen to their crude accents and dialects – I go as a mere listener to language.

Queen: Exactly – you listen. Walsingham knows of a certain brothel, somewhere south of the Thames, which he suspects is a nest of well-determined conspirators. He hath received rumours and very pregnant suggestions that there are serious preparations afoot to harm my person. I thought that with thy special talents and skills William, thou couldst visit this place – perhaps as a customer – and just glean what thou canst?

William: What does Your Majesty mean – my 'special' talents?

Queen: Thy acting skills and...

William: And?

Queen:....William, I know about Thomas Morton, I know why thou camest to London. But....but what I and Walsingham don't understand, is why thou and thy friend – who I believe was called Edward – disguised yourselves as women? Why wouldst thou need to conceal thy person if it wasn't for some evil purpose such as a plot against the Crown?

William: We were not concealing our persons, we were concealing our love.

Queen: Your love?

William: Yes – and our love was never a conspiracy against thy person.

Queen: Then why conceal it? Friendship was never a crime.

William: The face of our friendship was more than it could show to the world.

Queen: You mean it was a very private, loving friendship?

William: Yes, we enjoyed a very special, emotional intimacy.

Queen: That is as it should be between good friends, but still, why disguise yourselves as women? Truly J don't understand?

William: Our small home was as a stage upon which we could play any role or character that was our fancy. We both felt most comfortable together as women. Edward was my wife and J was his.

Queen: His husband?

William: Sometimes, and sometimes his wife.

Queen: Art thou saying, as bedfellows you – ?

William: Yes I am. We frequently consummated our love carnally, just as any pair wedded in matrimony would do.

Queen: But then I am surely correct to think thou hast committed an act which is contrary to all Biblical teaching, against the natural order of the world and of all good government?

William: Yes, many times. What thou callest 'Biblical teaching', good governance and the natural order, have – for over two thousand years – strangled, or rather ruled our understanding of love.

Queen: O come William, what is there to understand? There is love and there is lust. Dogs lust and mount in the streets. People do not.

William: Your Majesty, people do lust and love all the time – privately.

Queen: But the lust thou hadst for thy Edward and he for thee, was that really the imprint of love?

William: It was what it was Your Majesty, but it is not for kings or queens or the clergy to condemn it as anything else. The church has ever seen love as a carnal instrument, a way by which the one flesh of two people can bring forth children. Now I ask thee, can love not mean more than this? Can love not mean something beyond what it means? At birth Fortune smiled on me and gave to my soul a wonderful ambivalent alchemy which cares not if the object of my love is male or female – I was born ambisextrus. I care not who loves me as long as I am truly loved, and those I love care not who loves them as long as they are truly loved.

Queen: Thou hast spoken eloquently William and I will think on thy words. But if thou truly lovest the freedom to write thy plays, to act and compose thy poetry, then thou must help us. Thou asketh 'Can love not mean more than procreation?' Yes, we can love each other, as thou hast so convincingly put forth, but can we not also love the freedom our independence from Rome has given us? Where the boundaries of love are laid I know not, but for sure the love of Rome is bound by narrow walls of iron.

William: Indeed, love is not love which hates when it hatred finds, nor when it turns to rejoice and kill in the name of prejudice.

Queen: Ah William, is not this amazing world of ours so brim full of man's hatred, that oft we seem to spend our lives just ducking the blows and rages of someone else's madness? – and all just to stay alive for one more day! Can we not wonder what people might accomplish if we all were free of such constant distrust and terror?

William: I fear, Your Majesty, the future will surprise the future by forgetting the past. People have only ever seen what they need to see. What lies beyond their seeing has been expropriated and festooned with superstition by the Churches. Maybe one day a necromancer, an alchemist or some conjurer in logik will reveal the world to us with new eyes and we will see infinite wonders that astound and terrify us with their complex beauty.

Queen: So William, wilt thou help thy Queen? Wilt thou help England keep alive these flames which one day may awaken our island to the complex beauty of which thou speaketh?

William: I have but one request before I can consent to thy request.

Queen: And what is that prey?

William: To say sorry for Edward's death.

Queen: I can say with a heart full of true sincerity and contrition that I

am deeply sorry for Edward's torture and execution.

It should never have happened.

As recompense I have had Edward's

treatise on Power printed and bound.

[The Queen gives William a copy from beneath the table]

Walsingham thinks I am mad and one day this book will be

either my undoing or my successor's, but in the spirit of the

new age, surly we are nothing if we cannot rise to the

terrifying risks it may bring?

William [opening Edward's book and reading at random]: 'Paradise has

only ever stood in the shadow of swords – simply because the

shadows in men's minds have never given way to light.'

Queen: I have read his Treatise and there is much I disagree with.

But there is much, much more that unerringly hits my heart.

He had such an inward-looking eye which oft appears to see

into the very seams and creases of the soul.

But William, it is late! I must go!

256

[The Queen rises, as does William]

Come, give me thy hand. Remember, what thou doest for me

thou doest for a vision of England that we both share.

What can be accomplished, may depend on what we both dare.

[exeunt The Queen and William]

# ACT 4

## Scene i

[A tavern/brothel. William, dressed as a woman called Charlie, is sitting at a table. Next to him sits Jackie, a customer, who is very 'keen' on Charlie.]

**Jackie** [groping beneath the table]: Come on Charlie! I can see thy wantin' eyes! Let me stroke thy wantin' thighs!

**Charlie** [William]: Jackie! Thou art a rude rascal! Get thy hand out of my skirts! I'll let thee explore the high seas soon enough!

**Jackie:** If thou keepest me in these shallow waters too long, I'll run aground!

**Charlie:** Then don't put forth thy sails until high tide – get off me!

**Jackie:** If I don't raise my main sail soon, there'll be a flood at low tide an' no mistake! Please come upstairs!

**Charlie:** I've told you – when I'm ready and not before! Now tell me, who is that fine-looking captain whispering in the shadows over there? Dost thou know him?

**Jackie:** I've never 'ad the pleasure of his mast-head if dat's what thou meanest?

**Charlie:** No I don't! It's just that he looks like the praying type – what dost thou think?

Jackie: Nah! If there's any 'hole-liness' in 'im it's round the back!

Charlie: Jackie! Canst thou not take one breath without having visions

of sweaty lust!? What about this charmer with his back to

us? At that table? Dost thou know him? He's been keepin'

his voice so low I suspect he can't talk at all?

Jackie: Watch this! I'll show thee a pretty play.

[Making sure he's unobserved, Jackie takes a blank piece of paper from his jacket pocket and spreads it out on the table. He draws a few lines and writes a few words.]

Charlie: What art thou doing? Is that a chart of streets?

Jackie: Hush thy voice! The fox, see, must needs send the hounds barking

down an empty burrow. We wouldn't want 'em sniffing

around too close to 'ome now would we?

Charlie: Why Jackie speaketh thou in riddles?

Jasckie: For the same reason thou speaketh of high tides and putting

forth sails – to protect my, and thy, false modesty.

[Jackie finishes drawing and writing. He folds up the paper as small as he can. He then gets up and casually goes over to the table where the 'charmer' is sitting with his back to them. Unseen by all except William (and the audience) he surreptitiously drops the folded piece of paper into the charmer's jacket pocket. He then slaps the charmer on the back as though greeting a long lost friend. They talk a while. Jackie then leaves the table and saunters over to another part of the tavern where a group of serious-looking men are sitting and gives them the nod and casually wanders back to William and sits down.]

*Keep talkin' and watch!*

[Several of the serious-looking men get up and approach the 'charmer'. They take hold of him. A scuffle ensues. They pull the paper from the charmer's pocket, open it, nod at each other and drag the protesting charmer away.]

*Now Charlie, thou seest J's got power.*

*Charlie: Power!? How? What hast thou done?*

*Jackie: Sent a man first to hell then on to heaven. But come, wot J*

*want from thee now is upstairs. My ship's risen on a sudden*

*swell and J'm going to undress thy modesty, lift up my anchor*

*and ride thy unchartered waters!*

[Jackie takes William's hand and gently pulls him towards the door that leads upstairs. William acts very coquettish.]

*Charlie: O captain Jackie! What wouldst thou from me!? J barely*

*know how to swim! Jf J should struggle thou must promise*

*to dive in and save me!*

[All of what happens next, on the balcony and in the two adjoining rooms, the audience can observe. Jackie leads William upstairs to a balcony with many doors leading off to bedrooms. He pulls the now not-so-reluctant Charlie into a room. They embrace, but Jackie's passion is so fervent he quickly undresses and throws his clothes over the floor. Charlie, however, is slower and has only removed his shoes when two large, grim-looking men – who followed the pair upstairs – walk boldly into the room. Jackie shouts at them to leave, but the men suddenly grab Jackie, gag him and carry him struggling through a side door that leads into an adjoining room. Before they close the adjoining side door one of the men turns and shouts at William]

**Man: *Y*ou! *B*itch! *M*ove not!**

[After they close the adjoining side door William quickly moves to the door and listens]

**Man 1: *T*hou useless, squeakin' turd!**

**Man 2: *T*hou hast a mouth as wide as an 'hore's legs!**

**Man 1: *T*hy braggin' will bring tomorra's entertainment to nought!**

**Jackie: *I* 'aven't said a word! 'onest! *N*o one knows 'bout tomorra!**

**Man 2: *K*eep thy skulless voice down!**

**Man 1: *W*ot 'bout thy cock-friend in der next room!?**

**Jackie: *N*othin'! *I* swear!**

**Man 2: *D*er's only one way t'be sure.**

[The two men nod at each other and begin to strangle Jackie. William, who has been listening, realises the danger he faces and quickly removes his wig and women's clothes and throws them beneath the bed out of sight. Just as quickly he dresses in Jackie's male clothes left over the floor. He hastily puts his friend's jacket on and leaves the room. When they have finished murdering Jackie the two men toss his body onto a bed and re-enter the first room. They see that the 'woman' has gone and rush out onto the balcony where William – now unrecognisable as a man –is calmly approaching the stairs. One of the men grabs his shoulder]

**Man 1: *Y*ou seen a woman!**

**Man 2: *L*ong 'air – she'd 'ave bin in a hurry!**

William: *Yes! Stupid bitch nearly broke me leg! She wuz runnin' like as*

*she 'ad a hoard o'devils after her virginity!*

[The two men rush down the stairs, through the tavern and disappear out into the street. William calmly exits]

**Scene ii**

[The Queen's apartments. Enter Her Majesty and Walsingham in discussion]

Walsingham: *But Madam, thou hast recruited a godless sodomite!*

Queen: *Walsingham, I have in these last months since Christmas come*

*to see more than thou seeth.*

Wals: *I fear Your Majesty has been sorely influenced by that*

*seditious tome which I strictly counselled ought to be cast*

*into the flames from whence it sprang — not printed and bound!*

Queen: *Thou sayest 'sorely influenced', Walsingham, but I would rather*

*say 'thoughtfully excited'. Thy very own words were that our*

*stance against Rome is for a new freedom, a new*

*independence, but we cannot do this Walsingham if we*

*supress all new thinking — however provocative it may be.*

Wals: *But sodomy Your Majesty! It's despicable! Perverse! It's*

*utter depravity! Condemned by God's very own words!*

And...And we now have this sodomite from Stratford working for us!

Queen: Walsingham we are talking about saving the entire English nation from Papal rule! What has this got to do with what two friends do in their private bed? What wouldst thou do – remain 'pure' because thou didst not accept William's help, and so have England over-run by Spanish rats and thyself and thy family butchered in the streets as heretics? Thou hast seen with thine own eyes what happened in Paris on St. Bartholomew's. I would rather, Walsingham, accept the help of one intelligent, godless sodomite than have England subdued by an army of ignorant Catholic sodomites!

Wals: But we will be damned by God Your Majesty!

Queen: I suspect, Walsingham, the truth is, you and I would rather be damned by God, than hang from a gallows in Rome – and have all that we have achieved torched to the ground. And anyway, the word 'sodomy' sounds so frightful, it's so full of hate before it's even spoken. Can we not just call it love?

Wals: Your Majesty! Thou goest too far!

Queen: Then prey, come with me. Lift thy mind out of the Catholic past. Let us chart a different future into what thou once said are the 'unknown waters of freedom'.

Wals: I cannot, in all conscience, Your Majesty, chart a future based on sodomy.

Queen: O Walsingham! Don't frighten thyself with false conclusions. It would not be a future based on sodomy. It would be based on the rule of laws and a respect for whatever ways men or women choose to love each other. Does that sound so seditious?

Wals: No matter how 'free' they be, I fear the people are not ready for such unintuitive, disturbing thoughts.

Queen: Maybe one day Walsingham, the people will surprise even themselves. Good, Sir Francis, we will converse more on this matter again soon, but for now we must discuss the preparations for tomorrow's business at the Privy Council. I shall be at the Hampton Palace tonight. I would like to meet later after supper. Can you come?

Walse: Indeed Madam, I shall be there. I have already agreed the route and Lord Hunsdon wants to include a musikal fanfare as Your Majesty's carriage moves down the Strand.

Queen: Yes, but this is trifling – what about the Lord Chancellor, Sir Francis, what is he likely to want?

Walse: You approval for the building of three more vessels to patrol the Irish coast. He wishes to prevent even more Jesuits crawling down our backs.

Queen: And Lord Hunsdon wants musik?...

Walse: Indeed – he says thy people need to thrill not just at thy sight but at the sound of thy approaching.

Queen: Well, if the Lord Chancellor can afford it...

[exeunt The Queen and Walsingham]

### Scene iii

[A room at the rear of the theatre]

Jonesie: Will! Give me thy curse! J ain't seen thee this green since thine eyes first clapped on poor Eddie! What's 'appened?

William: They murdered him – whilest J listened from behind the door.

Hans: Den de door had thy life gerettet – J mean saved!

Jonesie: Who murdered who?

**William:** It was awful! Hast thou ever heard the sounds a man makes when he's being slowly strangled to death? And I was to be next!

**Hans:** Thou hadst kvick vits Villiam to put on his clothez.

**Jonesie:** But why did these men strangle 'im?

**William:** I heard them say something about his big mouth and tomorrow's entertainment, and Jackie – my friend – screamed that I knew nothing about tomorrow.

**Jonesie:** So they didn't do 'im in f'money then?

**William:** No.

**Hans:** Den they do in 'im for woman?

**William:** No, no. For some reason they didn't trust him. Just before they began to strangle him, one of them said 'there's only one way to be sure.'

**Jonesie:** Sounds certain like they wuz cappin 'is bottle f'good alright. But 'ere Will! I almost f'got! Now dis'll warm y'fingers as much as y'eart!

[Takes a quill carefully out of his pocket.]

Take a geezer at dis Will! This is an artifice of rarest genius – bought it from one of Hans's countrymen down the docks.

266

Hans: In my land vee call it 'ein Stylus'.

Jonesie: Special nib see – made o'dis thin, hard metal. Name y'battle and it'll stay as sharp and as trusty as a sword. You'll be able t'write verses from 'ere to the Moon and back and it'll keep as true as a bosun's whistle!

William: 'ein Stylus'? Now the pen will really be the sword whose truth may never falter.

Hans: Dis iz a nice jacket! Can J try, yes?

[Hans takes the jacket that belonged to Jackie and puts it on. He stands in front of a mirror]

Jz too tight in my shoulders – and it makes my sideback too big.

Jonesie: Yer backside! Thou art such a plonker Hans!

Hans: The collar iz a little too pricky-hard. Gug!? What's diss?

[Hans takes the jacket off and begins fiddling with the collar]

The Schneider put something in here zat makes the collar too stiffy. Ah got it!

[Hans slides a long, rolled-up piece of paper out from inside the collar]

Jonesie: What's that!? Let's see!

[Hans gives Jonesie the paper who spreads it out flat on the table]

Hans: Jt's drawing!

Jonsie: Like a map!

267

**William:** Hummm strange - before he was killed Jackie made a drawing which he dropped in the pocket of someone he wanted arrested. He said something about sending the hounds on a false trail. But why? And why hide this drawing on himself?

**Jonesie:** If this Jackie was as foxy as he sounds, I'd say he was one fox who didn't want the hounds sniffing around his legs?

**Hans:** Maybe he wuz – you know – because of diss?

**Jonesie:** Hans is right, this map's maybe the real reason his bottle was squeezed shut.

**William:** But what does it show? Is it a map?

**Jonesie:** What's this square thing? It's got the letters 'S T P' in the middle? And what's this cross?

**William:** And what does 'The Beach' mean between these lines?

**Jonseie:** 'The Beach' ? Could be somewhere on the coast? William! Me brother-in-law fishes off 'astings an' he swears not a month goes by without boats landing at night unloadin' dozens o' Jesuits! I bet this is a map showin' 'The Beach' where they land!

**Hans:** On Der Strant – der Beach?

Jonesie: These two lines are long- so it must be a long stretch of beach.

Hans: A long Strant?

William: But there's no sea? If this is supposed to be a beach, which

side of these lines is the sea?

Hans: And we are island – der is many Strants – I mean beaches.

William: I don't know. [Yawns] I'm too tired to think anymore. I've got

to get some rest.

Jonesie: Or it might mean nothin' and is just a piece of innocent paddin'

in the collar - and we is breaking our 'eads just over a scrap
o' paper.

Hans [yawns]: I sleep too. Tomorrow Villiam I must play the geist in

thy play - 'Ven I to sulphurous and tormenting flames must

render up myself.'

Jonesie: Hans – render up thyself to bed – I'll be there anon.

[exit Hans]

William: Jonesie?

Jonesie: Tell me.

William: Tonight I came too close to death – I shook hands with those

who would have yawned as they cut out my heart. I feel


eviscerated and yet my corpse still blinks and breathes.

Jonesie: J have just the thing to calm thy nerves.

[pours a drink and gives it to William]

Just the smell of this ale 'as been known to make birds

drop out o' the sky. Come, drink it down and get thee to bed. J

promise, tomorrow thou wilt wake up with thy legs running!

[exeunt William & Jonesie]

## Scene iv

[Hampton Court. Evening. The Queen with Henrietta, a Lady-in-Waiting ]

Henrietta: And in England we have ferocious lions that do sit in trees

and tweet like birds!

Queen: And cows that stand on two legs reciting the Psalms!

Henrietta: And honey spiders that spin threads of gold and at night

whisper poetry in our ears!

Queen: And flocks of English woolly fish that lie in the fields debating

philosophy!

Henrietta: O my Your Majesty! This fancy doth so wet my cheeks with

mirth!

Queen: This fancy doth so wet me where J must needs swift to my

commode!

Henrietta: Madam! Thou art the Queen! Thou canst not say such things!

Queen: If I cannot say such things Henrietta, I durst not be Queen!
                                        [enter Sir Francis Walsingham]
Wals: I am glad to find Your Majesty in such high spirits so late in

the evening.

Queen: What dost thou think Walsingham?

Wals: Your Majesty?

Queen: Do the English love woolly fish?

Henrietta: Or lions that roar with birdsong?

Queen: Or trees that grow downwards from the clouds?

Henrietta: Or streams that do flow upwards from the seas to the tops of

mountains?

Wals: Ah! You will turn things outside-in and downside-up – though I

cannot see for what purpose?

Queen: For the purpose of no purpose! Or if there is a reason it is to

play the advocate of stupidity so we may laugh at our serious

selves and allow our souls – for a brief pulse of time – to play

the frivolous fool.

Henrietta: Well said Your Majesty – the world as it is, is already too

overfull with long white-beards whose looks would turn a

lusty heart into a cauldron of ice.

Wals: The world as it is, Lady Henrietta, is too full of serious

madness which unfortunately far exceeds the frivolous variety

thou desirest.

Queen: So, which dost thou bring Walsingham, the serious or the
frivolous?

Wals: As you know Your Majesty, the affairs of state are always

serious – if they were frivolous then I would wear the

clothes of a jester and thou wouldst constantly dream of

dancing through palaces full of...of apple pies.

Queen: Methinks thou wouldst make a clever jester – but come! What is

the business I see hiding behind thy creased brows?

Wals: I have received fresh news from the Low Countries of a Papal-

instigated conspiracy involving a Scottish Duke – the Duke

of Lennox, a fire-breathing Catholic – some unnamed

northern English nobles and a bevy of Jesuits newly landed

from Ireland.

Queen: What!!?

Wals: There is no need for alarum Your Majesty, these are just

rumours, mere whisperings. I have already dispatched my

men to the northernmost border to ascertain their veracity.

Queen: Again these Jesuits do crawl and creep at my back! They are

like a disease of the bowels, pustulant growths worse than

the plague! The plague at least attacks and kills quickly! But

these vermin attack peoples' minds and spin erstwhile honest

men and women into such diabolical ecstasies they turn and

devour their own kind! These Jesuits are spiritual cannibals!

Wals: Madam calm thyself! Rest assured J have my fist around each

Jesuit's throat so completely, should they dare do anything

against thy person, J will personally desecrate their souls.

Queen: Thy passionate loyalty Sir Francis is commendable. J would

thou closeth thy fist so tight, their blackened tongues would

stick out as far as Rome!

Henrietta: Tush madam! Thou must rest for tomorrow's ceremony. All

this talk of cannibals and throats is unsettling and thou wilt

sleep fitfully if at all. Please may we retire to bed and leave

Sir Francis to his Jesuits?

Wals: Lady Henrietta counsels well Your Majesty. J will take my

leave. Please forgive the intrusion of my serious news.

Tonight I will try to dream myself a jester who knows

only how to bring good news.

Queen: Do not fret Walsingham, the good news thou canst bring me is

the bad news for mine enemies. Henrietta, thou art right, I am

tired. Goodnight Walsingham.

Tomorrow, matters serious and potent to the Council I bring,

I'm tired of being Queen, now I will be King!

Henrietta: Madam!

Queen: Just a little fanciful senselessness Henrietta, before we retire.

Wals: Goodnight Your Majesty.

[exit Walsingham shaking his head]

### Scene v

[The following morning. The room at the rear of the theatre. Enter William yawning. A cock crows. William glances out of the window up at the sun]

William: Thou art like me – a lazy cockerel. The sun is already high

above the roofs.

[He goes over to the table from the previous night and picks up the piece of paper and again puzzles over the 'map']

The Beach?.....ST P ?.....A Beach?

[He laughs to himself and imitates Hans's German accent]

Thou hast 'kvick vits Villiam!' 'Der Strant'!?

274

The Strand?  The Beach?

[He sits and begins to eat some breakfast.  Moments later Jonesie comes rushing through the door]

Jonesie: William! William! Art thou up!? Come! Hurry!

William: Why Jonesie! What's the matter!?

Jonesie: It's the Queen! She's coming! There's musicians and

performers all down the Strand to cheer her on her way!

Come on before thy lazy head misses the spectacle!

William: I have to eat something! Where is she now?

Jonesie: Her carriage 'as just entered St. Martin's ! She's goin' down

The Strand towards ST. Paul's! Come on! The crowds are

such a sight! The whole City is alive with colour and musik!

I'm not waitin'! Catch me up!

[Jonesie runs out. William stops eating, suddenly stands and snatches up
the paper]

William:....The Beach!...Der Strant!....The Strand!!!....ST P ...

ST.Paul's!!.....Jonesie!!!!!!!!........

[William races out after Jonesie]

# ACT 5

## Scene i

[A street lined with waiting crowds. The Queen's closed coach comes into view. Walsingham and some of his guards ride on horseback behind and beside the coach. The crowds wave and cheer. The Queen waves back. William suddenly appears running frantically through the crowd, shouting above the crowd's noise, trying to attract the Queen's attention.]

**William:** *Your Majesty!! Stop! Stop! Your Majesty!!*

[Walsingham, however, does see William and bellows out to his men in the crowd to 'Arrest that man!' The Queen notices nothing. William is manhandled by several of Walsingham's men. A fight ensues and William manages to struggle free and continues to run through the crowd and catches up to the Queen's coach. This time he screams out so loudly the Queen turns, recognises William and hears his frantic shouts]

*Your Majesty!! Avoid The Strand!! Do NOT go down The*

*Strand!!*

[Half a dozen or more of Walsingham's men surround William and overpower him. Walsingham bellows out for William to be taken to the Tower and he is carried away struggling. The Queen now tells the driver of her coach to drive through some gates into the closed courtyard of a house they are passing.]

**Walsingham:** *Your Majesty!? Why have you stopped here? The whole*

*of London is waiting for you!*

**Queen:** *The whole of London will just have to wait Walsingham – even*

*queens are sometimes indisposed – I need to use this house's*

*commode.*

Lady-of-the-House: This way Your Majesty. You do our 'umble

privy a great 'onour.

Queen: I thank thee. Pray, couldst thou attend me? I fear I will have

need of thy assistance. Walsingham, tell the crowds outside

I will return as soon as I've used this good woman's

commode – I'm sure they'll understand.

Walsingham: As you wish Your Majesty.                    [exit Walsingham]

Queen[to Lady- of-the-House]: Please do as I ask – there is little time. I

do not need thy commode. Instead I need thy help to divest

me of this dress as fast as thy speedy fingers can allow.

Lady-of-the-House: I will do my best Your Majesty.

Queen: Bravely said! Now listen while we work, there is more I would

like thee to do...

## Scene ii

[Crowd waiting for the Queen outside the House]

Woman 1: It takes me as long t'pick me nose as to 'ave a pee! She's bin an age in there!

Woman 2: Don't be a dumplin' ! She's the Queen! Royal wees 'as got t'be specialities o' the state!

Woman 3: Any'ow, wiv a dress the size of a rigged ship she'd never fit in a privy!

Woman 1: I'd 'ave peed meself wicked if it took me three days t'get me knickers down!

Woman 2: If thou saw a rich gent it'd take thee three seconds t'get thy knickers down!

Woman: O thou crusty bitch! O look out 'ere she comes! Long live yer Majesty!!

[The Queen's coach re-emerges from the House's closed courtyard. The Queen herself cannot be seen but her large, golden dress can – it fills the windows of the coach thus giving the impression to the crowds that the Queen is inside. Once the Queen's coach has returned to the street and all eyes are following its progress, two people emerge unnoticed on horseback from the courtyard of the House and follow the procession at some distance as it makes its way down The Strand. After a few minutes there is the sudden loud retort of a musket and immediately the Queen's coach explodes and disintegrates in a ball of fire.]

[William in chains, alone in a cell in The Tower. He is tempting a mouse to eat]

William: Come my little brother, eat. I seek only thy companionship and

thou seekest only the crumbs that fall from my mouth. Thou

dost not know it, but thou art truly closer to my heart than all

of devious humanity. Dost thou blunder and crusade about

the globe peddling thy petty obsessions? No. Dost thou

declare war against the shrews and moles because their god is

different to thine? No. Dost thou kill and call it an act of

love? No. Then dost thou proclaim thy truth as the one power

that shakes all mountains? I think not. What a piece of

ambiguous rubbish is man, that he can balance suns and stars

in one hand, yet clutch severed heads in the other! That he can

have a mind which tempts the darkest secrets of creation, yet

at the same time bring in giants and ghouls to explain what he

cannot understand? We ought to faint with the joys of insight

into our world — not be rendered blind and outraged by life's

cruel wisdom. Ahh....... Thou hast beautiful eyes little mouse

— they are full of simple, harmless fear - not the slippery, serpentine smiles of those who would so passionately be thy friend because thou art their next meal. Come eat! 'Though thou art right not to trust me – J am after all, human – a creature who sees trust as a weakness, a being who has always thrown wide the gates to reckless tyranny.

[There is the sound of keys in the cell door. Enter the Queen and Walsingham]

Your Majesty! Thou art alive!

Queen: William, J owe thee my life. England owes thee its Queen, and one day humanity will owe thee its future.

Wals: And J owe thee an apology.

[Both the Queen and Walsingham bow their heads before William. William is shocked.]

William: Nay! Please do not supplicate thy selves! That is how bad gods are born! J did only what J had to do. But pray tell me what happened after J was taken away? Why, Your Majesty, dost thou say thou owest me thy life?

Queen: Walsingham, have these chains removed this instant!

[Walsingham nods to the jailer who comes and releases William]

Queen: Your warning William led me to pretend I was in the carriage as it proceeded down The Strand. I was in fact on horseback dressed as a Duke far at the rear of the procession.

Wals: It seems apparent that one of the water barrels on Her Majesty's coach had instead been filled with gunpowder. A single musket shot was fired at the barrel causing it to explode.

Queen: I feel William thou hast snatched me from Death's closing teeth.

Wals: Indeed, Your Majesty, by the loving grace of God thou art safe.

Queen: By the grace of God and wild, human intuition.

William: Though one might ask, Sir Francis, if thy God is so all-powerful and loving, what was He doing when the traitors filled the barrel with gunpowder?

Wals: I know, William, thou wouldst tempt my beliefs with such blasphemous questions, but Divine Will is not something we humans were ever meant or born to understand.

William: A clever rebuttal Sir Francis, but it's one I could never accept.

Queen: Well this is a fine place – a prison cell in The Tower – to be

discoursing on the limits and existence or non-existence of

Divine Will ! Gentlemen, my father King Henry would be

very pleased to see what his act of defiance against Rome

hath released into the world, that such as we in such a place

can question the divine origins of ourselves without trying to

slit each other's throats. But come, let us leave The Tower

before Master jailor here decides to incarcerate and stretch

his guests for blasphemous misconduct.

What might, or might not, be said hereafter,

May for some bring sorrow, for others, laughter.

[exeunt Queen, Walsingham and William]

## Scene iv

[A stage in a theatre. A rehearsal. A man (Alex) is sitting precariously on the very edge of a high castle wall. It is clear he is contemplating suicide. Another man (Robert) is standing not far away trying to dissuade Alex not to throw himself to his death. William is sitting watching the two actors. Occasionally he suggests how they should stress certain aspects of the dialogue]

Alex: Back! I say!....Go! Go away! Leave me to die!

Robert: If I leave thee to die Alex, each day I live hereafter I will die

anew! I beg thee Alex, do not do this!

Alex: I have made my decision – now go!

(William: Don't forget Alex, you are angry and suicidal.)

Robert: Dost thou think some eternal darkness will grant thee peace?

Alex: What!? Just look at what thy 'eternal sunshine' has revealed!

Pah!

Thy words are hooks trying to fetter me to this world of

brutality and avarice! Leave me alone I say!

(William: Some sarcasm in the words 'eternal sunshine')

Robert: I see every reason to live and –

Alex: – and I see every reason to die! Don't come closer Robert! I

swear this is my last hour on earth and thou wilt not thwart

me!

Robert: Good! Then throw thyself down! Those rocks below gape as though they are rising from the mouth of a Behemoth! Go on! Leave me to live for the rest of my years a shattered, loveless wreck of a man whose only sleep is a nightmare pageant filled with images of thy broken corpse!

Alex: So thou wouldst have me live only for thy sake!? What splendid selflessness that is!

Robert: If I want thee to live it is because I love thee Alex.

Alex: Thou liest! Thou lovest only thyself! I feel it! Do not speak any more! Thy words only mock the truth!

Robert: The truth!? What truth!? Alex learn to look beyond thine own eyes!.....Good! Remain silent! Ignore me!....The truth I see is of a life wasted – of someone pouring nourishing milk into the sand, of someone burning bread as coal to keep warm in a hot summer.

Thou hast maybe three score years in which to do something to help change the world – but what instead hast thou chosen to do? Suicide Alex is no answer to the world's incessant cruelty. Yes I know how thou – how we – have suffered!

How this all god-fearing world is populated by power-zealots and religious gluttons who willingly slaughter their tender path through people's minds! And all in the name of a divine love! Dost thou think I don't know all this?

(William: Slight pause here.)

Sometimes I

ask myself, if I am to be godless in death why not in life too? The godful see themselves as either blessed or evil – probably they are both. I choose to be godless so I can be neither blessed nor evil. And yes, no matter what thou chooseth, there is still treason, torture and callous butchery on every corner – whether thou art godful or godless. Dost thou think I don't know how, such as we, are despised and cursed as unnatural dogs, as diabolic monsters who, they so think, spend every waking moment on our backs licking each other's anuses! I hate this every bit as much as thee Alex.

Alex: Then die with me! Come! We can stay united in death! And the world can go and rot in its righteousness!

Robert: Good. Let us cast our bodies together – give me thy hand!

[Hesitatingly Alex lifts his hand out to Robert. But when Robert is close enough he suddenly grabs Alex and pulls him away from the edge. They struggle furiously and almost topple. Alex then suddenly stops fighting and collapses sobbing into Robert's arms]

Alex:.....Let me go!....

Robert: Sssshh.........Ssshhh................

I too have oft reached out into the darkness before my eyes and struck at the cold emptiness – at the void which seemeth to mock at my humanity, to menace and laugh at my very soul. But never once have I been tempted to abdicate my life and kneel before death. Sometimes methinks what is abroad in this world, despite all the vivacious and colourful celebrations of life, is really the reverence and worship of death. What else could drive our obsession with heinous brutality, dominance and greed? But I refuse still to kneel to this bastard god – to any bastard god – because I know in my soul's deepest marrow, there will come a time when love shall reign supreme, a small moment when we shall step across a threshold in our hearts and finally walk free of our inhumanity.

[enter messenger for William]

Messenger: Sir? Art thou William, the writer of plays?

William: I am he. What wouldst thou?

Messenger: Sir, Her Majesty The Queen would like thee to attend her

at the Palace as soon as possible. She wants me to inform

you that she is poorly and urgently needs to impart some

advice pertaining to your safety.

William: My safety!?

Messenger: Yes Sir.

William: Good. I will come with you. [to the actors on stage] Excellent

gentlemen! We will continue tomorrow! The Queen has been

taken ill and I must to the Palace. Come.

[exeunt William and Messenger]

## Scene v

[William is ushered into the Queen's bedroom. She is clearly very ill]

Queen:....William!...

William: Your Majesty!.... Thou art so naughty!

Queen:...But..why William?

William: For not informing me sooner thou wast poorly.

Queen: J am not poorly William, J am dying. J have felt it for days.

My flame is fluttering – in here – the wick is about to fall

into the hot wax and...and J will grow cold.

William: Your Majesty, the flame thou hast lit in the hearts of so many

people – even when thou departest – will never burn out.

Queen: William do not flatter an old woman on her death bed. Listen to

me. Since Walsingham's death things at court have changed.

Thou must not perform this play of thine. Robert Cecil is

far worse than his father – he would torture his own child if

he thought it threatened his position. He is a puritan tyrant

and he...he is preparing to throw thee into The Tower.

William: The Tower!? But what for?

Queen: Sedition and...and blasphemy - both of which he has made a capitol

offence.

William: But he cannot know what is in my play — I've only just

finished writing the last scene?

Queen: William thou art still too naive — there are eyes and ears in the

very air thou breathest. Cecil has spies even in thy theatre —

how dost thou think I know about the play? One of Cecil's

spies is in my confidence. Please for my sake William — take

this as my last dying wish — leave London, go home, and take

thy play with thee. Thou hast done enough.

William: I cannot countermand my Queen's last wish, and, if the truth

be plain, I have of late oft felt drawn back to my roots.

Maybe it is time.

Queen: But William...

William: Your Majesty?

Queen: I have one more request...a request that might cause thee infinite

pain or joy.

William: Your Majesty has me puzzled— what is this request of infinite
pain?

Queen: When I die I want thee only to recite a eulogy as I lie at the

Westminster altar. But....

William: But?

Queen: But let it sing true and not be full of petty grandiloquence – only

thou canst do this. Have I thy promise?

William: Fear not Your Majesty, thou hast my promise already – it

lies enclosed within my heart, a vessel thou captured many

years ago.

Queen: Good. Now I must rest – I don't want thy infinite words to

blow out my flame too soon. Adieu William, my brave

friend.

William: Adieu, Your Majesty.

[exit William]

## Scene vi

[A room. Behind a desk, shuffling some papers, sits Robert Cecil, the Earl of Salisbury. Before him on the other side of the desk stands one of his spies]

Cecil: And you say the manuscript instructs the actor to say 'bastard

god' ?

Spy: Yes sir. But then he must clarify it by saying 'any bastard god'.

Cecil: Indeed! Good! Good, I can already hear his chains rattling! What

else?

Spy: The actor uses the expression 'religious gluttons' and – if I

understand it aright – the phrase 'licking each other's...'...

Cecil: Yes?...Each other's what?

Spy: I'm not sure what an 'anus' is sir?

Cecil: He says that!! Art thou sure he didn't say 'liking each other's – '

you know?

Spy: No your Grace, he definitely said 'licking'. Is an anus a type of

Oriental fruit from the New Word like the patata?

Cecil: The Patata!? Yes! Yes!. An Oriental fruit!?......I can't believe

this!...No! You dullard ! It's the poison of sodomy!!...

Now get out!!                                      [exit spy]

291

I will not have such a play as this spreading such abominable
filth throughout the City! God knows it is corrupt enough and
already over-ripe for a damnation far worse than Sodom and
Gomorrah! Such a play will just add horror upon horror!  But
Hush! Don't fret! Don't fret! Shhhh!... I will give them all
the sodomy they want! I will drive home the hot iron so deep
into their precious 'anus' their screams will make God in
heaven shiver !! That the Queen could have such a bestial
animal as this for a friend is shameless!
But shame never did wield much power –
– whether in the street, or in The Tower!

   Ha! Ha!

## Scene vii

[William is sitting up in bed reading a manuscript. Suddenly church bells all over the city begin slowly tolling. Without knocking Jonesie bursts in]

Jonesie: William! The old Queen's dead!! People's wandering about

like lost sheep! She's dead William!! Dead!

[runs out]

[William lets his papers fall on the bed and stares blankly before him. Eventually he says to himself]

William:  So Elizabeth thy flame finally is out.

Now J must find words to dispel the evil and doubt.

[There is a loud and impatient knock at his chamber door]

Hello?  Come in!                                    [enter a Messenger]

Messenger: The Earl of Salisbury demands your presence forthwith.

William: Has Robert Cecil, The Earl of Salisbury, ever heard of the

word 'Please' ?

Messenger: Jf you resist, my orders are to take you forcibly to The

Tower.

William: Where there is haste my friend, there hides the Devil. So

where is thy impatient master?

Messenger: J am to convey you to his chambers at once.

William: Certainly his chambers sound more hospitable than The Tower.

Good. But I hope you will allow me to put on my trousers

first? Or does the Earl of Salisbury want me in my night

gown?

Messenger: Dress and be quick! I will wait outside.

[exit Messenger]

### Scene viii

[The chambers of Robert Cecil, the Earl of Salisbury. Cecil sits behind a large
desk and William sits opposite]

Cecil:...You?....You?....

William: You?

Cecil: You...like men?

William: You're a man. I don't like you.

Cecil: Quite – I am blessed. What I mean is that you like men in a

way that is contrary to God's law?

William: You mean contrary to man's limited view of himself.

Cecil: You contradict God at your peril sir.

William: No, I contradict you at my peril.

Cecil: You indulge in...in the touching of men carnally which the Bible

expressly forbids.

William: The Bible, Sir Cecil, is the fountain of all blasphemy.

Cecil: How dare you say such a thing! You! – who have slept carnally with legions of Devils! I could have you roasted alive for slandering the Holy Book! How dare you!

William: If you roast alive all men who tell you the truth, you will have a world stuffed with obese liars – or cowards.

Cecil: God has written that only men and women are permitted to clasp carnally – yet you insult His laws every time you...you...

William: You?

Cecil:.....I...er...errr...Doth it not hurt?

William: Doth what not hurt?

Cecil: Thy fleshy affections?

William: Look, I...I think I understand your...curiosity Sir Cecil, but I fear I am not the person to help you. However, you did not bring me here to discuss the relationship between theology and carnal love. Why am I here? What do you want?

Cecil: Very well. I know Her Majesty – may God rest her soul – spoke with you a few days ago.

William: That's true.

Cecil: I also know she wanted you to eulogise her departure from this life - at her funeral in Westminster - to the nation's nobility.

William: That's right.

Cecil: I cannot and will not allow that. If you go anywhere near Westminster on the day of the Queen's funeral, I promise you, I will have you thrown into the most rat-infested dungeon in The Tower. I will not torture you, but if you survive, I will personally see to it that you remain in chains until the very darkness crawls into your eyes and turns them into balls of jelly.

William: You would do all that for me, if I try to say farewell to my Queen?

Cecil: You will not be so trite when you have to eat cockroaches to stay alive.

William: I am indebted to your clarity.        [William stands to leave]

Cecil: There is one more thing. I have banned your latest play - it is the work of a mind besotted with evil and debauchery, and if you ever dare stage it, either here in London or anywhere in England, it will give me yet one more reason to bed you with the rats in The Tower.

William: You know, hatred like yours must be very hard to bare.

Cecil: And the difference is, you do, but I don't, care.

You are free to go.                    [exit William]


## Scene ix

[Westminster Abbey. A large congregation of nobility. The Queen's open
sarcophagus is slightly raised on a bier before the altar at the head of the main
aisle]

A Prelate: In Nomine Padre. The Viscount of Essendene will lead

the eulogy. Viscount –

Viscount of Ess.: My lords, Ladies and members of the nobility of

this enshadowed land! Before me lies the sun of suns who

even in death doth shine a most noble light! Her Majesty was

a ship unparalleled of ships whose sails bosomed the skies

with glory! She was the engine of engines! The grand

cannon of all ordinances! Magnificent! Radiant! And blessed

with mountainous, concatenations of splendour! Yet alas!

Thou hast crossed the Big River never to return!

Thou hast left us high and dry!

Never to laugh, forever to cry!

Why didst thou have to die?

Though the end for us all is nigh,

Thou left without a sound or sigh,

Without one kiss or goodbye.

Thou, who placed the very sun in the sky,

Hast left us here with not one dry eye.

I ask our God, the one on High,

Not to dissemble, laugh or lie,

But to tell us plainly before we die –

Why? O why? O why?

Prelate: Thank you Viscount for your uplifting words – I am sure they

touched God himself. And now Queen Eleanor of Denmark

would like to say a few words.

[Queen Eleanor, a heavy black veil obscuring her face, approaches the sarcophagus. It is, of course, William – who, as his eulogy continues, makes less and less effort to disguise his voice]

Queen Eleanor[William]: This Queen, this friend was once my bitterest

enemy. Why?

Because neither she nor I could see how lost we both were in the immensity of the conflict that surrounded us. We were enemies not because she sought my obscure life, but because friendship was a luxury she found hard to trust. And who can blame her? For almost all of her reign, her own life was a struggle to survive between colossal forces.

These were forces that were so depraved and inhuman, so inspired by the goal of human degradation that, had they triumphed, the ensuing carnage would have turned this treasured isle of ours into a universal, raw hell – a land stagnant with blood and rank with tyranny.

Even as a child Elizabeth was thrown into a maelstrom of discontent and brutality, and yet out of this she brought forth a rare and precious idea. Our Virgin Queen gave birth to a notion far more important than heirs and babes, Elizabeth's womb guaranteed the conception, gestation and birth of liberty. This was a freedom not simply from Papal superstition and its deadly Inquisition; nor was it a freedom from Protestant torture – it was a freedom to see the future of her people on this tiny island as the future of all humanity. Some might say this was an arrogant freedom, one born from a desire to dominate and enslave. But to such people I say you do not understand the real meaning of the freedom to which Elizabeth gave birth. She once asked me, if man is born so innocent and clean, how does his mind become so encased in labyrinths of iron chains? – a question no one had ever before dared to ask.

Elizabeth, my Queen and friend, was no philosopher. What was really behind her question, what was really in her blood was the final emancipation and enlightenment of humanity. It was a vision of human freedom that was meant to liberate us from our dogmas and obsessions, our self- righteousness and zealotry, our arrogance and hatred.

She.....Ah! ...My!....My Queen!...My love!....

[At the far end of the central aisle William sees (and we see but not the congregation) the ghost of Thomas Morton walking towards him down the aisle. Thomas is dressed in a bridal gown but around his neck is a noose which trails far behind him on the ground as he walks. He is also carrying in his arms the severed head of Edward. In the horrified reactions of William that follow, the congregation are ruffled, but they put down William's sudden emotional behaviour as his being overcome with grief for the dead Queen.]

Thou wast my love!...Our love!....Our mother!.....I cannot

look upon this vision!.... It cuts through my soul like a

glowing knife! Away!.... This truth is too full of truth!...

 Thy meaning too full of meaning!!.....Help me!...I swear I

did love thee so, so much!...Thou wast my first and only

Queen! ...O my sweet!.... The past should fall from

our memory's precipice – not rise again!...Thou wast so

fair!... Here, taketh thou my heart with thee...

[As Thomas approaches the Queen's open sarcophagus, William slowly backs away in terror. But as he (and we) watch, Thomas seems to melt into the sarcophagus and disappear. William slowly regains his composure]

Elizabeth, thou...thou hast surrendered to a dark river;

We, thy people, are left still bracing the ebb and flood of

    our uncertain history.

But now there is a hope, a wish, filled it seems, with epic

    consent –

Thou hast cascaded liberty across our lips,

And if it survives it must be because of what we do with our

    freedom, not what our freedom does to us.

We must not let thy legacy be defined by our future,

Rather our future must be defined by thy legacy, thy life and

thy love.

We are all what thou hast given to us.

Prelate: Thank you Queen Eleanor of Denmark. And now the Requiem

sung by the Abbey choir.


## Scene x

[As a heavily veiled 'Queen of Denmark' leaves the Abbey, she is surrounded by Cecil's men. Cecil then confronts William]

Cecil: William of Stratford! You disobeyed my express command! J –

William: Who !? J'm afraid J do not know of whom you speak Sir? J

am Queen Eleanor of Denmark.

Cecil: Thou art no more the Queen of Denmark than is my cat! Thy

performance – though too full of excessive dripping of tears –

has, unfortunately, won thee much sympathy and –

[enter the Bishop of Westminster effusive with praise]

Bishop: Ah Queen Eleanor! May J be the first to congratulate thee on

such a splendid eulogy! J'm sure Sir Cecil would agree! Jt

was most uplifting and full – if J may be so bold – of a

future vision of humanity that was really inspiring! Listen,

I'm giving a little reception in my chambers behind the Abbey,

wilt thou join us? It would be a great honour! Splendid!

[William takes the Bishop's proffered arm and they walk off back towards the Abbey. As they leave the circle of Cecil's men, William turns his head and calls out to Cecil 'Meeeeow!' The Bishop and William laugh and proceed arm-in-arm into the Abbey]

Cecil [to one of his men]: Follow them. When the 'Queen' emerges, take

some men and get him out of the city. Return him to his native

Stratford and impress upon him that he is henceforth banished

from the capital and is to remain confined to within five miles

of his poxy town! Any infringement of this will result in his

immediate transfer to The Tower. Do you understand?

Man: Yes, your Grace.

Cecil: And......And I don't want him harmed – he may be a bestial

apostate with a flapping tongue, but underneath he is

irrelevant. Go!

        [exit Man]

Farewell Queen, I am the one only I can pity,

Underneath, thou art everything I dare not be.

## Scene xi

[A sunny day. William and Celine (Thomas Morton's sister) sit on a bench under a tree]

William: Thou do knowest Celine, the sorrow I feel for what happened all those years gone by, hath never left me?

Celine: William, thou wast not in error. Thou canst not blame thyself. I had always suspected Thomas and thee were very close, and in all honesty, I had never seen my brother so happy as when thou wast with him. He seemed so joyously transformed. As thou knowest Thomas and I were also very close – we were both so different from our awful bothers we sometimes harboured doubts as to our parentage. Our enraged father so inflamed Thomas's brothers against him, there wast little hope your happiness would ever last. I pleaded with them to let Thomas be, but father wast so replete with hate he became like a madman screaming that the honour of the family was a at risk.

William: So what became of thy family?

Celine: I only have survived. Father was killed by one of his many enemies not long after thou left, and of my six brothers two just left Stratford and disappeared – I think they feared they would meet the same fate as their father – and the other four died violent deaths in brawls and crime.

William: Yes, Anne hath told me as much.

Celine: Of course. But why?...er...

William: Why am I here? I so would like, Celine, to find where Thomas is buried. I have searched the churchyards, but there is nothing.

Celine: Thou wilt not find Thomas in consecrated ground William. The local clergy and priests – may God dam their souls – refused to bury him saying suicide was a sin and he was...well, they said that too was a sin.

William: So....So where is he buried?

Celine: I am the only one who knows – if it hadn't been for me his father and brothers would have left him to be eaten by foxes and cats. We're...We're sitting on him. He's below this bench. Oft do I come here and talk with him – it is my way of keeping him alive in my heart.

**William** [standing up]: Hast thou a spade?

**Celine:** What!? Thou canst not exhume him!

**William:** Please Celine! Don't be alarmed! I have been forbidden to

print or perform my last play – which in many ways concerns

Thomas. I only wish to bury my play with him. Wouldst

thou allow me to lay this small metal box in Thomas's last

resting place?

**Celine:** Of course.

[She fetches a spade and together they move the bench. William
digs a small but fairly deep hole. He kneels down and carefully
places the metal box into the hole, covers it over and replaces the
turf]

William, I will leave thee to make thy private peace with

Thomas. Strangely, from the instant he was interred, I feel

he hath been waiting for this very moment. How I, who still

live, can feel a deceased brother's thoughts, I know not, but

for so long they have rested here, in me, like a dark, clandestine

pain.


[exit Celine]

William: Thomas, thou hast been with me and I with thee these thirty

    more years.

    Thou knowest there is no end to love,

    For once it hath moved the waters of the soul, they are never

    again at rest.

    Thou knowest too that love is all we have to embrace the

    heartless, sinister void that embraces us,

    And the moment our love witnessed its reflection, mine in

    thy eyes and thine in mine,

    The void in us died and love took its first breath.

    Adieu, sweet Thomas, adieu.

FIN.

www.ingramcontent.com/pod-product-compliance
Lightning Source LLC
Chambersburg PA
CBHW030343020726
47493CB00003B/662